ISOBEL'S SON

M J Knox

With best wishes,
M.J. Knox.

Published by TWQ

ISBN: 978-0-9927667-0-2

For Henry, with love and gratitude for his unfailing support and encouragement

ISOBEL'S SON

March 2008 - The Offices of Fairfax and Lowther Solicitors

'Would you like a cup of tea or coffee, Tom, before we start?'

'Thanks, but no. I have to get back for afternoon surgery. I'm guessing this won't take long? We seemed to have covered everything. You've been a great help, Ronnie. Thank you for all you've done.'

'I am only too pleased to have been of service. I think you know what good friends Isobel and I were.'

Tom saw the older man's flicker of emotion as he sat down to pick up a file from the low table. Ronnie withdrew an envelope and looked again at Tom. This time his expression was controlled and professional.

'I have a letter here for you from your mother. She asked me to keep it for one month after her death and then to give it to you to read. She trusted me enough to tell me why she had written it and I know only what she said to me. I haven't read the letter but I must warn you that its contents will come as a shock. I am not going to say any more at this point. I feel you should read what she has to say. If you wish to talk to me after that, you will find me in the room across the landing. I will be alone in there, so just walk in.' He got up stiffly from his chair and handed the envelope to Tom. As he reached the door he turned to glance back. 'One thing I do know, Tom, is that Isobel loved you above anyone else. Keep that truth in your mind as you read her words.' He left the room and closed the door quietly behind him.

Tom glanced down at the envelope and at Isobel's flowing, well-formed letters in her black italic handwriting – just his name. His mouth felt dry. Ronnie Fairfax had warned him, said it would be a shock. He noticed a carafe of water on the table with a tumbler serving as a lid. He placed the envelope on the table, poured some water into the glass and stood up. Looking out of the large window, he watched the figures walking through the shaded square below and along the pavements, going about their daily business. He guessed that once he opened his mother's letter, nothing would be the same. He felt a compulsion to absorb the normality of the scene outside, fearful of it changing into a world that was different, less certain. He sat once more in the brown leather chair and opened the envelope. Inside were many pages of the closely written words of his mother.

'Darling Tom,

You will be reading this after my death and if you have heeded dear Ronnie's words (and I know he will have passed on my request for you to be alone when you read it) then you are no doubt sitting by the window in one of his old chairs and I expect Ronnie is not far away – I asked him to be near you – because, my dearest Tom – what you are about to read will not be easy for you. My heart is aching as I write this, for the pain I am about to inflict upon you. I have so many times thought of talking to you about the things I am telling you in this letter, but each time something stopped me. I am a coward, but this letter will be necessary if I never managed to pluck up the courage to talk to you directly and for that I ask for your understanding and forgiveness.'

Tom glanced at the top of the paper and saw there was no date. He returned to Isobel's words, conscious of his increasing pulse rate.

'I was always acutely aware that Edward was not a good father to you. Oh yes, he provided for us as a family and, at times, I think we even managed to behave towards each other as families should, but you know, as I do, that this was superficial. You were aware of the favouritism shown by Edward towards Sarah and, yes, I saw the hurt and confusion in your face when he patronised and humiliated you, which he did relentlessly, all the way through your childhood and right up until his death.

He couldn't even bring himself to offer praise or encouragement when you qualified in your chosen profession. I am so pleased that your work has brought you such fulfilment. You are a good doctor, Tom. I think, at last, with your beloved Alex, whose love and support have sustained you for so long, you have indeed found some peace and joy. For that I am thankful.

And it is because of this contentment in your life that I have held back from telling you something I should have told you a long time ago. As the years have gone by I have watched you develop and blossom into the man you are and of whom I am immensely proud and love more than you will ever know.

Now, I will stop trying to make excuses and offering utterly inadequate apologies and tell you what you need to know and may have begun to guess already.'

1

Her eyes scanned the beach. Pressing her toes into the soft, brown sugar sand, she studied her feet and waited. Bubblegum-pink toe nails peeped through the grains and sparkled as they caught the sunlight.

I don't suppose he'll even notice, she thought to herself. Oh well, Daddy liked them. Said they were, 'deliciously Hollywood', whatever that means.

The vast sky rose up from the calm, green-grey sea, which lay so far away you could hardly tell where the horizon ended. Isobel adjusted the straps of her blue cotton sun dress, looked down at her small breasts and thin legs and wondered for the thousandth time, why, why had he told her, of all people, that he loved her? 'I don't know,' she said out loud. She lay back into the yielding mattress of sand, warming now as the sun shone, and smiled. She closed her eyes and pictured him, felt him, savoured him.

When she sat up and glanced to her left, there he was, striding along the sand, the gentle breeze ruffling his hair. She watched him and her heart soared, her pulse raced, her face flushed. She took a deep breath as he came closer. He was tanned and sunny.

'Hello,' he said, smiling down at her.

'Hello,' she replied, looking up at his silhouette.

He sat down and tipped her chin towards his face. 'You look so lovely. I've have been watching you as I walked along the beach and I've been pinching myself and asking why someone like you should even give me the time of day let alone tell me that she loves me.'

Their eyes locked. They reached out and wrapped their warm limbs around each other. Salty kisses and tingling bodies touched and embraced, breathing together. The beach stayed empty and time seemed not to move as the sun rose and the sand beneath them grew warmer.

'You are so beautiful.'

'So are you,' she replied and they laughed. They broke apart suddenly, dusted the sand off each other and clambered up to run out and meet the far away, incoming tide.

They walked back hand in hand, stopping every now and then to look at the curly worm coils in the sand, or to pick up a strange shell. Their damp hair coarsened and skin smarted in the salty air as clouds built up. Inland, the greens of the trees and the reds and umbers of the roofs took on sharper, brighter hues against the darkening sky, reminding her of Bill's paintings. As they left the sea behind, she recognised the figure of her father; slight, bespectacled and wrapped in his favourite old scarf.

His cry carried on the wind, which was building up rapidly, as the sun lost its brilliance and its heat. It seemed only in this sanctuary that was North Norfolk could the elements change quite so swiftly and dramatically.

'Belle!' His voice reached them on the now buffeting wind. 'Come on. We have to go.'

They quickened their pace and released their hands from each other's, reluctantly, but with the silent acknowledgement that her father would not approve. As they approached the older man, he appraised them, looking closely at his daughter as if to check for any signs of damage.

'Right, we'd better be off then. Have you got your shoes? You can comb that hair in the car.'

'Oh Daddy, don't be so grumpy. I've got my bag and my shoes and I'll tidy myself up on the way.'

She didn't add that, as it was her dead mother's grave the two of them were going to visit, no-one would be commenting on her appearance. She turned her face to the young man by her side and smiled.

'See you later?'

He smiled back. 'I'm working till closing time tonight, but I'm not starting till five, so perhaps I'll see you when you get back?'

They darted quizzical glances at her father.

'Daddy?'

'What?'

'Will we be back before five?'

Her father directed his solemn gaze at them both. 'We might ... and we might not ... difficult to say, really.'

She smiled. She knew that meant they would be back before five.

'See you later, Bill,' she said laughing and looking at him waiting. 'I'll call round to your house when we get back.'

He grinned, relieved. 'See you later.'

He turned and walked away from them. He began to whistle as he strode up to the dunes, through the sand couch and marram grass and down to where he had left his bike. Then, still whistling, he set off along the narrow road, lined on each side with reed beds and beyond them, the marshes and on to the village.

'Come on Daddy. Let's take the flowers you've picked for Mummy. You'll feel better when you've had a chat with her.'

Thomas knew this to be true. Painful as it was, he did seem to derive some pleasure and peace from their regular visits to Peggy's grave. He looked at Isobel and, as always, smiled at her youthful energy and sparkle. He loved her very much but he knew she sometimes felt suffocated by his over-protectiveness. He acknowledged to himself that he could not expect his daughter to mourn the loss of her mother for as long as he would. Now, a year after Peggy's untimely death, he still felt bereft and lonely. Isobel was sixteen and beautiful and had a life ahead of her. Why should he draw her into his grief?

As if sensing her father's thoughts, Isobel linked her arm through his as they made their way to his shiny, black Morris Minor. Bought the year before Peggy had died, this car had carried Thomas and

Isobel on their many visits to the hospital and on a few occasions, when the pain was less severe and Peggy had been allowed home, it had taken her and Thomas on gentle coastal and country sojourns through the undulating fields and byways of North and West Norfolk.

He and Peggy had married in 1925 not long after he had moved to the small seaside town to take over the chemist shop in the High Street. He had been one of the evacuated soldiers, from the deadly trenches of France in 1916, suffering from severe pneumonia and carrying the piece of shrapnel that was to remain embedded in his chest for the rest of his life. Following his recovery he had taken up his place at Cambridge and buried himself in his studies and love of the sciences, obtaining a first class pharmacology degree. His health had suffered and his full strength was never fully restored but his absolute dedication to his studies had afforded him some distraction from the terrifying flash-backs.

Peggy was the youngest of four children of the Methodist minister and his wife, who continued to call their youngest child by the name they had bestowed upon her - Margaret. She worked as a secretary in the offices of a small firm of architects. She and Thomas met at a dance in the church hall. He, the quiet, studious Cambridge graduate and she, the lively, somewhat rebellious and very pretty local girl, who took it upon herself to show Thomas all around the town and the surrounding beauty spots, having quite made up her mind that he was the man for her. It was to be nine years before Isobel was born. They had wondered at this tiny being who brought such joy into their lives. Clinging together through the war, protecting their child from what seemed to be an ever more frightening world, the three of them had survived.

Now, after five frugal years of peace, Thomas bore his grief and the responsibility for his daughter's well-being with grace, but with deep concern for her future.

Isobel was lost in thought on the short journey along the coast road to the small churchyard. I'll have to tell Daddy, she decided. I don't want to come to the grave so often. I'll come on my own sometimes, or with him on special days like birthdays, or Christmas. Thomas cast a sideways glance at his unusually subdued daughter, her dark hair obscuring most of her profile as she gazed down at her hands.

'What is it, Belle?'

'What is what?'

'There's something bothering you. I can tell. Do you want to tell me what it is?'

'Not really.' Isobel mumbled into her chest.

Thomas knew his daughter well and also knew that if he let it go and appeared not in the least curious she would start to talk. 'That's alright then,' he stated and looked ahead at the road.

Isobel looked at her father. He seemed to be concentrating on his driving. After a moment she blurted out, 'Daddy, I've got something to ask you.'

Her father wondered if this was something to do with William Harvey, the young man Isobel had been spending more and more time with, and his heartbeat quickened a little with anxiety. 'Alright' he said steadily. 'Go ahead.'

They were approaching the churchyard and Isobel felt this was completely the wrong moment to say what she had to say.

'It'll wait. We're nearly here.'

A narrow gravel pathway wound its way through the tombstones, some of which perched precariously at impossible angles, as if they would collapse, were they touched. As they drew round to the back of the small flint stone church and walked towards the far corner of the graveyard, the occasional sound of passing cars on the road softened. The silence in that shaded and serene spot was broken only by the sound of the occasional bird, chirruping amongst the inevitable yew trees, planted hundreds of years before and guarding the church against the elements. Peggy's resting place lay close to the hornbeam hedge marking the boundary of the churchyard. Beyond it were fields, sometimes golden with wheat and sometimes lying fallow. Today the buff coloured crop contrasted with the dark greens of hedges and the changing skies overhead cast moving shadows across the field.

Isobel watched her father remove the old flowers from the small vase at the head of the grave. He tipped the dregs of stale water out on to the grass beside him and then poured, from a thermos flask, fresh water for the roses from their garden. Isobel had watched her father do this every week for the past year and recently had begun to feel superfluous. She was sad that her mother had died and she missed her sometimes, but her grief was now less palpable, less intense. Her father was still a long way from a place in the future, perhaps, when he would be able to think back on his life with Peggy and remember the good times. His grief was still raw and this regular and ritualistic pilgrimage to his dead wife's grave was something he needed. As she had begun to do over the last few weeks, Isobel hovered at the grave until the flowers were arranged to Thomas's satisfaction and then she quietly walked away out of earshot. This was outwardly to allow her father some moments on his own to say whatever he wanted to his dead wife, but mostly because Isobel found it increasingly embarrassing to witness his distress.

Her thoughts wandered to Bill and reluctantly to the prospect of his departure. Too soon he would be going to London to study art. He had been accepted by the Royal Academy and she knew how prestigious that was. She was pleased for him but dreaded his going. Why did he have to leave her when they had only just found each other? She flopped down on a grassy mound and leaned against the cool bark of a tree. She closed her eyes, conjuring up his face, his smile, his tousled hair, windswept and sun-kissed, laughing and then tender as he wrapped her small frame into his strong arms. They had often stood like that, gazing out to sea, for ages, but what had seemed like no time at all to them. Even at sixteen she knew that his promise of returning regularly to see her was unlikely to be realised and her heart ached at the bleak prospect of weeks or more likely months without seeing him or feeling him close to her.

They had grown up in the same area, just a few miles away from each other and had never met, until Bill called into her father's shop when she was helping out behind the counter. He had smiled at her as she fumbled with his change and dropped coins which had rolled all over the place. She remembered blushing to the roots of her hair which, at the insistence of her father, was tied neatly in a bun at the nape of her neck. She had to wear a crisp white coat over her clothes too, which she hated and which made her feel felt lumpy and uncomfortable. On that first meeting he had come for Aspirin for his mother. Over the next few weeks he had turned up more and more frequently on some pretext or another – more Aspirin, throat sweets, Milk of Magnesia – till her father had commented.

'That young man seems to be in here rather a lot. His family must suffer from multiple ailments, or they are a bunch of hypochondriacs!'

Isobel, her eyes closed, recalled how they had met on the beach one evening and how they had talked and walked until the sun was almost lost over the horizon and the beach had emptied of dog walkers and tourists and a massive sky hovered over them and the sand beneath their bare feet had become cold. He had kissed her goodnight, outside her house, gently tilting her chin up towards his face. Isobel indulged herself and re-lived the shining moments they had shared.

Thomas looked down at his daughter, at the smile playing about her mouth. How young and vulnerable she seemed. 'Belle,' he said softly.

On the short journey home from the graveyard, neither of them spoke, seemingly lost in their own thoughts. It was in the kitchen while helping to prepare their evening meal that Isobel told her father she would prefer not to visit her mother's grave every time he went. He straightened up from lifting a dish from the oven, placed it on the hob and turning to look at her, smiled. 'I thought that's what you were going to say to me.'

'Daddy, I'm sorry. It's just that ... '

Her father put his hand up to stop her. 'Belle, you don't have to explain. I understand. I will go when I need to and you can come along whenever you want and I shan't hold it against you. I know you loved your mother and she would understand too.'

She went to him and gave him a kiss on his bristly cheek. 'Thanks Daddy. Are you sure?'

'Yes,' he replied firmly, looking into her eyes. 'I am.'

And with that the subject was closed, quite comfortably, for both of them.

The weeks passed by. The summer ended. Bill left for London and a new life. Perhaps because of Isobel's age, combined with Bill's complete and utter absorption with London, his work, new challenges, different and exciting people, their short but intense relationship came to an end. Isobel, who had declared ever-lasting love for him on their final evening together, thought her heart would break. Bill had told her he loved her and she had believed him, but as time went on she began to accept that she would lose him.

She and her father carried on, each with a pain deep inside. His, tempered with precious memories, futile regrets and sad resignation, and hers with vivid and almost tangible recollections of the young man who had utterly and completely stolen her heart. The two of them went for long, soothing walks by the sea. The ever-changing sky, the immense sweep of the beaches, sometimes with no other person in sight, and the water, with its myriad patterns of tides, familiar to them, but not to visitors, calmed or invigorated them. These moments always lifted them out of their despondency and reminded them of the magnitude of the world around them.

Bill's visits home became less and less frequent. The pain of his departures never lessened but as time went on they stopped writing to each other. They moved on into their separate worlds.

2

Would it be today? With a sudden, sharp certainty, he felt it would and put his foot down on the accelerator. The road shone in front of him like slate coloured silk, shimmering and moving, reflecting the oppressive sky that shifted and rolled overhead. The silhouettes of leafless trees stretched their branches above him; noduled, arthritic fingers, straining to touch each other across the narrow, winding country road; on through the soulless suburbs and along the brightly lit dual carriageway. He parked, grateful for the fact that Out Patient clinics had finished, which meant there were spaces He checked his phone – no message – and turned it off. Striding towards the massive, newly built atrium of the main entrance, he was conscious of a rising sense of foreboding. This walk to the Victorian wing of his old teaching hospital was so familiar. Today he was oblivious of his surroundings as he quickened his pace. Through the vast space, a cross between a motorway service station and an airport terminal, with almost as many eating outlets and shops, past a group of clinically obese members of staff tucking into their pies and chips and down the long corridor, disregarding the works of art on the walls and, in sculpture form, squatting in the small courtyard gardens outside. He was brought abruptly to a halt as a trolley laden with boxes blocked his way while the porter tried to manoeuvre the turn to the lifts.

The faint but recognisable odour assaulted his nostrils. Even with all the cleaning regulations, the undeniable fact was that old peoples' wards clung on to that sickly, stale smell of soiled beds and disintegrating bodies. He knew, more than most, that this was still the unglamorous end of the National Health Service. Dutifully rubbing some antiseptic gel into his hands, he moved aside as a doctor swung through the open door and, without a glance at the gel dispenser, rushed down the corridor. As he entered the ward, to his relief, he saw Kim, the nurse he knew and respected. He approached the nurses' station and Kim looked up. Tom knew then that his mother had died. It was something in Kim's expression – compassion maybe - and an almost imperceptible shaking of his head.

'I'm so sorry, Tom, I'm afraid your mother died a few moments ago. We tried to call you, but there was no reply from your mobile number, or your home number.' Tom recalled turning off his mobile as he had parked the car. So, it was today, after all.

'Are you OK? Would you like a moment to yourself – or shall I take you to her? She's still in the same side ward. I was with her when she died.' Tom looked at the tired face of this sensitive and kind person, who he knew from watching him, worked very hard to keep, not just the patients in his care comfortable and safe, but who supported and encouraged his team of nurses and the inexperienced and terrified junior doctors on his ward. He was grateful that Kim knew better than to try and console him by saying that his mother had died peacefully, but he was glad that she had not been alone in the end.

'I'm fine, thank you. I had this feeling, just now, on my way here, that I'd be too late. It happens so often doesn't it?'

Kim nodded. 'Yes, indeed. Strange, isn't it?'

The two were familiar with the scenario of relatives or friends who had either arrived too late, or who had been persuaded to 'pop out' for a cup of tea or for some fresh air, only to discover on their return that their loved one had died in their absence.

'I'll go to her then,' Tom said.

Kim led the way, passing a couple of nurses who glanced empathetically at the tall man on his way to see his dead mother. They had just tidied her up and made her 'presentable', knowing that her son was on his way. He had come every day.

The side ward was decorated in 1980's drab pink, blotchy wallpaper, with a faded and peeling flowered frieze at waist level. Someone had thoughtfully opened the window and sprayed some powerful air freshener around. It had always been an acrid citronella when he was training, but this had been replaced by a chemical sort of lavender. As he drew close to the bed he realised that this was not enough to mask the smell of infected wounds.

Kim silently left the room and closed the door. Tom looked at the small figure of his mother. The nurses had crossed her hands over her chest and placed a Bible and some limp freesias in a grubby, green plastic vase, on the table at the foot of the bed. Tom felt like two separate people as he looked, for the last time, at this woman, his mother, who had loved and supported him all his life, often through difficult and demanding times and who had always believed in him and encouraged him. On the one hand he was her son, and on the other he was a doctor, fully aware of the clinical details of the traumas she had endured over the last few weeks; the agony of a ruptured bowel, the faecal peritonitis, which, together with the stroke during surgery, had finally killed her. This intensely private and gracious woman had died a horrible death, slipping into unconsciousness in the side ward in the last few days. Tom had visited her every day, in Intensive Care and then in this room, and watched as she had gradually faded away from him and the increasingly remote possibility of a life which would have been hard for her to bear. Disabled by the stroke and living with a colostomy would not have been a life that she would have wanted.

He knew that it was his mother's absolute and often irrational fear of hospitals, and indeed the medical profession as a whole, that had prevented her from seeking help when she was in acute pain. This phobia, coupled with the attitude of his late father, had caused his mother to avoid medical investigations even when Tom had reasoned with her, as a doctor and as her son, to seek help. He wondered why, as an ex-nurse, she should hold such fears. Now, she was no longer with him. The church-candle wax skin was drawn tightly over her cheek bones and her mouth gaped slightly, her eyes sunken. Only her hands looked the same; hands that he suddenly remembered, he used to play with, removing and trying on her rings and then putting them carefully on the right fingers, while they sat together watching some children's programme on the television, or when she read to him. He could hear her soft, deep voice, reading with such expression and using different voices and accents for all the characters, so that they came alive in his young mind. He looked at the hands and felt a wave of deep sadness wash over him. His eyes ached and hot tears trickled down his face.

'Oh, Mum. I'm sorry I wasn't here. I love you,' he murmured, knowing that she could not hear him anymore, or ever again, but having to say it anyway. He bent towards her and kissed her forehead. 'Goodbye, goodbye, Mum,' he whispered as his tears fell on to her face. He straightened up and took a final look at her body. If only he had been able to intervene and make her seek treatment, if only ...

He knew that many people felt remorse, guilt even, when their parents died and why should he be an exception? It was so different from how he had felt when his father had died. He pushed away the thoughts of his father and walked slowly to the door; one last glance back at the tiny form in the bed and he left the room. Kim was waiting for him, as Tom knew he would be.

'Alright?' he asked.

'Yeah, thanks for all you did, Kim. You've been great ... you and your team. I wish there were more like you.'

'It was a privilege. I'm just sorry she's gone. We did our best for her. Professor Fraser asked me to give you his best wishes and his condolences. He's sorry he wasn't able to be here to see you himself, but he did ring and he asked me to be sure to pass on his message.'

'That's kind of him. Will you thank him too? He's a good man. He must be nearing retirement now,' Tom replied, feeling affection, as always, for his old teacher and mentor. 'Well, I'll head off. There is quite a lot to do, isn't there, when someone dies.'

'Indeed there is,' said Kim. 'We'll be taking her down to the mortuary as soon as you leave, so if you want to see her again, that's who to ring. OK?'

'Thanks again, Kim.' They shook hands and Tom walked to the door, passing other side rooms with frail and lonely people in them, waiting to go home or to die, whichever came first. He rubbed the antiseptic gel into his hands and left the ward.

He walked the same corridors as when he had come in and it was only when he had passed through the smoke screen provided by shivering patients in dressing gowns and some of their visitors, anxiously puffing away, just outside the main entrance, that he inhaled deeply the cold damp air. He gulped it in until his chest hurt. The car was cold and a fine drizzle needed intermittent wind screen wipers to clear his way. His neck was aching. He eased back against the head rest and lowered his shoulders.

Driving through the yellow street lights and eventually into the dark lanes towards his home, the headlights picked out the shimmering road once again. He suddenly remembered, with remarkable clarity, what the roads reminded him of – the colour of his mother's shiny, dark grey evening dress and himself watching her put on her discreet diamond jewellery and apply her lipstick in front of her dressing table mirror. He must have been about nine or ten, at a time when his parents went to dinners and cocktail parties – always to be told that it was, 'to do with Daddy's work.'

Using his hands-free he called Alex. 'Hi, it's me.'
'Were you in time?'

'No, but I had a feeling I wouldn't be.'

'Oh Tom, I'm so sorry.'

'Yeah, so am I. At least Kim was with her and I actually believe him. To be honest, she wasn't aware. I won't be more than about half an hour.'

'I'll have food ready.'

Tom realised he was hungry and that he really needed to get there, pour a drink and be enveloped in the comfort of his home.

'Tom, Sarah rang. Your phone was off. She'll be here in the morning, but she said she'll go straight to your Mum's place. I told her she was welcome here, but she said she'd rather go there and did Eileen still have a key.'

'Right, how did she sound? I'll call her to tell her Mum's gone. She never answers her phone. I don't want to tell her by just leaving a message'

Alex waited and then said steadily, 'Just get home. We'll talk then. There's nothing you can do till she gets here.'

'Yeah, I know, it's just so ... '

'I know. Drive carefully.'

Tom gripped the wheel and peered out into the night. His thoughts were jumbled. Had the surgery staff managed to get the locum? Alex will know, of course. He must ring the undertaker tomorrow. Oh God, Sarah! She had flown over from the States for their father's funeral and the relief when she had left had been immense. Where had it all gone so wrong? He sighed deeply as he reflected on his troubled relationship with his only sister. There had been no response to his repeated calls to her asking her to ring him back.

He was getting nearer home now. Unseen small houses and cottages, built with old, mellow Warwickshire red bricks and grey slate roofs, nestled in the blackened countryside and along the roadsides. At last his house fell into view. The curtains and blinds were still open and Alex had turned the garden and porch lights on. A warm glow from these lit his way and welcomed him home. As he approached the front door he could see Alex in the sitting room putting logs on the fire. Quite suddenly, he felt a lump in his throat and pain behind his eyes. He opened the door. Alex came out of the sitting room and simply held his arms out to him. Tom felt the strong, warm, enveloping embrace and the soothing words as he wept silently into Alex's shoulder.

'Come on, I've poured you a drink and food's nearly ready.' Alex helped him off with his coat and drew him into the sitting room. A glass of red wine was by the fire and Tom flopped into the deep armchair and kicked off his shoes.

'Thanks, Alex. I'm so glad to be home.' He smiled wanly at the calm figure watching him with gentle concern in his dark eyes.

The two men sat opposite each other as Tom talked about his mother and his last moments with her body. Alex listened and looked at his partner's weary face. Over supper, they ran through the list of things to be done the next day. As Tom had known he would, Alex had organised a locum. Frank, who stood in for them at the surgery on a regular basis and was liked by the patients, was going to cover all Tom's surgeries for the next week and could stay on for a couple of days after that, if necessary. Then, he had stated, with some relish, he was off to drive across Australia, with his wife, Mary; something they had wanted to do for years and now that their children were self-sufficient, they were, at last, off on their adventure.

'I wonder how she'll be ... Sarah, I mean,' Tom mused.

'You do know, Tom. She'll be like she always is, probably worse. Last time she was genuinely in mourning for your Dad. This time, you're no doubt going be on the receiving end of all her anger at Isobel. I'm quite surprised she's bothered to come over at all, especially as she doesn't know Isobel has died yet.'

'I know. It is odd. She no doubt has her reasons. D'you know, in all the years since Dad died, she hasn't contacted me once? The only times we've

29

spoken have been when I've called her. I'm not going to put up with her behaviour if she's on some vendetta of her own.'

Alex had heard these determined words about Sarah before and he knew how much it cost Tom to utter them. They did not hide the hurt he knew Tom felt. He looked across at the slim, tall man opposite, leaning back in his chair, sipping wine and focusing on some middle-distance speck across the room, as he narrowed his eyes, so vividly blue, even in the soft lamp light. Alex watched him run his elegant fingers through his short, thick, grey hair. He knew Tom was bracing himself for the next few days, tired as he was. Alex got up and took the plates through to the kitchen and loaded the dishwasher. Outside the rain had stopped and the clouds had cleared to reveal a multitude of twinkling stars. He stood at the window, looking out at the ghostly garden, the raindrops on the shrubs and potted plants which had hung on through winter, illuminated by the garden lights and the moon.

Wrapping a long woollen scarf around his neck he poured himself another glass of wine and stepped outside. His breath was visible in the sharp night air. He looked up, through the trees, to the stars and drank a silent toast to Isobel Gabriel, who had been so unwavering in her support and love for him and Tom. Now she was gone. He wondered how Tom would take it. Sarah would be here for a while, until after the funeral at least. A swift shudder of anxiety passed through him at the thought of what undoubtedly lay ahead.

Tom was sitting resting his head on the back of the chair, eyes closed, when Alex went back into the sitting room. He drew the heavy curtains and locked the doors. He and Tom had lived for five years in the Victorian house, described as a 'cottage' in the estate agent's glossy brochure, he remembered, with a wry smile. A cottage implied a small dwelling, but this house had space and had felt big as they had gradually re-decorated and furnished the rooms, enjoying bringing warmth and character, with treasures found in local reclamation yards and antique shops. They had settled into village life, or rather on the periphery of that way of life - just enough to be polite - but managing to retain the privacy they both craved, happy at the end of the day to leave their busy town practice and all the challenges of a surgery situated on the edge of a large housing estate.

They had worked together as partners, building what had been a rundown practice, into a new, thriving medical centre, offering a range of services. Suzie, their part-time partner, was essential, as most of the women who came to the surgery requested a female doctor. They employed two practice nurses and a team of four receptionists and Doug, a rather formidable, but highly efficient practice manager. The Community team of nurses and other Primary Care professionals were on site in the newly built premises and most of the time everything ticked along smoothly. They were meeting their targets, so keeping the Government happy and they felt that they delivered professional and easily accessible care to their patients.

As a result, they were both wiped out on many occasions, but somehow their relationship remained in balance – strong and supportive. Alex knew that Tom would not want to take time off, but he also knew that he needed to. Over the last week, as Isobel's condition had deteriorated, Tom had travelled each day, after surgeries, to be with her. Now Sarah would be around and Alex knew that Tom would need even more support. Sarah had always managed to get under Tom's skin. Alex had never quite fathomed out what exactly caused this friction between the two siblings, but over the years had often felt relief that Sarah lived so far away and that they rarely met. He struggled sometimes to remain passive when she hurt the man he loved. He switched off the lights and wandered back into the sitting room. The fire was fading now. Tom's eyes were fixed on the disappearing red glow, his wine left unfinished.

Alex gently shook Tom's arm.

'Come on - sleep.'

3

Tom opened his eyes and within seconds his heart was racing. He swung his legs over the side of the bed, aware, without glancing at the clock, that he had overslept. As his brain cleared, he realised Alex had gone off to morning surgery, and that he didn't need to. The image of his mother, lying with her hands crossed over her chest and the Bible at the end of the bed, flashed through his mind. He stayed sitting for a moment, collecting his thoughts. Today he had things to do and Sarah to meet. He grabbed his dressing gown from behind the door and padded downstairs to the kitchen. A note from Alex saying he would catch up with him later lay on the table. Tom switched the kettle on and spooned some coffee into the cafetiere. He went into the study and turned on the computer. Checking the arrivals, he saw that Sarah's flight had landed on time, which meant that she would be on her way by train to their mother's house. Tom knew it would never occur to Sarah to call him and ask for a lift from the airport or the station.

Half an hour later, Tom had drunk coffee, eaten some toast, shaved and showered. Throwing on warm and comfortable clothes he gathered up his keys and set off for his mother's house. He stopped at the village store on the way. At least he could make sure the house was warm and that there was some fresh bread, milk and fruit for Sarah. He bought some soup as well, to be on the safe side. Isobel's house was the one she had shared with her husband for forty years and where she had stayed for the last fifteen years on her own since his death. Over many years she had sympathetically restored the house and had coaxed and nurtured the large back garden until it was the most beautiful and tranquil space, filled with sweet-smelling, quintessentially English flowers, trees and shrubs. It was the house that Tom and Sarah had grown up in and most of the careful upkeep had paid off once they had passed the age of playing with friends in the garden. Isobel had been more than content to allow toys and footballs and all the messy detritus of childhood to take precedence over horticultural excellence. They had attended the local schools and stayed in the house until they had left to pursue their careers. Sarah had chosen London where she had studied law. She now worked in America for a pre-eminent and well established Boston firm. Tom had stayed in the Midlands to study medicine.

Tom parked the car at the front of the tall, cream, stuccoed Regency house. The 'Sold' sign was stuck into the ground beside the elegant wrought iron railings. Well, he thought, at least this was sorted before Mum died. Was it relief or just sadness that he felt when he thought of the small ground floor flat that she had been about to move into? They had almost argued over her decision to sell the house, but she had been insistent that she no longer wanted to live in such a large place and really looked forward to living somewhere more manageable. The flat they had found was indeed very suitable for someone on their own. They hadn't signed a contract, following the advice of the estate agent that they should sell the big house first; that it would sell quickly. He had families looking for just this sort of period house with good schools nearby. He had proved to be an optimist and the slow-down in house sales had meant that they had settled for less than the original asking price. Everything had then happened very quickly. The next step would have been signing the contract on the flat. Now, that would not happen, but the big house was going to have a new life, with children once more.

Tom turned the key and entered. The unexpected smell of fresh coffee wafted towards him. He heard a radio playing softly in the kitchen at the end of the long hallway. A large suitcase stood by the bottom of the stairs ... Sarah. He felt a tightening knot in his stomach. And at the same time, irritation with himself, that his sister could still have this effect on him. How the hell had she got here so soon.

'Hello!' he called. 'Sarah?' He walked towards the kitchen, where he saw his sister sitting at the table, both hands wrapped around a mug of coffee, gazing out of the window to the garden.

'Who else.' she said. 'Surprised to see me?'

'Well, yes, I am. I thought you only landed this morning.'

'I did. I was working in New York, so I flew from Newark to Birmingham, picked up a car and here I am. Eileen gave me the key and actually, I was hoping to close my eyes before calling you as I'm dead on my feet, but you've buggered that up, surprise, surprise, so you may as well tell me the latest. I was planning to go and see Mum after I'd rested and showered.'

Tom looked at her, noticing the sleek, unruffled clothes, the glossy, dark hair and immaculate makeup, even though she had just come off an overnight flight. No offer of a hug or a kiss on the cheek to greet him, just her usual caustic tone and sardonic expression. It was suddenly tempting just to state, 'Mum's dead,' but Tom knew he couldn't do that, so he went to Sarah and bent down to kiss her cool, moisturised cheek, catching a hint of her perfume as he did so.

'Hi, Sarah, good to see you. I just presumed you'd come to Heathrow and get here a bit later. I've brought some milk and stuff.'

'No need,' Sarah sighed. 'I'll call in somewhere on the way back from the hospital.'

Tom sat down opposite his sister and looked at her closely. Sarah looked back and narrowed her eyes as she studied his face.

'Sarah. I'm afraid Mum died yesterday evening. I'm so sorry you weren't here, but she was very peaceful at the en ... '

'What! Why the bloody hell didn't you tell me to come over earlier?' She stood up and strode across

36

the kitchen to the sink. Clattering her mug on to the draining board, she turned back towards Tom, tension in every part of her. 'You're a bloody doctor, for God's sake. Surely you could have seen this coming and told me to get the hell over here!'

'Actually, I couldn't. She deteriorated very quickly, Sarah. The last couple of times I left you a message to try and warn you that she was sinking fast, there was no reply. And I tried to speak to you last night. I thought it would be better to tell you myself ... not just leave another message.'

'Well, I came as quickly as I could. My God, Tom, if you'd warned me earlier I could have re-scheduled. Of course, you no doubt wanted to be with her on your own. Why does that surprise me! So, our mother's dying moments were with her darling son – how sweet!'

'Actually, no, I arrived too late.' Tom stated quietly, immediately regretting the words.

Sarah stared at her brother. 'Christ Almighty, Tom. You're not that far from the hospital. You're a doctor. You had been going in regularly ... and she died alone?' She spat the words at him. 'Well, I'm bloody glad you're not my doctor!'

Turning back to the sink she ran water into the mug and then swung round again. 'Was *anyone* with her?'

Tom looked sadly at her. 'Yes, Kim, one of the nurses. He'd been really good to Mum and he's a good nurse.'

'Well, good for Kim!' Sarah replied, her words heavy with sarcasm.

A tangible silence fell between them. Tom looked at her back as she busied herself drying her mug, twisting the tea towel vigorously round and round the inside.

'We have to talk, Sarah. There's a lot to sort out. I was on my way to the undertaker, so do you want to come with me?'

'Why? What's the point? You know what to do. I need to collect some stuff from here. Have you been through her papers?' Sarah stared at her brother.

'No, not yet,' and suddenly angry, 'she only died last night, Sarah!'

There was another stiff moment of silence between them and then Sarah moved towards the sitting room, her heels clicking on the tiled floor and speaking over her shoulder. 'Have you got the key to Mum's desk? I can't see it anywhere.'

'No, but I can get it. She kept it hidden in a fake tin of baked beans at the back of the cupboard.' Tom smiled as he thought of Isobel tucking valuables into bags of rice and flour and then forgetting about them. More than once he had found her emptying these bags into bowls in an attempt to find a key or a piece of jewellery, that she swore was safer there while she was away visiting friends, or on holiday.

'Do you remember, Sarah, how Mum used to hide things in ... '

'Yes, yes. I don't need to hear it all again, Tom. We really do need to find all the legal stuff in here. The sooner the funeral is over the sooner we can move on. Thank God the bloody house sale has gone through. Come on, Tom, cough it up. Let's get cracking.'

Tom went to find the tin he knew held the key to his mother's desk, taken aback, not for the first time, at his sister's brittle lack of sensitivity.

'Was there something in particular you wanted to find?' he asked as he fished around in the cupboard.

'Not really, but you know how organised Mum was. She is bound to have left some instructions for us in the event of her death.'

Tom accepted this without commenting further. Whatever his sister had in mind, he really didn't care. She had always gone her own way and he had to agree this time – their mother had been very organised and neat and tidy. He heard Sarah's outburst as he found the key.

'For God's sake, Tom, step into the real world, will you! My God! It was bad enough growing up with you. Can't you, for once, think about how I might be feeling right now?'

Tom resignedly stayed quiet. For too many years he had worried about what Sarah was feeling and only in the last few years had he accepted that theirs was never going to be a close relationship. He felt great sadness and regret, but he also knew that Sarah's coldness towards him was of her own choosing and for her own unfathomable reasons.

Sarah waited by the elegant, eighteenth century, French mahogany desk, so cherished by their mother, who had inherited if from her grandmother. Isobel was of the generation of women who still wrote letters regularly to her friends all over the world. Fleetingly, Sarah felt a pang of nostalgia and recalled standing next to her mother, as a small girl, asking who she was writing to and her mother explaining about someone called Bunty, who lived a long way away in South Africa and who had been at school with Isobel. All her mother's friends seemed to have funny names – Dottie, Biddy, Hettie - but then there was Mary, which was a name that Sarah knew from friends of her own. It was Mary who went to live in Tasmania. She had asked where that was and Isobel had got out the atlas to show her and Sarah had watched her mother cry as she wrote to that friend. Sarah had collected stamps from the letters received by her mother and had placed them, with extreme care and orderliness, in a large stamp album which she guarded possessively from her brother.

She shook herself out of her reverie and glanced up as Tom walked in with the key. Sarah was only too aware that she hurt people, especially those closest to her, but somehow the more she acknowledged uncomfortable truths about herself, the more she shrugged them off and concentrated on the practicalities of her deliberately busy life. She was irritated even by the sight of Tom – not his fault, of course – but it had always been so. When they were growing up, Sarah had been intensely jealous of her young brother and this jealousy had never been addressed openly by their parents. She had manipulated their father quite blatantly, and used him as an ally, always knowing that she could melt his heart when it suited her to do so. On the other hand, Isobel, in her quiet way, had always seemed able to see through Sarah, as if she knew what Sarah was thinking. Sarah had bullied and blackmailed Tom over many years when they were small – pinching or kicking him when no one was looking, hiding his favourite toys, threatening to tell their parents when Tom was persuaded, by Sarah, to steal some chocolate from the sweet cupboard – little, seemingly inconsequential things, that lots of siblings get up to, but which terrified the quiet, sensitive little boy. Isobel had quite firmly drawn an invisible, protective arm around him, in an attempt to shield him from his self-contained and domineering sister, whom Isobel loved and whom she knew was not quite as confident as she appeared. What Sarah had resented most of all was her mother's protection of Tom. Edward's fatherly love for her was not enough. She knew as she got older and when she left the family home that Isobel had also tried to protect Tom from their father.

Tom unlocked the desk and lowered the front down, revealing the tidy contents. Sarah stared at the few neatly piled pieces of paper and envelopes. 'She has had a tidy-up! I don't remember it ever looking so empty.'

Tom had been under the impression that Isobel had been putting her house in order ever since their father had died.

'Sarah,' he said, quite suddenly not wanting to be part of this search through his mother's papers. 'I really have to collect the death certificate and contact the solicitor ... you know ... all that sort of stuff. If you're sure you don't want to come with me, I think I'll go and get that over with. Will you be OK here? I'm sure you can sort out a few things on your own.'

'Well, it looks like Mum has done that for us, doesn't it? I mean there's nothing here.' Sarah pulled open the drawers, all of which were empty. Tom paused by the front door and called back, knowing what his sister's response would be, but still feeling he should offer.

'You know you are welcome to stay with Alex and me?' There was no reply from Sarah. 'Well, at least come and have a meal while you're here ... perhaps?' Why am I doing this, he mused. I know what she'll say!

'Tom,' Sarah came to the sitting room door. She looked at him with a thinly veiled expression of exasperation on her face. 'I'm knackered after the flight and, to be honest, I've got a pile of papers to go through. I've booked myself into a hotel. This place is cold! I don't suppose I'll need to be here for long if you get your act together and we sort the funeral quickly.

'Right,' Tom said as he opened the front door. I'll be back as soon as I can. Have you got a mobile number you can use over here, just in case?'

They exchanged numbers and Tom stepped out into the dank February air. He walked to his car, closing the gate behind him, conscious of a sense of release to be out of the house and away from Sarah.

Sarah watched him go and then turned back to the desk. She sat down with a sigh and began the process of sorting through her mother's documents. She knew she had been hard on Tom and that he was feeling the loss of their mother more deeply than she was, but she also knew that in time he would be fine and he and Alex would resume what she perceived to be their idyllic life together. The bitter bile of jealousy seeped into her once more. She tried to suppress it, but a gush of emotion quite suddenly overcame her and hot, angry, unwanted tears scalded her eyes. The papers became blurred and her head thumped.

'Oh, God. Not now!' She got up, the chair tumbling backwards to the floor as she stalked through to the kitchen and, struggling with the heavy lock on the back door, stepped out into the tranquil garden, gasping and gulping in an attempt to stem the flood of tears. She stood still, breathing deeply and at last, evenly, mustering up all the techniques she could recall from her years of therapy. Through the turmoil in her head she gave a wry smile to herself as she thought, not for the first time, of the vast fortune she had given to various counsellors, psychotherapists, gurus, healers and many more practitioners over the last few years.

She turned back into the kitchen, reached into her bag and retrieved a packet of cigarettes. Clutching her lighter she once again stepped into the garden. She inhaled deeply, steadfastly refusing to let the guilty feelings invade. She gazed around her mother's handiwork, beautiful, even in winter. Isobel had had such a knack of placing plants and shrubs in just the right place and had chosen them carefully so that even today there was colour. Sarah only knew one or two by name and, perversely, spent the next half an hour trying to identify them. She gave up after jasmine and snowdrops. She thought of her Boston apartment, with no garden and inside, just some glossy, green houseplants, carefully chosen by her friend, Stella, an interior designer and which were only kept alive because Juliana, her cleaner, cared for them.

Five days later, remarkably quickly, considering the usual backlog of bodies for disposal in the winter months, Isobel was cremated. She had written a carefully worded letter to Sarah and Tom expressing her wish for a quiet funeral. The young curate from one of the local churches had made the effort to talk to Tom and Sarah about their mother and officiated with sensitivity and wise understanding beyond her tender years. Tom was touched at the number of people who managed to attend and at the tributes and genuinely affectionate words spoken about his mother. Many of her friends had died in recent years, but she had continued to sing in a local community choir and had, for many years, held regular meetings of her reading group, which had always included younger people. The choir had asked if they could sing at her funeral, and in the absence of any formal service, this wonderful sound held the whole procedure together, for which Tom was grateful. One of the young men who had attended the reading group for the last couple of years and who had sometimes accompanied Isobel to Cheltenham or Hay, to indulge their passion for literature, read some words he had written in her memory and his obvious grief at the loss of this older woman seemed to touch everyone there. Sarah seemed satisfied that the whole occasion had passed off smoothly. There was a small and short gathering of people after the cremation which was when they both were reminded that their mother had been held in high esteem and genuine affection by all those she knew.

Much to Sarah's indignation, but not to her surprise, Tom and the family solicitor were the executors of Isobel's will. Nothing out of the ordinary emerged from it, with all Isobel's assets being divided equally between her two children, with a few hundred pounds to a couple of charities. Isobel had requested that her ashes be scattered by the sea in North Norfolk. Tom and Sarah were surprised that this most undemanding of women should have stated her request quite so specifically, but concluded that as Norfolk was where their mother had been born and had always talked of so fondly, it made sense.

'You'll have to do that bit on your own, Tom,' Sarah stated emphatically. 'I've got to get back and to be perfectly honest I don't go along with all this nonsense of scattering ashes.' Tom knew this to be true and would have been amazed if Sarah had said anything different.

The next day he approached Sarah as she was preparing to leave, keeping his voice deliberately light, to avoid putting any pressure on her. He knew the probable response but a small glimmer of hope persuaded him to ask her anyway.

'Sarah, why don't you come and have supper with Alex and me tonight? Goodness knows when we'll see you again and it would be nice to have an evening together.'

Sarah looked at her brother, noting the lines around his eyes and across his forehead. Despite this, he still looked very like the boy she had grown up with; the bright blue eyes, the curly hair, which she had so envied when she had hated her own lank, dark hair. She recalled looking at Tom's thick, long eyelashes, with the same envy and a deep sense of injustice that her brother should be blessed with these and other attributes; his kindness and generous attitude towards people, which she could never master. She sighed and pushed away her images of the past, as she had done for so long now that it required little effort. She immediately felt in control once more.

'I think not, Tom. Thanks all the same. I spoke to Alex at the funeral and I have decided to stay near the airport tonight anyway.'

Tom knew not to try and persuade Sarah. He felt again the deep sadness that came over him when he thought about his sister, for so long removed from his life, by her own choice. Sarah gathered up the few old photographs she had decided, at the last moment, to take with her. Tom had invited her to look through these at her leisure and to take whatever she wanted. She had opted for one of her parents on their wedding day and two or three of the family on holiday – sunny, squinting pictures - no others. He wondered if she realised how much her rejection of him hurt.

'You have the rest if you want. I can't see the point of keeping masses of old photos myself. I can remember all I need to.'

She turned away from him and busied herself folding Isobel's clothes to take to the charity shop. Tom watched her, knowing this was her way of coping, and making himself respect her for it.

He had tried, as had their mother, over the years, to offer support and love, but somehow, she had not ever been able to relate to them, nor indeed, he felt sure, to anyone close to her now. With a heavy heart he faced the fact that they seemed to be drifting ever more apart. He knew that with the death of their mother it was unlikely they would meet again and this realisation made him desperate.

'Sarah, I know you have your own way of coping and I respect that, but ... '

She swung round to face him, her eyes black with emotion.

'If you know, Tom, then why do you persist in trying to make me talk to you; fall back into some cosy, sibling relationship? I manage - OK? That's all I have to do - and carry on with the work I happen sometimes to quite enjoy. I don't have to take on relationships to make other people happy. I have to survive this God–awful life in the best way I can. Let me go back to my life and you get on with yours!' She paused and looked at him, softening slightly. 'Tom, it's not as if we have ever been close, is it? Bloody horrible things happening in our lives are not going to make us suddenly become comfortable with each other ... however much you would like that. You have got to stop trying to make things better, just so you can feel more comfortable. I should have thought, as a doctor, you would have realised by now that actually sometimes you just can't!'

He walked with her out of their family home to the car. She turned and looked up at him. Light drizzle fell softly and somewhere a police car siren wailed.

'Bye, Tom.' Sarah reached up and kissed him on the cheek. He put his arms around her and held her stiff, unyielding body to him for a moment.

'Bye, Sarah,' he mumbled into her hair. 'Look after yourself. Keep in touch. I'll email you?'

'Yep, sure,' she replied as she extricated herself and got into the driving seat.

Tom stepped back from the kerb and watched as she drove off down the road. He felt desolate. His eyes filled with tears. The ache in his throat was almost welcome. It was physical pain and he needed it. After Sarah's car had turned the corner at the bottom of the road, he made his way into the house, closed the front door, stepped over the packing boxes and sat at the kitchen table.

He had long ago ceased to receive Sarah's words as a personal affront. He had learned to accept that her behaviour and attitudes were her responsibility and not his, nor anyone else's, for that matter. But, even now, he held on to a glimmer of hope that she would unbend and allow herself to be closer to him.

He reflected on Sarah's harsh words and acknowledged that there was truth in what she had said about him always wanting to make things better. He knew that this irritated people and he really did not know why he felt this way. He knew enough psychology to understand that his father's cold and distant attitude towards him had moulded his character to some extent, but also that his mother had always given him all the love and security any child could wish for. Was this need to make things better why he had gone into medicine, he wondered, not for the first time. Alex had often told him that there was nothing wrong with wanting to help and that more people should be like that. They had talked many times over the years about family relationships

He rose from the table, glanced around and said out loud, 'Oh Mum, how did you manage to be so calm and wise and loyal to all your family?' He shook himself. 'Right - time to go.' He loaded up the car with the boxes for the charity shop, locked the house and set off. The feeling of resignation about Sarah was a familiar one and Tom knew he now had to concentrate on the remaining business surrounding his mother's death and then to get back to work. He missed the bustle of the surgery and the privilege of seeing people who had come to him in need. Tom and Alex had both worked with health professionals who were quite simply in the wrong job. These were the doctors and nurses who somehow managed to climb up the professional ladder without showing any compassion towards the people in their care. The arrogance of some of them was astounding and the lack of empathy distressing to witness. Tom remembered how relieved he was when he had worked alongside Alex and seen someone who maintained such an honest and sensitive approach to those in his care.

Their surgery was a training practice and so had regular visits from medical students to gain experience in Primary Care and have the opportunity of seeing 'real patients'. Tom and Alex both enjoyed this aspect of their work and attended the regular training sessions for post-graduate doctors. They often came across students who were obviously doing and saying all the right things to a patient –

going through the motions as they had been taught – but by rote. Then, just occasionally, a student would engage with the patient and communicate as if they really cared. Tom and Alex had got to the stage where they could pretty much spot a potentially 'good doctor' as they walked into the room. Much to their satisfaction the numbers of this type of person were slowly increasing. The students who had been pushed into medicine, usually by ambitious parents, quite often by parents who themselves were in the medical profession, were often the ones who struggled with the patient-doctor relationship, as their preconception of how a doctor behaves was invariably their parents' view.

Having off-loaded his mother's belongings at the charity shop, Tom headed for the surgery. As he drove along the quiet roads the thin February sun crept out from behind heavy clouds. By the time he pulled into the surgery car park his head had cleared and he felt more than ready for the practice meeting which he knew would have started. He entered the staff room and saw his colleagues munching away on the fresh sandwiches which were always bought from the delicatessen down the road. They all looked up at him and in their own way offered support, with tentative smiles, a nod of the head, or just a gentle, 'Hi Tom.' He had received cards or letters from each of them and a rambling rose to plant in the garden in memory of Isobel – tender and thoughtful gestures for which he was grateful. He pulled up a chair next to Alex and accepted food and a strong coffee gratefully, suddenly realising he was famished.

4

Thomas Armstrong was well known and well liked in the small coastal town. He was the only chemist and had built up a strong feeling of trust and respect with his many regular customers. After Peggy's death, he had been astonished at the outpouring of kind wishes and deeds, sometimes from the most unexpected of sources – people whom he hardly knew. Despite having been aware of his late wife's increasingly ambivalent attitude towards the church, Thomas found great solace in the welcoming and unquestioning haven it presented after her death. He played the old reed organ and spent increasing amounts of time keeping at arm's length the older and unattached women, all eager to care for him. He still visited Peggy's grave but as time went on he became more at peace and able to embrace life without her.

And then the day he had been dreading arrived. Isobel burst into the shop, the bell clanging, as she slammed the door behind her.

51

'I've been accepted!' She beamed at her father. Thomas smiled and calmly took the letter from her to scan the page and read the words telling him that his daughter would be leaving.

'Congratulations, Belle. It's a wonderful hospital and I know you'll enjoy Cambridge.'

Six months later, Isobel was gazing out of the window of her small room in the Nurses' Home, which overlooked the entrance to the mortuary. She had realised very soon after arriving in Cambridge that her father was going to be alright without her. She knew there was no shortage of people to offer support and companionship. The days spent together, on his occasional visits, were treasured. She allowed her father to show her around, even though she was increasingly familiar with all the sights and Cambridge never failed to charm them.

Nursing suited Isobel, despite the stringent rules and regulations. She made friends who were to last a lifetime. She indulged in brief and light-hearted romances with a range of men, mostly undergraduates, whom she outgrew and who disappeared for long stretches between terms, leaving Cambridge to revel in its quiet, gentle pace of life. There were doctors, of course, but Isobel found them generally to be rather full of their own importance and always with a slightly distracted air when you tried to engage in conversation with them, as if their minds were actually on something else. There seemed to be an unspoken class issue too. Isobel formed the opinion that, for some of the people she worked with, the daughter of a chemist from a seaside town in Norfolk did not quite fit the bill.

She spent her first stretch of night duty on the Ear, Nose and Throat Ward. Despite her loathing of sleeping in the day, she found the peace of the hospital at night a welcome change from the bustle of day duty. As a first year student nurse her job was to care for the small patients in one large room of the ward. These were the 'T's and A's' – children who had had their tonsils and adenoids removed. They had their temperatures and pulses taken every thirty minutes until midnight and then hourly. With ten hot and restless little bodies to keep calm and comfortable in their cream painted metal beds, all with cot sides up, Isobel had her work cut out. The smell of that room, the dried blood, the occasional post-operative haemorrhage, sometimes a particularly fragile and terrified child, and the memories of one particular night, stayed with Isobel. For ever afterwards she could recall the atmosphere in that room and the snoring, snuffling, sleeping children. Every now and then the Staff Nurse in charge would require Isobel to assist her with adult patients in the other rooms. Isobel was terrified of the man with the tracheostomy and watched in admiration as her colleague used the suction machine to remove mucus from his increasingly bubbling wind pipe. As she progressed through her training Isobel often reflected on her first spell of 'nights' and recalled how unsure and insecure she had been then.

It was after a day of fitful sleep on the last Saturday of January 1953, that she heard, in the buzz of conversation in the dining room, about the tidal flooding of the East coast of England. Isobel had not checked her pigeon hole, so was unaware of the note someone had put in it, to say that her father had phoned to say he was fine. She ran to the telephone kiosk in the nurses' home to ring him. Hearing his voice, calm and measured, was such a relief.

'I'm fine, my dear and so is the shop. We're fortunate. Home is safe too. Good job we live on the hill. The houses by the marshes are flooded. We are doing all we can to help. Now, don't you worry. I'm alright. You get on with your important work too.'

At her meal break, in the early hours, more news had trickled in and by the next day everyone was talking about it. There had been hundreds of deaths and many servicemen, including the Americans still based near the small town where her father's chemist shop was located, had struggled for hours, trying to reach people. Isobel spoke again to her father at the shop. The sea front of the town had been badly damaged, the fairground completely swept away and even the railway line had been submerged for a time. Isobel wanted desperately to go home, but knew, even as she asked, that Home Sister would not agree.

'Nurse Armstrong, there are people who have no choice but to go to their loved ones and try to rebuild their lost homes and start afresh. Be thankful that you and your father are safe. Your first duty is to your patients – here in this hospital.'

That night, as Isobel gazed down at her charges, who were all mending now, in the straightforward way of children, she thought of the people on the East coast of England and said a silent prayer for them.

There were invitations pinned on the notice board in the nurses' home, inviting them to dances at the RAF station, which was situated a few miles out of Cambridge. It was at one of these dances, in 1956, that Isobel met the man she was to marry. Edward Gabriel stood out from the crowd of senior officers who were surveying the dancers. He was by far the most attractive man in the packed mess that served as a dance hall for these hectic events. Isobel had spotted him and so had her friends. He had dark curly hair and treacle brown eyes and Isobel couldn't quite believe her luck when she watched him approach, immaculate in his Squadron Leader's uniform, which seemed to her to be far smarter than anyone else's. He reached the small group of friends she was with and looked directly at her.

'Hello. I'm Edward. Would you like to dance?'

A year later they were married in the Methodist church in her home town; Isobel's dainty frame enshrouded in a full-skirted dress of ivory silk taffeta with a sweetheart neckline and her dark shiny hair held back from her face by a delicate seed pearl headdress and the long veil her mother had worn in 1925. The ladies of the church had insisted on arranging the flowers and so the whole place was filled with the scent of lilies, roses, stocks and Norfolk lavender. Edward had finished his time in the RAF and was working as a director of his father's engineering firm in the Midlands.

After the reception in the hotel overlooking the sea, Isobel, Edward and Thomas went to the small churchyard in the nearby village, where Isobel laid her bouquet on her mother's grave and said a silent goodbye. She knew she would not be visiting that little corner of her past life very often. She found the hug from her father, as they bade each other a tearful goodbye, almost overwhelmingly sad. They left him there at the lytch gate, with a brave smile on his face and a hand raised in farewell, as Edward put his foot down and his Glacier Blue MGA Roadster – a wedding present from his father - roared off down the hedge-lined road to their honeymoon. Edward's father had slapped his son on the back and in his jokey, singularly insensitive way, had remarked bombastically that, 'a man needs to have *some* fun after he gets married!'

It was a whirlwind of glamorous hotels and sights to see, starting with their first night in Claridges in an immaculately shining Art Deco suite. They went on to Nice, which was hot and crowded. As if Edward had known that this would be the case they ended their travels in the mountains of Switzerland, where the air was sweet and the crowds less pressing. Isobel felt she could breathe at last. They relished in free and uninhibited sex, tumbling into bed, or sharing a bath or shower at whatever time of day they wanted and talking together on long walks in the mountains. Isobel felt happy and exhilarated. She suddenly felt stunningly attractive and glowing. The hotel staff were delighted to have the young honeymoon couple in their care and smiled benignly and knowingly each time they saw them.

It was not long after their return to England and to the Midlands that Isobel felt, deep inside, the unwelcome and uncomfortable stirrings of doubt and discontent. At first everything had been busy and exciting. She showed a natural flair for home-making and a much admired talent for interior design. The handsome house was lovingly furnished and decorated, holding on to its grace and character. Isobel had given up trying to persuade Edward that she could do some nursing, that she had too much time on her hands. Edward's response was at first gentle and persuasive, but as time went on he became increasingly adamant and impatient with his wife, whom he now realised was more spirited than he had thought and could even be quite opinionated. This did not sit comfortably with Edward, nor, he was sure, with his friends and business acquaintances who dined with them. In fact, most of these people admired Isobel's spirit and found her a refreshingly informed and interesting conversationalist.

Isobel attended cookery lessons at Edward's insistence, even though she was a competent cook and loved experimenting with food. Edward's mother, Helen, had booked Isobel on to the short Cordon Bleu course in London.

'Think of it as my little wedding present to you, my dear. You will have to cook for Edward's foreign visitors just like I have for Arthur.'

This dainty, compliant woman, described by Edward's father, when he had first met her, as a 'pretty little thing', was delighted to have a daughter-in-law. She had almost given up hoping that Edward would settle down and was relieved that he had at last found himself a wife - at the grand old age of thirty five.

Isobel survived the rigours and petty rules of the cookery classes. Why she had to learn the French names for everything she did not understand. She would never use them at home. She found some of the cooking fascinating and some quite repulsive. Quite at home with fish dishes, she felt distinctly squeamish about handling sweetbreads or liver and kidney. Moments of freedom were filled with late dashes into a gallery or museum. She had insisted to Edward that she could stay with her old nursing friend, Mary, who worked as a Staff Nurse at St Thomas's, rather than at Edward's parents' pied-a-terre, a colourless and claustrophobic flat in a Victorian mansion block in Chelsea. Edward and his parents indulged what they felt was Isobel's lack of confidence in a city environment, because, after all, they surmised, she was quite an innocent, having been brought up in Norfolk.

Mary and Isobel shared a comfortable and laughter-filled time. Mary had arranged her shifts so that they could spend as much time together as possible. They went to the cinema to see 'The Barretts of Wimpole Street'.

'Bill Travers is gorgeous. Completely wrong for that part, mind you! I wonder if I'll ever meet someone tall, dark and handsome.' Mary mused. 'It's alright for you, Izzy. You already have! Edward is very good looking!'

'Yes, he is.' Isobel said quietly.

Cheap but tasty evening meals were eaten, either in a small, Greek, family restaurant nearby, or by the fire in Mary's tiny but cosy flat.

'I never, ever want to cook, or eat, or even see, anything in aspic, ever again!' Isobel stated between mouthfuls of Mary's attempt at a cheese omelette. 'This is so delicious!'

They chatted about their training and the fun they had had, the sad and difficult moments and the nicknames everyone was given. No one kept their full name but some were kinder than others. Isobel had grown bored with the old, 'Isobel necessary on a bicycle?' comment and had got used to being called 'Izzy' but she felt for her friend whose nickname from day one in their Preliminary Training School was 'Mare.' She knew that some of their set delighted in using this name because (and even Isobel could not deny this) Mary did have large teeth and did have a habit of throwing her head back and letting forth a whinnying sort of laugh. Mary, who was not as impervious to this mockery as she appeared, just got on with her life, as she always had. London suited her. Isobel recognised a new-found confidence and contentment. She could not help envying Mary's freedom, despite her long shifts at the hospital, to live her life the way she wanted. Their time together passed all too quickly.

Mary looked carefully at Isobel as they waited for the train.

'I wish you could stay longer, Izzy.'

Isobel smiled at the tall, kind person, with her wild, chestnut hair tumbling around her head. She recalled how it was always escaping from the ridiculous caps they had had to wear, causing Ward Sisters throughout the hospital to complain.

'Me too.' Isobel hugged Mary, tears welling up. She blinked them away.

'I'll come again, and you must come and stay with us.'

The two young women held on to their embrace as the train pulled in to the platform.

'Bye, Mary. Thank you so much for everything. I'll write, and please, let's meet again soon.'

Mary watched as Isobel found her compartment. Edward had insisted she travel First Class. Isobel came to the open window. They both smiled bravely at each other for the few awkward moments when there can be no meaningful conversation because of the noise. Isobel reached out to hold hands. She smiled brightly as the wheels began to turn. Mary watched until she could not see Isobel's wave any longer. Turning to walk out and into London's busy streets, she reflected on the past week. She knew that she and Izzy would remain friends forever, despite their lives going in such different directions. They had that bond, often found between nurses – a sisterhood and lasting and genuine fondness for each other. As she breathed in the crisp air, her niggling concern for what she considered an already stifling set of relationships in Izzy's life was countered by the sudden and liberating sense of freedom in her own.

Edward was waiting by the car as Isobel walked out of the station. He took her case and kissed her, giving her shoulder a little squeeze.

'Well, here you are. How was the cooking?' He did not wait for a reply.

'Looking forward to some decent meals now! Hope you can remember everything they've taught you. Mother and Pa are coming round for dinner tomorrow so you can show off your new skills.'

5

When Isobel found she was pregnant, Edward was delighted, as were his parents. They all fussed around her as if she was an invalid. Helen had only just hung on to her babies and had ended up having caesarean sections. She was in terror of anything medical and considered pregnancy to be an illness. During the queasy first three months Isobel didn't mind their over-attentiveness, but at around fourteen weeks into the pregnancy she began to feel more energised and took to walking every day, sometimes for miles, through green parks and around the older areas of the pretty Regency town. On a blisteringly hot day in the long summer of 1959, their daughter was born in the Maternity Wing of the local hospital. The labour was long but uncomplicated. Isobel was supported by a wise and capable Scottish midwife, who soothed, coaxed and guided the new mother with great patience and expertise. Not until she was satisfied that both mother and baby were clean and tidy did Nurse invite Edward into the ward.

'You can come in now Mr Gabriel.' She beamed, her cheeks shining and ruddy from her efforts.

'What is it?'

The midwife, used to all sorts of reactions from the fathers of the precious new lives she helped into the world, looked him in the eye and said calmly, 'Congratulations, Mr Gabriel, you have a beautiful wee girl.'

Edward glanced at the tightly bound infant, at the minute pink face and then at Isobel, propped up against the white pillows, wan but smiling, her eyes bright with something he did not recognise. She had a new look about her. He leaned over her to kiss her forehead. She smelt different – scrubbed, clinical. He felt alienated from this person – these people – the nurse, the baby and his wife. He was intruding.

Isobel looked up at him, raising her face, reaching out her arm to touch him, but Edward moved away towards the door. He turned to face the three females in the warm, white room.

'Well done, darling. Better get some sleep. I'll pop back later. Mother will want to meet the new arrival, I'm sure.' He opened the door and was gone.

Slow tears trickled down Isobel's cheeks. She smiled through them at the nurse.

'Don't worry, dear. He just needs time to get used to the idea. Some men are a bit frightened of hospitals and all that sort of stuff. He'll be right as rain in no time - just you see.'

Enveloping the small, starfish fingers in her hand, Isobel gazed in wonder at her daughter.

'Hello, Sarah. I'm your Mummy.' She kissed the tiny hand and wiped her tears.

For the first few weeks of Sarah's life Edward barely acknowledged her existence. He felt, in any case, that this was not a place for men. His mother bustled around and knitted shawls and cardigans for her granddaughter, which Isobel received with grace, tactfully making sure the baby wore these items whenever Helen visited. Sarah took up her time and with each day Isobel felt more confident as a mother, discovering that her nursing training had been a good preparation. She did not panic if the baby woke early or cried for no apparent reason. She grew calmer and more competent while Edward worked long hours. He began to travel more frequently for his father's machine tool company. He was responsible for the export of their goods and this involved trips to North America and Europe. Isobel had accompanied him just once, towards the end of the first year of their marriage. They were away for three weeks in Connecticut where they had renewed the fun and intimacy of their honeymoon. After that Edward travelled alone. Like a rock that is slowly but relentlessly worn away under a constant drip of water, their relationship deteriorated, in small, barely perceptible ways. It was only separately and in their own hearts that this was admitted. On the surface, theirs was perceived to be a successful marriage by their friends and acquaintances.

Thomas, whose health was increasingly frail, drove carefully from Norfolk to meet the new baby and to spend some precious time with his daughter. With frequent breaks, either to rest his eyes or to drink some hot tea from his Thermos flask and eat some of the sandwiches, prepared for him by one of his devoted ladies from the church, the journey took him most of the day. When Isobel had suggested he travel by train, Thomas had declined, stating that if he was going to collapse and die on the journey, he would prefer to do it in the privacy of his car and not on public transport. Isobel was only too aware that her father's health was failing. She knew he was coming to see her now because he might not live much longer and the prospect of losing him made the future look bleak.

Thomas sat in an armchair and held Sarah in his arms, supported by a pillow, to take her weight. He looked down into her face and spoke softly to her. He told her about her grandmother, Peggy and about the sea and the whelk sheds and the fishing boats. Isobel took some photographs. These became treasured possessions that she kept in her desk all her life. A few weeks later Thomas died. He was alone in his house, sitting in his favourite chair, listening to the radio, when his heart, having struggled for many years following his wartime chest injuries, simply stopped beating. One of the church ladies found him the following morning and, after ringing the doctor, rang Isobel.

Edward drove his wife and child to Norfolk. The roadster had been sold and a more substantial family saloon acquired while Isobel was pregnant. Isobel needed to spend some time in her father's house sorting through his papers and making decisions about the sale of her old home. Edward had no choice but to look after his daughter. He walked along the lanes, self-consciously pushing Sarah in her pram. On one glorious autumn day when the sun still radiated warmth and the sea was calm, sitting on a bench, looking out over the salt marshes, he had lifted her out and placed her on his knee facing him. He studied her dainty features, noticing for the first time that her eyes were dark like his. Quite suddenly, Sarah smiled. Edward stared and found himself smiling back. An unfamiliar rush of tenderness engulfed him. It was a shock but he liked it. She smiled again, penetrating, inscrutable eyes looking right through him. He lifted her to his face and kissed her downy cheek. She gurgled and nestled her soft head into his neck. From that intimate moment, Edward was besotted with his daughter. As Isobel grieved for her father, Edward spent as much of his spare time as he could, playing and even giving a bottle to Sarah. As she grew, this attachment began to exclude Isobel more and more. Edward would take Sarah to his parents' house, arriving back home late. When Isobel pointed out that it was way past Sarah's bedtime, Edward would dismiss her concerns, stating that he knew what he was doing and that his parents were Sarah's only grandparents and it was important for him to spend time with his child. As she grew, Sarah began to understand that her father would indulge her every whim. Her mother would not.

Isobel loved her child but was worn down by Edward's smothering possessiveness of his daughter and his increasing and obvious irritation with his wife. She felt tired and unwanted most of the time. Mary rang her regularly, and on one occasion, sensing her friend's low spirits, more by what Isobel did not say than what she did, suggested that perhaps Isobel should take a holiday by the sea. She knew how much Isobel missed the coast and the wide, calming skies of Norfolk. Isobel was not sure if she would feel comfortable now in the place where she had grown up, but Mary offered to join her for a couple of days. Isobel began to think more definitely about the possibility of a break.

6

As the bitter, frozen winter came to an end in 1963, Edward's father suffered a massive brain haemorrhage and never regained consciousness. His wife, Helen, died a few months later. Edward's gentle mother simply faded away. She stopped eating and died a month after increasing pain and nausea forced her to see a doctor. She had ignored a lump in her breast and must have been ill for a long time, as the cancer was widespread. The family company was struggling and was under threat of a take-over. In an attempt to boost exports Edward set off once more for the USA and then on to South Africa.

Isobel decided to go to Norfolk to breathe clean air and to visit her parents' graves, to walk with the push chair and play on the beach with Sarah. One of her father's friends rented out a small house overlooking the marsh and the sea beyond. It was considered to be the best spot for watching the sunsets over the West-facing stretch of coast unique to that part of the North Norfolk. Edward had insisted that Isobel should sell her father's house, pointing out that he found Norfolk a 'God-forsaken place' and in any case the seaside family home where he had spent all his holidays was in Cornwall and, in his view, far more beautiful and interesting. As he frequently pointed out, they were lucky to have it. Isobel acknowledged it was indeed an impressive house, situated high above the sea, but in her heart she knew where she felt most at home.

Edward had reluctantly agreed to Isobel having driving lessons. Much to his surprise she had passed first time and become a proficient driver. She drove her father's prized Morris Minor. She told Edward she was going to Norfolk. He tried to persuade her to go to the house in Cornwall but Isobel stood firm.

'You're mad! What the hell do you see in that place? The sea is freezing, there's hardly ever any sun and at least you don't get flooded out in Cornwall,' he had sneered. He was unhappy at leaving Sarah and genuinely felt she would have a better time in Cornwall.

The day after Edward left for America. Isobel loaded the car with her daughter, a couple of cases and a few bits of food for that evening and set off. Sarah's long sleep allowed her thoughts free rein. She still loved her husband but had resigned herself to the fact that it was not the love she had dreamed of. As Edward's relationship with Sarah had improved on one level, in that he was devoted to her, on another, it was suffocating – not just for Sarah, who was too young to understand, but for Isobel who felt trapped and powerless.

She felt liberated as she drove towards the coast. Into her mind came memories of Bill. She wondered where he was now. When she had been back to see her father and they had chatted about this and that, he had invariably mentioned Bill. Isobel wondered sometimes if her father deliberately talked about him just to see her reaction. He was an intuitive man and had always had an uncanny knack of seeing through her. He had passed on any news that had come his way. Bill's parents, having retired from the hotel they had run for many years, were living in a bungalow on the coast road just outside the town. Bill had finished his course in London and had moved to Italy. Thomas thought he was in Florence, teaching at the university there. He had married an Italian woman and only made rare visits to his elderly parents. Isobel recalled the seemingly endless warm sunshine and the empty stretches of sand, the lost innocence of those days with Bill. She smiled but felt sad with nostalgia for her first love.

She concentrated on the road. The rest of the journey was taken up with singing nursery rhymes and telling stories to Sarah who had awoken and was fractious and demanding. They stopped in Wisbech for a snack and arrived at the house overlooking the marsh by early evening. Isobel looked at the old flint, stone and timber house. She had seen it before, tucked away, when she had walked down to the Staithe to look at the boats. Now, she was eager to see inside. There were stone steps leading up to the front door, underneath which was a storage area with room for a small car behind large wooden doors. This meant that from the main room of the house there was an uninterrupted view of sky, marsh and the sea

Leaving Sarah in the car, she carried their luggage up the steps, returning a couple of times until everything was in. By this time Sarah was protesting loudly at being left waiting.

'Come on, darling; let's get you out of there. Look, we can see the boats.'

Sarah's dark eyes followed her mother's pointing finger and she stared at the water. The sun was low and glowed pink and orange, throwing shimmers of colour between the small boats that were bobbing up and down at their moorings. The tinkle of halyards knocking against the masts accompanied the sea gulls' cries. A few people were carrying equipment from their vessels to walk up towards the road and the parking area by the side of the sailing club. In high summer there would be many more holiday makers but this early it was still quiet. Isobel helped Sarah up the steps. In the sitting room there was a vase of flowers on the table. A note from the owners welcomed her to their house. Closing the bottom half of the stable door, Isobel turned to Sarah.

'Let's have a look round, shall we? The little girl followed her mother as she checked the layout of the old building. There were two bedrooms and a smaller box room, in which there was a single bed and pretty, flowered, cotton curtains. Old pictures of Winnie the Pooh hung on the walls and a small but well-stocked toy box stood in the corner. Next to this was another room with a built-in captain's bed encased in tongue and grooved wood which, like all the woodwork, had been painted a washy, duck egg blue. The small window looked out across the Staithe and the boats. The biggest bedroom shared the same view but through a much larger window, which had wooden shutters and a white gauze curtain, ruffling slightly in the breeze. Looking round the room Isobel felt immediately at home. The capacious wooden bed had been made up with crisp white cotton sheets and pastel coloured blankets, topped with a faded but freshly laundered patchwork quilt. White cotton towels were hanging on an old, bleached, wooden towel stand beside the wash basin and sweet smelling tablets of soap filled a green glass jar. The small bathroom was next to the box room and similarly decorated. Isobel felt, quite suddenly, that she was glad she had sold her father's house. She relished the welcome sense of freedom.

Sarah had found another box of toys and was contentedly exploring it by the enormous window of the sitting room. This afforded anyone in that room the panoramic view over marshes and sea. Isobel gazed for a moment to revel in the soft pink of the sky. In the distance she could just make out the silhouetted shapes of the old whelk sheds. They brought memories flooding back, of happy days, with her father, chatting to the fishermen and even on a few occasions, being allowed to go out with them for an hour or two. At one end of this cosy room, which was simply furnished but with plump cushions in all sorts of fabrics providing colours and textures to complement the white washed walls, there was a bottle green, enamelled, pot-bellied stove, beside which was a large basket of logs. Instructions on how to light the stove were written on a sheet of card propped up on the brick fireplace. Isobel unloaded food and clothes and set about lighting the stove. She and Sarah had a sumptuous supper of beans on toast. Food shopping was for the next day. By mid evening, Sarah had been fed, bathed and tucked up in the little bed. She had settled quite quickly with a few extra stories and Isobel's soft stroking of her forehead.

Mary was due to arrive at about eight o'clock. She had insisted that she would not need feeding as she would have a large lunch at the hospital and would eat a sandwich on the way. Isobel was looking forward to spending time with her friend and found herself wishing Mary could stay more than a couple of days. She checked on Sarah and that the spare bedroom was fresh and dry, appreciative of the thoughtful, welcoming touches of small jugs of fresh flowers in each room. She knew that a woman who lived nearby was employed by Hugh and Laura, the owners, to keep the place in order while they were away on their travels, which was all winter and into the spring. Their own children, all adults now, but whom Isobel could vaguely recall playing with as a child, used the house too, so it was never allowed to become damp and cold.

She stepped outside to the top of the steps and leaned on the wooden hand rail. Inhaling deeply, she smelt the sea. She closed her eyes against sudden tears. Her heart felt full of memories of her childhood and adolescence.

'Oh, for goodness sake!' she muttered. Taking another deep breath and pressing her hands to her eyes, she turned back into the house. She lit the lamps which gave out a soft glow and sinking into the battered old sofa she switched on the radio. She was jolted awake by the sound of Mary coming up the steps.

'Izzy, are you there? Give me a hand, will you?'

The two women hugged each other.

'Mary, you look wonderful! How was the journey?' Isobel was surprised to see a difference in Mary's appearance, subtle but nevertheless, a change. Her hair was shorter and her curls bounced and shone. Her eyes were bright – with something Isobel could not decipher.

'And you look peaky. The journey was fine.' Mary studied Isobel as they carried her bag and a box of what appeared mostly to be bottles into the kitchen. 'You OK?'

'Yes, I'm fine. Glad to have got here. It was a long journey for Sarah.'

'Yes, of course. And how is my Goddaughter?'

'She's fast asleep. Come on, I'll show you your room and you can have a look in on her too.'

A few minutes later Mary was unloading her box of goodies.

'I know you'll be amazed at my domesticity but I've made a cake – and – a shepherd's pie for tomorrow!' she announced with a flourish. 'But, first things first. Let's have a large gin!'

Two G and T's later, Isobel had assured Mary that everything was ticking along in her life perfectly well and there was no need to worry about her. She moved the focus of their conversation.

'So, how are things with you? You really do look very well and, actually, Mary, you look sort of different. It's not just your hair, which I love, by the way. It really suits you. It's something else. Have you been trying make-up, because if you have, it works! I've never seen you so ... oh, I don't know ... sort of shining!'

Her friend smiled. It was then that Isobel realised. Mary had met someone. Mary, who everyone thought would end up married to nursing and becoming Chief Nursing Officer, at least.

'You've met someone. I'm right, aren't I?'

Mary beamed. 'Yes, you're right. I knew you'd guess, but I was going to tell you anyway. In fact, I could hardly wait to see you. I really wanted to tell you face to face.'

Over the next hour or so, Mary proceeded to tell Isobel about the man she had met; the man she was going to marry. Isobel was amazed to learn that he was a doctor.

'Mary, we swore we would never marry a doctor!'

Mary threw back her head and gave her whinnying laugh.

'I know, I know, but Robert is different. He's not like some of the ones we came across. He is kind and gentle and fantastic with patients and he's handsome and funny and – well – just wonderful. I can't believe he loves me – me of all people!'

Isobel crossed the room and embraced her. 'Oh, Mary, I'm so thrilled for you. You deserve to have someone good. I hope you will be very happy. I know you will. When are you getting married?'

'Well, sooner rather than later. We have to sort out when is best for both of us, but you will be the first to know, Izzy. Please will you be my Matron of Honour?'

'Of course I will. What about your sisters though?'

'Oh, don't worry. They'll be my bridesmaids and the boys will be ushers. That's if I can persuade any of them to dress up!'

'You're not wearing an engagement ring.'

'No. Our shifts have been really awkward, but we are going to choose one next week.

It was after midnight when they went to sleep. The gins and the happy conversation helped Isobel to sleep soundly.

Sarah's usual morning prattle, followed by persistent pats on her mother's face and cries of 'Mummy, wake up!' roused her at seven o'clock. The three of them had breakfast together, Sarah absolutely delighted to have Mary's undivided attention. The spring sunshine felt warm on their backs as they set out to the village shop. The two friends chatted amiably about this and that, but mostly about Mary's plans. Sarah demanded occasional attention but on the whole seemed content to pad alongside looking at the hedgerows. They called at the fishmongers on the main road with his large wooden blackboard propped up outside, still decorated with the painted fish and crabs that seemed to Isobel to have been there forever. Isobel knew the shop well and proudly showed her landlubber companion the impressive display of locally caught fish, crabs, lobster and intriguing collection of smaller shell fish.

After lunch they set off for the beach. A cool breeze from the sea reminded them that it was still early in the season and they were glad of their windcheaters and warm trousers. Still, they dug holes in the sand and carried endless buckets of water from the sea, up the beach to watch it disappear into the hole. Sarah ran around, laughing and shrieking if a wave came anywhere near. As it was a Sunday, there were a few other small children nearby who unselfconsciously joined Sarah in her squeals and acrobatics by the water's edge. Supervising adults watched from their sheltered spots on the sand or wandered along by the water keeping a close eye on their children or grandchildren. Mary broached the subject of Edward, innocently enquiring about his work. She had observed Isobel while appearing to be looking around at the scenery or the children. She was not taken in by Isobel's nonchalant comments and reassurances that all was well. She also knew that until and unless Isobel wished to open up there was nothing she could do.

Shepherd's pie eaten and small child bathed and settled into bed, Isobel and Mary sat again in the comfy chairs, sipping gin and reminiscing about the old days at their training hospital in Cambridge. As always they ended up laughing until the tears ran down their faces. In bed, Isobel pushed away the disquieting pangs of envy as she acknowledged how Mary really did seem to have found a deep and profound love.

Mary left early the next morning.

'Are you sure you are alright?'

Isobel looked up and directly into Mary's eyes. She was determined not to burst Mary's bubble of happiness.

'Of course I am. See, just two days of this sea air and I'm already feeling full of energy. Now, off you go and drive carefully. Tell that gorgeous man of yours that I can't wait to meet him!'

They hugged each other once more. Isobel was touched that Mary had come at all. It was obvious now that she was desperate to get back to Robert. She and Sarah waved as Mary's battered old Austin drove up towards the road and out of sight.

7

Monday was quiet on the beach. The weekend visitors and local people with jobs to go to had disappeared. Isobel and Sarah walked out to firm sand, as the tide was out, and splashed in the puddles. Isobel threw a ball and Sarah ran to pick it up like an excitable puppy. A small girl came running over to Sarah. They eyed each other up for a moment with shy smiles. Suddenly, Sarah shrieked and threw the ball and off they went giggling and shouting to each other. Isobel was struck by the two heads close together as they poked around in the puddles. They both had such dark hair. Sarah's straight page-boy cut next to a mop of tight, almost black curls. She caught them in this pose with her camera and laughed out loud at their antics. Dark clouds appeared from nowhere and changed the atmosphere. The two little girls looked around for adults. Isobel was just beginning to wonder where on earth this child's parents, or perhaps grandparents were, when she saw her start to run away from Sarah, shouting,

'Papa, Papa!' The rain was coming down now, hoods were being pulled up and the few dog-walkers leaned forward against the sudden squally wind, whistled for their pets and aimed for their cars.

Isobel didn't bother with her hood. She loved the seaside rain and in any case the hood would not have stayed up with her hands needed to help Sarah. She peered across the beach, blinking raindrops from her eyelashes, to be sure the little curly-headed child had found her 'Papa.' It was then that she saw him. He swept the little girl up into his arms and held her close. He looked over to Isobel and smiled. Her heart seemed to miss a beat and she stopped on the spot, rain now trickling down the inside of her waterproof top. He stood still too. They looked at each other, each holding their daughters, each locked in the moment.

Sarah began to complain.

'Mummy, I'm cold!' Her small hand reached up to turn her mother's gaze towards her own. 'Mummy!'

'Alright, darling. We're going.' She forced herself to bend down and pick up the bucket and spades, eyes still focused on the only other two people now on the beach. He was walking towards them. She felt flushed and panicky. He reached them, just as the shower stopped, as suddenly as it had started. Mercifully, both children squirmed themselves down on to the sand, grabbed their buckets and spades and ran off as if there had been no interruption to their play. Isobel and Bill looked at each other.

'Isobel.' His voice was the same.

'Hello, Bill.' Did she sound the same to him?

'How are you? You look well. Are you here on holiday?'

She smiled and so did he. Without warning, he took a step forward, held her shoulders and kissed her wet face, first one cheek and then the other.

'It's good to see you after all this time.'

Isobel wobbled slightly and stepped back from him. She felt as though she might fall over. He put his hand under her elbow to steady her.

'Yes, it's good to see you too.' She smiled again. 'I'm well and yes, I'm here with my daughter for a short holiday.'

'Where are you staying? I was sorry to hear that your father had died. I heard that his house had been sold. Did you know his chemist shop is now a tea room?'

'Thank you. M,mm, I know about the shop. Actually, I haven't been to the town. We're staying at the Staithe, in the Harrison's house, you know, on the water's edge?'

'Oh yes, I know it - great views for painting.'

The rain started again. They gathered up their daughters and strode over the beach to the small car park. Heavy grey clouds descended and the rain hardened. Isobel suddenly couldn't bear to go back to the house without talking more to him. She wanted to know why he was here and for how long. What had happened in the last twelve years? Who was with him? Their cars were the only ones left in the boggy car park. She turned towards him after helping Sarah into the back of the car. He straightened up from doing the same task. Once more their eyes locked. Her voice shook as she blurted out, 'If you're not in a hurry, would you like to come back with us for a hot drink?' It was all she could muster up. He did not hesitate.

'That would be nice, thank you.'

All the way back Isobel tormented herself with doubts about her rash invitation. She felt nervous and guilty, as if Edward were watching from afar. She tried to rationalise her decision. It was only a cup of coffee. The children obviously liked each other. She and Bill would just chat about their lives since they had last met and then go their separate ways.

The process of getting two wet and now irritable children up into the house and then peeling off waterproofs, depositing the detritus of the beach by the door, took some time.

'What's your daughter's name?'

'Caterina – and yours?'

'Sarah. I'll get them a drink and a biscuit, if that's OK with you?'

'Of course. Can I help?'

'No, it's fine. Have a look round if you like. I can see why artists rent this place. There's a stack of old paintings over there. I think one of the Harrisons may paint. Tea or coffee?'

Isobel went into the kitchen. Cold drips were falling on to her shoulders. She grabbed a towel and rubbed her hair. While the kettle boiled she went to her bedroom, changed her now sodden jumper for a dry one and ran a comb through her hair. Glancing in the mirror she saw her cheeks were flushed and her eyes bright. Bill was squatting by the pictures, shoulders damp from his wet hair too.

Isobel threw him a towel.

'Here.' she said, smiling. 'You're soaked!'

He took the towel and attacked his hair, still the colour of straw, she noticed. He watched her.

'You look very sleek. Thank your lucky stars you don't have this mop!' His blue eyes shone. Isobel turned sharply to the kitchen. He was standing holding a painting when she came back into the room.

'Well, well! This is one of mine!' he came and sat beside her on the sofa. She looked at the picture. The delicate, watery tones and the sharp, fine lines of the boats were captured exactly. If she had found the time to look through the paintings she knew she would have recognised his.

'This is really bad, you know,' he said. 'Long time ago, I suppose.' He stood and replaced the picture with the others, accepted his mug of coffee and sat in an armchair. The two little girls drank their juice and munched on their biscuits, gabbling away to each other; Sarah, intrigued by Caterina's effortless ability to switch from English to Italian and back again and Caterina, deliberately throwing in Italian words just to make her new friend laugh.

'Caterina is such a pretty name.'

'Yes, Italian. I live there now – have done for years.'

Isobel felt as if a shadow passed over her heart. She knew he had gone to Italy. Why should she be surprised? Something stopped her from asking about Caterina's mother. Bill leaned back in the chair and stretched his long legs, feet encased in thick woolly socks. He took a deep breath before he spoke again.

'Caterina's mother ... my wife ... Flavia ... died.'
He glanced sharply at his daughter as if suddenly
realising she might hear and at the age of five would
understand. He need not have worried; Sarah had
Caterina's hand and was taking her to the toys in the
bedroom. Isobel saw the grief cross his face.

'I am sorry. That must be dreadful for you and
Caterina.'

'Well, it was horrific when it happened, of course,
but it's five years now and Caterina never knew her,
so her Italian grandmother, her 'Nonna,' has been
more of a mother figure really.' He leaned forward,
studying the mug in his hands. 'Flavia died
immediately after giving birth. It is rare but it still
happens. There was nothing they could do. She just
bled to death.'

Isobel leaned towards him and took his hand. He
looked at her and she recognised the anger, confusion
and desolation she had seen so many times when she
was nursing. He nodded, smiled a sad little smile and
squeezed her hand in thanks. He was glad she hadn't
tried to offer words of comfort. He was aware of her
sensitivity towards him and felt warmth from it.

They both sat back then and realised there was
much they could talk about. Over the next hour
Isobel answered his questions about her life and he
told her that he had gone to Italy after finishing at the
Royal Academy. He had travelled for a while,
picking up the language and then taken up a teaching
post at the University in Florence and, yes, he agreed,
what a wonderful place to be. There he had met
Flavia. She ran a sweetshop in the centre of the city
where she made chocolates and other delicacies. It

was a thriving business. She and Bill had found a small fifth floor apartment five minutes away. It was cosy and romantic. It was fortunate that her parents lived nearby. Grief-stricken as they were, they had generously embraced Bill and their adored Caterina.

Isobel listened intently, trying to conjure up the picture of them. She felt sad for Bill and especially for little Caterina. She wondered if they came to England often. As if he had read her thoughts, Bill added, 'We don't come back here much. This is really a duty call as Mum and Dad are getting a bit frail. Actually, I think they find us a bit much. To be honest I feel strange in this place now. How about you?'

'I love it here but I know what you mean. Edward won't come here anyway. His family have a place in Cornwall that they've always gone to. It's lovely but I think I'm a Norfolk girl deep down and always will be.'

They both laughed. He relaxed back in the chair once more and watched her sipping her coffee.

'You haven't changed, Isobel. I thought about you and I know I was really bad at keeping in touch when I went to London. We were so young. You were so young. I should have written more. Did you hate me?'

'No.'

Sarah ran into the room shrieking and threw herself at Isobel's legs. Caterina followed and did exactly the same to her father.

'Mummy, Mummy, Catina, Catina!'

'Papa, Papa, Sera, Sera!'

'It seems they know each other's names then.' Bill laughed as he lifted Caterina to his knee. 'We'd better go. Mum will have lunch ready for us. I dread to think what it'll be. She's quite confused so it could be anything!' The rain had stopped and through the big window bright sunshine cast swathes of silver-leaf reflections on the patchy wet marsh. He studied the scene. 'That is something I do miss. There is nowhere in the world with light like this. I might manage a few sketches while I'm here.' And then, glancing at Caterina, he laughed ruefully. 'Or perhaps not!'

Isobel retrieved the wellies and waterproofs and brought them to Bill. Sarah began to cry. Isobel picked her up.

'I don't think she wants Caterina to go.'

Bill looked at her. 'If you're not doing anything tomorrow, shall we give them another run on the beach? That's if it's not pouring, of course.'

8

They met each afternoon for the next three days. Sarah and Caterina played and ran about on the beach, oblivious of the cool breezes which intruded into the long warm spells. Bill sketched quick, accurate impressions of the landscape and of Isobel and the children. His soft pencil flew across the pages, capturing forever, moments and movements that would otherwise be lost in fading memories.

They talked about their past, the present and what they hoped for the future. Isobel still felt guilty and troubled, as if she was betraying her husband, but driven by a deeper need, to be close to this man, to feel again the sensations of that time they had shared thirteen years ago. Bill had told her that he doubted if he and Caterina would return to Norfolk, except, he supposed, for his parents' funerals. Their life in Florence was settling into a comfortable pattern and he was beginning to meet new people. He did not elaborate but Isobel imagined that this meant women.

Why was she surprised to hear this? Why was she surprised it made her feel sad?

They found themselves touching as they walked; at first just an accidental brushing of an arm or hand but then more deliberate contact, a shared hug with the girls, or catching hold of each other when chasing around. Late in the afternoon, on the Thursday of that week, they all tumbled into the house by the water; sandy, damp and exhilarated by the fresh, bracing air. On the previous days Bill had taken a protesting Caterina back to his parents but with each day their presence there felt more uncomfortable. Caterina was inhibited, her natural exuberance curbed by the elderly couple, who had grown used to what their son perceived as a rather dull and monotonous routine. He did appreciate that they relished some peace after all their years in the hotel business.

This afternoon he and Isobel had decided to share an evening meal and let the girls have their bath together as a treat. Bill was meant to be supervising the bathing and judging from the sounds of splashing and shrieking in the bathroom, was failing abysmally, but Isobel loved to hear Sarah so happy. The light was changing and she was shaking sand out of towels and shoes at the top of the outside steps. The tide was in and she watched a small boat being tied up at the water's edge close to the house. She recognised the man lifting out his haul of mackerel. He was the eldest son of a family of fishermen, the Shillings, known by everyone locally. Isobel and her father had gone out with them in their boat a couple of times.

'Hello; Michael!' she shouted.

He looked up, squinting in the faint, rosy sunlight.

'Hello. Oh, hello. Its Isobel isn't it? Fancy seeing you here after all this time.' His strong Norfolk burr and big smile were warm and friendly. 'On holiday then?'

'Yes, just this week. Are those mackerel I see?'

'They are indeed. D'you want some then?'

'Ooh, yes please. Hang on. I'll get my purse.'

Michael waited at the bottom of the steps with the plump fish, their pearlized skins with their distinctive black markings glistening in the crate.

'How many then?'

'Four please. How much?'

'Shilling each and they are beauties. Will you have them tonight?'

'No, for breakfast. How lovely. I always remember my mother just spreading butter on them and grilling them.'

Michael turned his weather-beaten, kindly face to hers and grinned. 'That's right. They don't need anything fancy.'

She paid him and took the fish. 'Thank you, Michael. Good to see you. How's the family?'

'Oh they're all fine thanks. Better get off. All the best.'

No questions; just a few friendly and unintrusive words. He turned and checked his boat before disappearing off with his fish. Isobel knew he would be in The Anchor and playing darts within the hour. At the top of the steps two small faces peeped around the door.

'Look what I've got,' she held aloft the fish and climbed the steps.

The sea air had cast its soporific spell on the children and they fell asleep sooner than either of the adults had hoped for. The wood burned steadily in the stove as the light outside turned to inky velvet, strewn with diamond stars. Bill had found a wine shop on the main road a few miles away and they sat sipping fruity Italian wine, their hunger satisfied by Isobel's chicken casserole. Bill drained his glass and got to his feet. He looked down at Isobel. 'We have to go, I guess. Mum and Dad will be expecting us back.'

Isobel stood up and spoke the words she had been pushing away all day. 'Why don't you stay? The girls are sound asleep. It seems a pity to disturb them.'

They stayed where they were for just a moment and then took a step towards each other. Isobel looked up at Bill. He returned her gaze, searching her face. He reached out to touch her hair. Isobel felt her legs go weak. She knew that in the next moments she would make a decision, the consequences of which, she would have to live with for the rest of her life. They wrapped arms around each other and their first tentative kisses became searching and urgent. Isobel thought she would not be able to stand for much longer as Bill kissed her neck. They pulled apart, laughing suddenly.

'Do you want to stay?'

'Yes ... but ... '

'Then stay.'

He kissed her again.

'I have to let Mum and Dad know we won't be back tonight. I'll call them from the phone on the main road. Are you sure, Isobel? It's different for me.'

She nodded, smiling. 'What will you say to them? You can't say you're here.'

'I know. I'll tell them we have been out driving and to save a long journey home we are staying in a B and B down the coast. I'm sure they'll be happy to have a quiet evening and no noisy little girl waking them too early in the morning!'

Bill slipped out into the dark and Isobel took a deep breath. She checked both sleeping children and paced restlessly until she heard his footsteps. They settled on the sofa and drank the rest of the wine, savouring the feel of each other and the anticipation of what was to come. By the time they fell into bed their need for each other was so intense it was almost unbearable. And yet, later, entwined in each other's arms as they began to fall asleep, they each wept silently and separately for lost loves.

As the sun stole through the cotton curtains, they were awoken by small hands stroking their faces; one little girl on each side of the bed, loud stage whispers pulling them away from sleep.

'Papa, Papa, wake up!'

'Mummy, Mummy, wake up!' echoed Sarah, giggling.

Isobel sat bolt upright in horror. Sarah was now looking curiously from Bill to her and back again. What on earth was she going to say to her daughter? She leapt out of the bed and rushed through to the kitchen, desperately relieved that she had put her pyjamas back on during the night.

'Come along girls,' she called, her voice sounding shrill and artificial. 'Let's get you both a drink.'

The two children padded after her.

'Why is Bill in your bed, Mummy?' piped Sarah. Isobel kept her back to them as she sought desperately for some suitable words. Bill's voice cut in.

'Because, you two were fast asleep in your beds and we didn't want to wake you. There isn't another bed so I took a little corner of your Mummy's bed so I could sleep too.'

He had appeared in the sitting room doorway, fully dressed and looking unperturbed.

'Come on then, who's going to be dressed first and come out with me to see the boats?'

Sarah and Caterina disappeared and scrambled into their clothes as Bill put his arms around Isobel, who was transfixed by the sink in a state of near panic.

'You OK? He asked into her neck.

'Oh God, I'm not sure! What if she says something to Edward?'

'She probably won't. You know how they are at this age. They really only think of the moment – and that is going to be looking at the boats and eating a delicious mackerel breakfast'

Isobel watched them scampering down the steps and running towards the boats bobbing about. Bill strode after them. Her heart sank as she wondered how she would cope if Sarah said anything when Edward got home. She was too young to be expected to keep a secret. While the fish was grilling, Isobel allowed herself a moment of reflection on the night.

Part of her felt exhilarated and excited but niggling away in the pit of her stomach was a deep anxiety.

The girls chattered away as the mackerel were eaten. Isobel registered vaguely some surprise that Sarah had eaten it so readily. It was Caterina's influence of course. Bill and she glanced at each other from time to time; he trying to fathom her thoughts and she nervously smiling in a vain attempt to push her worries away. They had only a moment to hold each other while the children carried various possessions to the cars.

'Are you sure you are alright?' he said, and kissed her.

'No,' she mumbled into his chest, clinging to him.

'I'm sorry, Isobel. It is my fault. I shouldn't have stayed.'

She looked at him with eyes shiny from tears. 'It is not your fault, Bill. I'm a grown woman and I wanted you to be with me. And it was ... wonderful.'

He kissed her again. 'Yes, it was ... and you are very beautiful ... and very, very sexy!'

She laughed, embarrassed, but pleased. 'So are you!'

'Goodbye, Isobel. I hope all goes well for you.' His voice was gentle as he held her tightly. It sounded such a final farewell.

They stood and waved as Bill and Caterina drove off. Both little girls were crying loudly in protest. Isobel cried inside, as a brief, beautiful part of her life disappeared out of sight.

There was no point in staying any longer. The magic spell had been broken. Somehow, and only by placating Sarah with sweets, she managed to clear the house and load the car. The final task of visiting her parents' grave was performed perfunctorily. Isobel had never seen the point of graves. When people were gone, they were gone and the sight of graves which had been neglected, with dead flowers stuck into rusty vases, she found quite depressing. Her Mother had always said that graveyards were good places to choose a name for your baby. Isobel thought wryly of this notion as she passed the headstones - 'Alfred' and 'Hilda', 'Gladys' and 'Stanley'. Her Father had asked to be buried by the side of Peggy. Isobel removed the empty stone vase, its metal lid punctured with holes for the absent flower stems and dropped it into the rubbish bin in the corner of the churchyard. She knew, as they drove up the gentle, gorse-lined hill, leading away from the coast, that she would not return to Norfolk.

9

Two weeks later, when Isobel and Sarah had settled into their routine, Edward arrived back from South Africa. Isobel had been preparing for his return. She had struggled to come to terms with the fact that Bill had gone - again. She did not regret their time together. It was as if she had needed to prove to herself that he really had loved her all those years ago. She knew it was not exactly going to enhance her marriage but probably nothing would. She had a daughter to think of and a home to run.

Edward came into the hall, calling, 'Hello, I'm back!'

Sarah ran from the kitchen and was swept up into his arms. 'Daddy, Daddy!' She showered his face with kisses and wrapped her small arms tightly around his neck.

'Hello, Sugarplum. How's my little girl then?'

They made a fuss of each other and then he lowered Sarah to the floor and looked at Isobel. She took a step towards him.

'Hello, darling,' he said hesitantly, his eyes scouring her face. He looked weary after the long flight. She noticed the watchfulness and felt a brief stab of remorse. In that moment she knew Bill had gone for good and that she would work to make her marriage survive. She put her hands up to his face.

'Hello, Edward. You look tired. We've missed you.'

His dark eyes searched hers.

'Have you?'

'Yes, yes!' cried Sarah, pulling at his jacket. 'We have!'

Their kiss was a brush of lips and no more as Sarah pulled her father into the kitchen to see the fairy cakes she and Isobel had made in his honour.

Sarah eventually fell asleep; her dark eyes so like his own, had grown heavy, but only after one more story had been read. Edward inwardly cringed with embarrassment when he performed this task but Sarah did not seem to notice and listened in rapt silence. He kissed her forehead and gently settled the eiderdown around her small frame, then tiptoed out of the room and down the stairs to join Isobel.

Isobel recalled, while Edward was upstairs, some words of advice her mother had given her years earlier, when Isobel had been asking about marriage and love and staying with one person for ages. Peggy rarely gave advice, leaving Thomas to pass on words of wisdom to their daughter. Perhaps that was why her words had remained in Isobel's mind.

'People shouldn't worry if they have a few secrets to take with them to their graves. Just occasionally - but only just occasionally - it doesn't do to tell the truth if it means the other person will be hurt. You have to learn to live with that secret and keep your own counsel.'

Isobel remembered wondering what secrets her Mother must have had, but did not dare ask. Her Mother, in any case, had walked out of the room and busied herself somewhere else in the house. She never repeated her words, nor offered any other advice.

They were sipping drinks by the fire in the sitting room, the dusk falling quietly outside.

'So, how was Norfolk?' Edward asked.

'Lovely, as always, but I know you don't believe me,' Isobel laughed. 'We had a lot of fresh air and fun on the beach. I think it did us both good actually. How was your trip ... successful?'

'Not brilliant. We're struggling a bit.' Edward rose to pour another Scotch, sat back in his chair and glanced lazily around the room. 'You've done a good job in here, Isobel. If we're not going to have more children, perhaps you could start up a little business – interior design or something.'

Isobel was astonished. Two subjects that Edward had never raised before had just been thrown at her.

'Well, I suppose we will have more children, don't you? But I could get a job. I'd still like to go back into nursing.'

Edward drained his glass. 'What the hell for? Awful hours, rotten pay. No, you could work from one of the upstairs rooms, I thought. That way you'd still be able to see to Sarah, and me, and the house.'

Isobel gave a brittle laugh, genuinely aghast at his tone. 'Edward, you sound like a Victorian patriarch! It is 1963 for goodness sake!'

He stared into his tumbler for a moment then looked at her with a wry smile. 'I did a bit, didn't I?'

The smiles that passed between them were warmer than they had been for a while. In bed, Edward seemed eager to please her. Isobel pushed the secret she was carrying to the back of her mind. The two of them lost all other thoughts and on that night, at least, revived their early passion for each other.

Edward returned to work, Isobel got on with the house redecorations and Sarah attended a small private nursery three mornings a week. When Isobel began to feel rising and bitter nausea in the mornings, she knew straight away, but decided to wait until she had been to the doctor, before telling anyone she was pregnant. When the pregnancy was confirmed Edward was genuinely pleased and told everyone. The baby was due at the end of the year and Isobel sailed serenely through the summer and autumn, only feeling heavy and cumbersome in the last few weeks. In September they went to Cambridge to attend Mary and Robert's joyful and very Scottish wedding, resplendent with kilts and bagpipes, in honour of Robert's ancestry.

'Bloody hell! They're all bonkers!' Edward declared, amongst the applause which followed an incomprehensible speech by Mary's eccentric, academic father. Isobel saw, with a pang of envy, the way Robert and Mary looked at each other, the loving, boisterous siblings and the support of the parents. Mary had insisted that, despite Isobel's pregnancy, she should still be there as her Matron of Honour. Isobel bloomed in her pale green satin and delighted in the vision of her dearest friend as a radiant bride, but the day was bitter-sweet. On a visit in the summer, Mary had told Isobel that she and Robert would be emigrating to Tasmania after the wedding. They were joining a new family doctors' practice in Hobart.

A sadness hung over Isobel for some weeks after they had gone but nature's preparatory hormonal activity took over and she soon began to organise the bedroom for the new baby. Sarah was beside herself with excitement and repeatedly checked the room and the tiny clothes, incredulous but intrigued at the thought that she had once worn some of them. One afternoon, early in December, Isobel was sitting with her feet up, reading a story to Sarah, when a stabbing pain shot through her lower back, making her cry out. Sarah jumped and looked terrified.

'It's alright, darling. It was just a funny pain in my back. It has gone now.'

Sarah studied her mother and jumped violently again when Isobel cried out as a searing pain shot across her abdomen and suddenly her waters broke. Sarah burst into tears and stared in horror at the wet patch seeping into the sitting room carpet.

'Mummy, Mummy, what is that?'

Isobel, summoning up strength from somewhere, managed to speak in a near normal voice. 'Don't worry Sarah. It's just the baby coming. Can you pass me the telephone from that table over there – look?'

Sarah backed away towards the table, her wide eyes transfixed by the damp chair and carpet. She carried the telephone to her mother and cautiously put it on the side table. Isobel suppressed a cry as she asked Sarah for her handbag from the kitchen. The little girl, speechless now, ran to the kitchen, grabbed the bag and thrust it at Isobel. She stepped back to survey this strange, frightening scene as Isobel rang the midwife.

'I won't be with you for at least an hour, my dear,' the midwife declared cheerily. 'I'm with my other due lady and baby's just been born.'

'Oh, God!' Isobel cried into the phone.

The midwife said she would call the ambulance for her and Isobel was to call her husband or someone to look after Sarah. Isobel dialled Edward's number.

'I'm sorry, Mrs Gabriel, your husband is in a meeting. Can I take a message?'

Isobel forced the words out between agonised cries of pain.

'Tell him I'm in labour and the ambulance is on its way and he must come home to look after Sarah. Hurry please!'

Susan Jeffries, the imperturbable PA, looked down the telephone receiver in horror. Good Lord, why didn't these wives get themselves organised! Mr Gabriel was not going to be impressed at being interrupted. Another scream pierced the air. Susan felt mildly sick.

'Very well, Mrs Gabriel. I'll see what I can do.'

'Don't bloody well see what you can do, just bloody well get him – now!'

Susan dropped the telephone and ran to the boardroom. Isobel, realising that Edward would not be home before the arrival of an ambulance, decided to call her new neighbour, Eileen, who had offered help with anything at all if she was ever needed. Eileen responded calmly and swiftly to Isobel's frantic telephone call. She let herself in. She and Isobel had decided to give each other a key to their respective homes – in case of emergencies. She calmed Sarah down and fetched Isobel's overnight bag with the baby things in that had been prepared only the day before.

Isobel's son arrived twenty minutes after she was transported to the hospital by the siren-wailing, blue light-flashing ambulance. Edward was excluded from the delivery room as everything was happening in such a rush and Sarah clung to him from the moment he arrived. Eileen slipped quietly away and went to their house where she spent some considerable time washing the chair and carpet.

Thomas George Gabriel's father and sister came into the room as the midwife handed him to Isobel. He was wrapped in a white hospital blanket and when Sarah looked at him he yawned widely and gave a little whimper. She was entranced and touching his downy cheek with her chubby fingers she said, in the playing voice she used for her dolls and teddies, 'You naughty baby. You made Mummy cry and wet her knickers!'

Isobel gave a weak smile. Edward roared with laughter.

'Well, that was all a bit dramatic and unexpected wasn't it? He looks a good size considering he's early. By the way, you nearly gave Susan Jeffries a heart attack!'

As the first few weeks passed, Isobel's niggling doubt became a full-blown, alarming matter of fact. When the true colour came through there was absolutely no doubt. The crystal clear, cornflower blue was devastatingly and irrevocably the blue of his father's eyes. Edward seemed not to have noticed his son's eyes any more than the rest of his new-born body. He was delighted to have a son but really felt that these early weeks were the mother's responsibility. He looked forward to teaching Tom to swim and play cricket and golf. His work kept him away from home until Sarah was either in bed or at least ready in her pyjamas. For Sarah, the novelty of a new baby brother soon wore off. He was a noisy nuisance and took up a lot of her Mother's time.

Sarah caught chickenpox in the spring of 1964 and despite still being breast fed Tom succumbed too. Edward had been roped in to settle Sarah into bed with a story while Isobel comforted a grizzly baby. Sarah insisted on looking at every picture for what seemed to Edward to take ages. Quite suddenly, while she was studying one of children on a beach, she piped, 'There's Catina! There's Catina! Look, Daddy, there's Catina!'

Edward looked at the book and smiled. 'What's 'Catina,' darling?'

Sarah pointed to a small dark haired girl in the picture. 'There she is. She played with me. She's my friend.'

'Oh, I see, at nursery you mean?' Edward went to turn the page.

Sarah stopped him. 'No, not nursery; at the seaside with Mummy! Catina and her Daddy.'

'I see - someone you played with on the beach.' Edward turned the page, eager to finish the story and go downstairs for a drink. Sarah looked solemnly at him. 'And she did come to our house and she did sleep in Mary's bed ... and Bill did sleep in Mummy's bed 'cos' Mary did go home and Catina did sleep in that bed.'

Edward looked at his daughter. 'What did you just say, Sarah, that someone called Bill slept in Mummy's bed?'

'Yes. Come on, Daddy more story, more story!' Sarah tugged at his sleeve.

Somehow he got to the end of the book, kissed Sarah's forehead, dimmed the light and stepped on to the landing. He could hear Isobel soothing Tom. They had agreed when she was pregnant the first time, that if they had a daughter, Edward could choose his favourite name and if they had a son, it would be Isobel's choice. In the end Isobel had named Tom after her father – not a name Edward particularly liked - but he had stuck to their agreement. Now, as he walked downstairs he tried to think of words that could be used to find out why their daughter had just told him that someone called Bill had slept in Isobel's bed. His mouth felt dry and his head as if it would burst. He poured himself a large Scotch. The sitting room was quiet, with just the lamps on and soft fabrics glowing in the fire light. The comfort he always felt on returning home was now invaded with dark, unsolicited thoughts and doubts. The room became oppressive. He opened the

French windows and stepped outside into the crisp, enveloping darkness. The whisky burned his throat as he gulped it down. His thoughts veered wildly between Isobel, still the most beautiful and loving woman he had ever met, and the women he had casually slept with over the years. He thought of Enid, in Cape Town, who demanded nothing from him except discreet sex and quite a lot of money. From the bottom of the frosty lawn he could see into his home; warm, welcoming and safe. What the hell was he doing standing, freezing to death, with such a painful ache in his throat that he could hardly bear it, with tears that would not come and with an all–consuming feeling of despair threatening to overwhelm him, so that he wanted to fall to the ground and weep like a child.

Isobel was leaning back in the big chair by the fire. Edward saw a beautiful woman, raven hair tucked behind her ears and falling to her shoulders. Her eyes were closed and dark eyelashes cast faint shadows across her cheek bones. He knew she was tired. He loved her. He could not bear to think that someone else had held her, discovered her body, kissed her and been kissed in return. He sat down opposite her and waited. It was only a few moments later when Isobel opened her eyes. She looked directly at him and smiled. Edward stared back.

'Who's Bill?'

Isobel sat up. He looked like a frightened child. She knew in that moment that whatever she said would affect their lives and, perhaps more importantly, those of their children. Nevertheless, she held back. She needed to know what Edward knew.

'Bill?'

'Yes, Bill!'

'Why are you asking me?'

'Why do you think?'

She saw the anguish in his eyes. He saw the caution in hers. He stood up and went to pour himself another whisky. Isobel watched him.

'Can you pour me one?'

When he had handed a tumbler to her he sat down again - rigid, on the edge of the seat – unable to look at her.

'Sarah told me.' He felt compelled to hear what he dreaded hearing and so paved the way for Isobel to reveal her secrets. 'She said that her friend, Cat something and someone called Bill, had slept with you in Norfolk; Bill in Mummy's bed!' His voice broke and he coughed roughly and swallowed, staring into his glass.

Isobel spoke softly. 'It's true. He did.'

She watched as his shoulders hunched even more and his head lowered. The silence that fell was punctuated only by the crackling of the fire. Isobel rose and went towards Edward. She knelt at his feet and looked into his downturned face. She saw the tears and put her hand up to wipe them away. He grasped her hand, pulled it to his lips and held it there.

'Edward. I'm sorry. It only happened once. He was my first boyfriend and his wife had died and he was lonely and ... so was I. I'm not making excuses. I don't deny that it happened ... once ... but it is never going to happen again.'

They had talked for a long time, each holding on to secrets. In the end it was as if they had made an unspoken pact - to stay together, no matter what.

10

Edward never mentioned his occasional and casual relationships with women which had taken place on his travels. He spent a final night with Enid and then said goodbye. His travels became less frequent as the business shrank and was eventually taken over. It had entered his mind, as he watched the new baby develop, that Tom might not be his son, but this painful realisation he was not prepared openly to acknowledge. If Isobel had humiliated him in private she was certainly not going to humiliate him in public. Instead, he detached himself from Tom as far as possible.

When the whisky pulled him into more maudlin reflections, he thought about his parents and how his mother had fussed around his father and entertained his clients from abroad, always unquestioningly accepting her husband's egotistic insensitivity. Arthur had always needed to feel powerful and was quick to belittle others, even his wife and son, when it suited him. Separated from his parents, at the age of seven, when he had been sent away to the same disciplinarian school to which, mystifyingly, he had insisted on sending Edward, he was also a man damaged by war. Arthur had survived the carnage of the bloody French battlefields of the Great War. He was resolute in his insistence that one should never talk about it, other than to say what a damned fine job he and his loyal team of men had made of it all. Edward's older brother, George, had been killed in action in 1941 and that was never referred to either. For his part, Edward had borne the 'sweat, blood and tears' of the Second World War with a mixture of grim perseverance and outward displays of derring do. His aeronautical acrobatics had won him admiration from other crews and his reputation with women only added to his image of a fearless and glamorous hero.

He resented the closeness of Isobel to her son and felt unable to shake off the burden of jealousy and suspicion, to engage with Tom. He was honest enough with himself to concede that it was not Tom's fault and he needed Isobel. To his work colleagues and international customers and certainly to their close friends, Edward presented the comfortable picture of a successful, talented and fulfilled family man and Isobel was crucial to all this. She was the perfect hostess and everyone liked her. Isobel never mentioned the other women in Edward's life, whom she had known about over the years. She had decided on the journey home after her night with Bill that she would not. Nor did she tell her husband that he was not Tom's biological father. To the outside world they appeared to be a stable and contented family.

Edward had been right about Isobel's aptitude for interior design. At first, their friends asked for her advice and then, as more and more people heard about her, people she did not know contacted her for help. In the town the woman who owned a home furnishings shop asked Isobel if she would be prepared to design for customers and she would provide training and pay for any courses Isobel needed to attend. Isobel found that, with time on her hands, when Sarah and Tom were at school, she relished the work and so began a firm friendship and eventually a partnership with Claudia, the proprietor and for Isobel, a welcome release from domesticity.

In one area of their lives, and crucially for Tom, Isobel's feelings prevailed – not because Edward respected her strong objections to children being sent away to school – but because their financial position did not afford them that opportunity. The business was not thriving and Isobel pointed out the sacrifices Edward would have to make if they were to fund Tom's education. It had never entered Edward's mind to suggest that their daughter be educated in the same way but he felt strongly that Tom should be sent to his old school. His reluctant acceptance that this would not happen served only to fuel further his animosity towards Tom.

Tom grew into a sensitive and gentle boy. He adored Sarah, despite her indifference to him, and increasingly, her antagonism. Sarah never grew out of the jealousy she felt for this curly haired, blue eyed little boy, whom everyone seemed to adore. She knew she charmed her father, but eventually, his over-attentiveness towards her began to grate. As she grew up, she hated the way he still treated her as his little girl. It was as if he did not want her to mature and her teenage years were turbulent for everyone in the house.

Tom was frightened of his father. Edward found Tom irritating. The bond between Isobel and her son seemed to him to be responsible for Tom's distinct lack of interest in two of Edward's passions – rugby and golf. Tom became a talented tennis player – much to his father's disdain. Edward had always hated tennis, a sport at which he had never excelled. As the years passed, Edward and Sarah, in their Machiavellian ways, succeeded in making Tom's life confusing and, on occasions, very unhappy. Tom struggled to understand what he was doing to provoke such animosity. Isobel intervened whenever possible and blazing family rows would sometimes ensue.

Isobel and Sarah maintained an uneasy relationship for most of the time. Just occasionally Sarah would let her guard down and Mother and daughter would share closer moments, but these were short-lived. When Sarah went to university, having sailed through her exams, Isobel knew that her daughter was gone for good. Edward consoled himself, on losing his daughter, as he saw it, by spending more time at the golf club and drinking more whisky. The truth was he was bored with his life and felt rejected by his daughter. He found Tom's presence at home something to be endured. There was no possible way he was ever going to understand this boy, so he continued not to try. By the time Tom left to study medicine, Edward had more or less washed his hands of anything to do with him. He was scathing about the medical profession, referring to them all as 'quacks.' He complained about the costs involved in the long training Tom would undertake, but Isobel had saved all the years she had been working and resolutely defended both her children's choice of careers. She encouraged their independence and kept in contact with them. Tom came home at regular intervals, Sarah less so.

Despite his and Isobel's unspoken agreement that the subject would not be discussed, Edward knew that there had been times when Isobel had wanted to talk to him about Tom's father, but he also knew, with absolute conviction, that if this agreement was ever broken, it would destroy him. While it was never talked about he could carry on. As far as his friends, and previously his colleagues, were concerned, Tom was his son, a successful doctor. Sarah did not know, of course, and he had insisted that she should not be told; far better to keep this bloody awful, humiliating secret just between himself and Isobel. He took early retirement with a generous pension and spent more time on the golf course.

He supposed he still loved Isobel. She was certainly stunning to look at. She was a devoted mother. She had supported him all their married life and had been a proficient and charming hostess to their visitors. He knew he owed her much. She could have left him and gone off with Bill - whoever he was - but she had chosen to stay with him, Edward. In his more generous moods he acknowledged that his life would have been the poorer without Isobel. In most ways their life together had been a success. The strong physical attraction which had been so exciting in the early days had suffered around the time when Edward had looked at Tom and realised the truth. He supposed a lot of their contemporaries went through difficult times. He was not sure because no-one he knew would ever talk about that sort of thing. Travelling had helped to ease the strain and Isobel had been very loving on his return. She still excited him even now. All in all, things could have been worse.

Some evenings, with his tightened up thoughts released through the exquisite escapism of his favourite malt whisky, Edward would allow himself to think back. Sarah had broken his heart, of course, when she went swanning off to the States. Actually, she had moved away, physically and emotionally, from him over a period of years. He had refused to see it until one day she had screamed at him to leave her alone. He could still remember the hurt and the anger he had felt. All her life he had indulged her and given her his support and to see her, eyes flaring, mouth twisted into a disfiguring snarl, practically spitting at him, was truly shocking. She had accused him of suffocating her with his control. He had thought of it as his love and devotion. He loved her more than anyone else. She was, quite simply, perfect.

It was when she went to London that he knew he had lost her to the world. She would be successful.

He would continue to fund her and do everything he could to support her and try to see her as often as possible, but she was not a little girl any more. Edward struggled with that. He could not bear to think of Sarah with a man. He knew too well what men were like. So, most of the time, he pushed those thoughts out of his head and concentrated on his work and his golf.

Edward sensed Tom's homosexuality but could not bear to have it confirmed. He found a bitter-sweet consolation in convincing himself that no *real* son of his would ever have become a 'Nancy-Boy'. When Tom and Alex came to the house for a meal, Edward would be sure to eat at the golf club. On one occasion, when he was caught unawares, because Isobel had forgotten to tell him, Edward had managed to hold back from speaking out loud his prejudices and his ignorance but he had extricated himself as soon as possible, feeling a deep revulsion. He had gone straight to his study, poured himself a very large whisky and then another and then gone upstairs and stripped off his clothes, which he threw into the laundry basket, unable to bear the thought of wearing them again until they were laundered. He had stood under a scalding shower until the water had begun to run cold. After rigorous drying with a towel, he had put on clean pyjamas, dressing gown and slippers and shut himself in his study with the whisky bottle and a biography of one of England's great explorers.

11

Isobel stood back to appraise her arrangement of tulips. Since the piano had gone to Tom and Alex's home she had had to find a new place for her flowers and family photographs. All the years she had used the polished top of the baby grand for these items she had felt a pang of guilt. Her parents had always assured her that nothing should ever be placed on the top of a piano. In their small seaside house the old upright had remained free of clutter. When Edward's Mother had insisted Isobel have the beautiful Bechstein, because her arthritis prevented her from playing any more, Isobel had been reluctant to accept such a priceless gift. Helen, in her quiet but determined way, had insisted. She was thrilled that Edward had married someone who would play her treasured piano.

'You can always pass it on if one of your own children plays. I like to think it will stay in the family.'

Helen had never commented on the photographs and flowers, reflected in the smooth mirror of the ebony veneer, but had always listened appreciatively to Isobel's playing; a smile softening her tight, tired face as she closed her eyes, her small frame resting in the dense cushions of the sofa.

The brightly coloured arrangement satisfied Isobel's artistic eye. The old Denby jug which held them, sat securely on her late mother's linen and lace mat. Around this, on the oval table by the window, encased in various silver or ceramic frames were photographs of family members; faded sepia ones capturing both sets of parents in their youth and brighter, coloured childhood ones of Sarah and Tom. One picture of herself and Edward on their honeymoon, laughing and carefree, with the mountains forming a romantic backdrop, caused a fleeting sadness when she dusted it, but she always brushed her feelings aside and moved on to the others. Edward had not noticed a small oval frame with a recent picture of Tom and Alex, smiling at the camera, in their skiing hats, with sunglasses perched on their heads, reflecting the bright sun and clear sky. Isobel loved the picture and always smiled as she saw the joy in her son's eyes. The most recent picture of Sarah was of her looking very beautiful; her dark hair shining. She was in a black dress and wearing pearls at her neck and ears; her expression impassive as ever. A shadow passed over Isobel when she looked at her daughter. Would she ever be able to reach her and hold her the way she could Tom? Her heart felt heavy as she replaced this picture.

Edward and she were expecting some friends for supper that evening. They were golfing friends of Edward's but Isobel had met them when she had reluctantly attended a couple of social events at the clubhouse. She took one last glance around the room and it was as she walked through the cool hall towards the kitchen that the telephone rang.

'Hello.'

A male voice at the other end spoke loudly. 'Is that you, Isobel?'

'Yes, it is.' Isobel was not sure, but she thought it sounded like Gilbert, who was coming for supper.

'Well, er, Isobel, m'dear. It's Gilbert here and, well, I'm afraid this is going to come as a bit of a shock, but, you see, Edward, well, he's gone to the hospital ... the General, they said. He collapsed on the fairway, you see.'

There was silence for a moment. Isobel sat on the small chair.

'You there, m'dear?'

'Yes, yes, I'm here.'

'Didn't know if you'd like me to take you to the hospital ... or maybe your son could? He's a doctor and all that, you know ... ' His blustering voice faded away.

'Yes, thank you. I'll call Tom. Do you know what happened?'

'No, no, 'fraid not. I'd just arrived and the ambulance was already there, you see. I said I'd ring you. It was all a bit chaotic really.'

Isobel took a deep breath. 'Thank you, Gilbert. It was kind of you to ring me. If you don't mind, I'll call Tom. He'll be at the surgery.'

'All right, m'dear. Let me know if I can be of any help. Give my best to Edward when you see him. That's if he, er ... I mean, you know ... '

'I will, Gilbert and thank you again.'

Isobel realised Tom would be seeing patients. She went into the kitchen, poured a glass of water and gulped it down. She locked the back door, grabbed her coat, bag and keys, slammed the front door shut and ran to her car. With shaking hands she switched on the ignition and set off at speed for the hospital. The lights were against her and as she waited at each set her thoughts veered wildly between the possibilities which lay ahead. The nurse in her had already gone through the most likely causes of her husband's collapse, none of which she wanted to acknowledge.

'Please let me find a space!' she pleaded out loud, as she reached the hospital car park. There were none. At one end of the car park, close to the buildings, were half a dozen short-stay spaces. Ignoring the 'Twenty minutes for Emergency Use Only' sign, she swung into a slot. She locked the car and walked briskly to the Emergency entrance. He would have been taken there. The woman behind the glass screen continued talking on the telephone for some minutes until Isobel said loudly,

'My husband has just been brought in. He collapsed.'

The woman glanced up at Isobel. She spoke quickly into the receiver.

'I'll have to go. I'll catch you later.' Then, glancing up, she spoke in a dull, disinterested monotone. 'Alright, sweetheart.' She was at least thirty years younger than Isobel. 'What name is it?'

Isobel gave all the details as patiently as she could and the woman told her to wait on one of the red chairs while she found out what was happening. Isobel sat on a red plastic chair and watched as the woman left her seat and disappeared down the corridor. Around her were members of the public, waiting, in various stages of discomfort. An old man suddenly vomited on to the floor and slid off his chair into the foul smelling, blood stained products of his stomach. Isobel was about to call a nurse when one came along and called for help. Isobel watched detachedly as they lifted the man on to a trolley and wheeled him away. No-one came to clean the floor as the minutes ticked by.

Isobel was on the point of going down the corridor to see for herself what was happening, when a doctor came towards her, accompanied by a Sister. Isobel knew that senior nursing staff only accompanied a doctor to see relatives when there was something bad to report. She stood and watched them approach as if in slow motion. She saw their mouths moving but did not hear their words. She simply knew that Edward had gone. She closed her eyes. She felt a firm grip on her arm and, opening her eyes, saw the kindly face of the nurse.

'Come along, Mrs Gabriel. There is a private room for us to sit in.' She guided Isobel, who could not feel the floor beneath her feet, and could not hear the hospital sounds all around her, to a small room, furnished with a sofa and some armchairs. This is the room where they tell you someone has died, Isobel thought. The young doctor sat opposite Isobel and the nurse sat beside her on the sofa. Isobel looked from one to the other and thought of Tom telling relatives that their loved one has died. She saw the doctor was terrified. Had he told anyone before, she wondered.

'Edward is dead, isn't he.' The flat statement – not a question - sounded loud and blunt to her own ears.

The door suddenly creaked open and in came the receptionist with a tray of tea. She smiled a deeply compassionate smile at Isobel.

'Here you are, lovey. This'll help.' She closed the door very slowly and gently behind her.

The doctor leaned forward in his chair. 'Yes, Mrs Gabriel, I'm afraid your husband died on arrival at the hospital.'

He coughed awkwardly and she saw bright tears in his eyes and irrationally she wanted to hold his hand and comfort him.

'The ambulance crew and all of us here did everything we could but I'm afraid it was a massive heart attack. We could not save him. I'm so sorry.' His face was flushed, she noticed.

She pictured them trying to restart Edward's heart and to get him breathing again. She wondered if he had felt pain. She remembered a patient, years ago, whose ribs had broken under the force of the compressions.

'Do you think he was in a lot of pain?' She knew the answer would be the same whatever had happened and wondered why she had asked it. Surprisingly, this doctor avoided the usual platitudes and said simply,

'I don't know, I'm afraid. I just know that he had gone by the time the ambulance pulled up. We still tried, but ... '

Isobel looked at him and smiled. How strange the need to comfort the bearer of bad news.

'I know you did all you could and I am grateful that you tried.'

The nurse proffered a plastic cup of tea. Isobel took it and noticed her hand shaking. Edward hated plastic cups; plastic anything really. She took a sip. It was thick with sugar. She replaced it on the tray.

'I'm afraid I have to leave you now, Mrs Gabriel, but Sister will stay with you. Perhaps there is someone you would like us to contact for you?'

Isobel remembered that doctors always moved on as soon as possible, leaving the nurses to console and comfort. She could see that, despite his brief, inadvertent display of emotion only a moment ago, as he opened the door, his mind had already left her behind.

The nurse touched Isobel's arm. 'Would you like to go and see your husband Mrs Gabriel? Is there anyone you'd like us to contact for you?'

'Yes ... I should like to see him please ... and ... no ... thank you. There is no-one to contact. Not just yet.'

'My name's Carol. Just ask for me if you need anything.' The nurse stood and leaving the room, promised to be back in a minute. Ten minutes later, full of apologies, she returned. Isobel had been bracing herself. As they walked down the corridor towards the side room, she recalled in her mind the bodies she had laid out. Performing the last offices, they had been taught, was the last service the nurse could offer a person and it was to be done in pairs, in silence and with tender respect. They won't have had time to do it all, she mused. They will just have tidied him up a bit ... for me.

The room was cool and lit only by the angle poise lamp at the top of the bed. They had turned its glow towards the wall slightly. Edward's long body lay beneath a white sheet. He looked like one of the figures lying prone on a tomb in a country church somewhere, the folds of the sheet draping the sides of the bed. The nurse took her elbow and guided her towards Edward. She looked anxiously into Isobel's face, searching for signs of distress or imminent collapse. Isobel looked at her.

'Thank you. I'll be fine. Perhaps I could be alone with him?'

'Of course, I'll be just outside if you need me.'

Isobel sat on the plastic chair. He was pale, with the beginnings of mottled, purple blotches gathering around one side of his neck. The stillness of death always surprised her. She moved the sheet and took his rapidly cooling hand; the hand that had held her, aroused her, admonished and, once or twice, threatened her. It held no power now. Isobel looked at the closed eyes. They would never see her again. He would no longer be a part of her life. He would no longer be a part of Tom's or Sarah's lives. She would not be taking him home. She would not have another conversation with him. They would not share a bed again. She would be alone in their home. He had gone. She closed her eyes and saw him at that first dance, in his uniform, coming towards her and saying his name. She replaced his hand, straightened the sheet, stood and leaned forward to kiss his cheek.

'Goodbye, Edward.' No tears came. Her eyes felt gritty, her throat dry as she left the room. This time, walking along the corridor, her legs felt heavy and the sounds around her, acute, exaggerated, intrusive. Carol caught up with her, touching her arm.

'Mrs Gabriel.' She sounded anxious. 'Are you alright? Is someone coming to pick you up?'

Isobel turned to smile at her. 'No, but thank you. You've been very kind. I'm quite alright, really. I should like to go home and I'll call my son and my daughter from there.'

'But are you OK to drive? You've just had a terrible shock.'

'I'm fine, really.' She placed her hand briefly over Carol's which was still resting on her forearm. How strange to feel such affinity and yet we don't know each other and will probably never meet again. She pre-empted Carol's question.

'I know we have to pick up a death certificate after the post mortem, don't we? I was a nurse you see, so I know there has to be a post mortem with an unexpected death, doesn't there?' She suddenly stopped and turned once more to Carol. 'And yes, my husband carried a donor card so please proceed with whatever you need to do. I'm afraid I can't remember what can be used in this sort of situation, but I hope Edward can be of some use ... to someone ... '

Carol looked at this small dignified woman, still obviously in a state of shock and yet so composed. 'Thank you, Mrs Gabriel, but I need you to come to my office, just for a moment, to sign some forms.'

'If they can wait till tomorrow, I should like my son to come back. I need to go home.'

Carol could see that Isobel's composure was being held together by a very fine thread and nothing needed doing right then and there. The donor card had already been seen and whatever could be used would be. They had reached the automatic doors. Isobel took a deep breath as a cool breeze blew in.

'Thank you, Carol. You've been very kind.'

Carol held back from insisting that Isobel remain at the hospital until someone came to fetch her, but made a mental note to telephone her at home within the hour.

Despite being familiar with hospital life, Isobel was always glad to leave and welcomed the feeling of release as she put distance between her and that enclosed, clinical world; never more so than at that moment. She concentrated on the traffic as she drove through the busy roads to her home. As she pulled up, Eileen, laden with shopping bags, was mounting her front door steps. She waved cheerily at Isobel. Isobel smiled back. Eileen waited to speak to her. Isobel knew that if she had to say out loud that Edward was dead she would break down, and yet there seemed no way out.

'Hello, Isobel. How's things?' Eileen's cheerful Scottish accent rang out. Isobel locked her car and walked towards her neighbour who immediately reacted to Isobel's drawn face.

'What is it? Oh, my dear!' She lowered her bags and came down the steps. 'Isobel, what is it?'

Isobel felt such an ache in her throat that she could barely speak. She swallowed painfully and felt her mouth begin to shake. With a great effort she made herself say the words out loud. 'Edward died today.'

Eileen wrapped her in her arms and held her, saying nothing. Isobel felt her legs go weak and silent tears fall down her cheeks. Eileen gently took the keys from Isobel's hand and led her up into her house, guessing, correctly, that Isobel would not wish to be taken into someone else's home. She took Isobel's jacket off her and guided her to the large sofa in the sitting room.

'There, you lie down here and I'll get you something to drink and then you can tell me what happened.'

Isobel put up no resistance. She laid her head back into the deep cushions and closed her hot eyes. She could hear Eileen going out of the front door, leaving it open and then a few minutes later returning and moving around in the kitchen.

Perhaps if I just lie here I will float away as well, she thought. Where was Edward now? She knew the answer to that and thought of him being cut open, or maybe his corneas being removed. They would be alright for transplant even if his organs weren't. How long after death was it that you had before they were no use to anyone? Would the post mortem mean they wouldn't be able to take anything? She couldn't remember. They would tell her she expected. Eileen came into the room with a mug of tea.

'Here you are. Drink this.'

Isobel sat up and cradled the hot mug in her suddenly cold hands. 'Thank you, Eileen.'

The plump little Scotswoman sat opposite and waited. Isobel told her what had happened. Eileen could not bring herself to feel sorry Edward had died. Of course it was sad when a life ended, but there had been no love lost between herself and Edward Gabriel, oh no. On the contrary, they had barely managed to be civil to each other on the few occasions they had met. Eileen hated snobs and Edward hated outspoken and opinionated women, especially those he felt were lower down the social spectrum. Eileen did feel concern and compassion for her friend, now looking pale and drawn. 'Have you phoned Tom?'

'No. I wanted to come home first. I'll ring him now.' She put her mug down on the side table and rose to go to the phone in the hall. It rang. She jumped and looked at Eileen in sudden panic. Eileen spoke firmly.

'It's OK. I'll get it.'

Carol's voice on the other end asked if Isobel was alright.

'She's OK thank you. I'm her neighbour and I'm not leaving her until her son gets here. It was kind of you to ring, Sister.' Eileen moved back to the kitchen as Isobel dialled the surgery number.

12

The blustery showers and biting April wind, which heralded the morning of Edward's funeral, persisted until they were seated in the unimaginatively designed municipal crematorium. As the first hymn began, the sun broke through, and a shaft of thin light caught the pale oak coffin as it rested in front of them. Isobel, with Sarah and Tom on either side of her, gazed at the arrangement of spring flowers, their delicate blues, yellows and pinks cushioned by the soft greens of foliage. She wondered if she looked smaller today; diminished, as so many newly widowed women she had seen. She sat up straight, composing herself and feeling the warmth of Tom's coat against her shoulder. Alex was sitting next to Tom at her insistence. He had offered to sit in the row behind them but Isobel knew how much her son needed his partner that day. Sarah, her beautiful perfume wafting subtly as she moved, surprised her, suddenly and movingly, by linking her arm through Isobel's. Glancing at her daughter's profile, Isobel saw the strained expression and wondered what Sarah was thinking as she bade farewell to her father. Close to them sat friends; a few who knew Edward and Isobel as a couple and Isobel's own friends whom Edward had never really acknowledged; Eileen, of course, and Claudia from the shop. Touchingly, some of Isobel's friends from the community choir and her reading group had turned up to offer their support and condolences. And Ronnie Fairfax, looking gaunt and weary, his wife, Annie, in the local hospice, close to death.

Much against Isobel's better judgement, and only because she knew Edward would have wanted it, she had agreed, after consulting Sarah and Tom, that members of the RAF Association and the Royal British Legion should be allowed to honour one of their own. This they did in the form of eulogies, mercifully short and the singing of their requested hymn, 'I vow to thee my Country.' Finally, as the coffin disappeared behind the olive green velvet curtains, a lone bugler played the Last Post.

Isobel endured what she felt amounted to a somewhat nationalistic display with some degree of discomfort. Tom and Sarah shared their Mother's unease but knew their father would have been pleased and, indeed, there were many friends of his in the chapel that day - men who had seen war in all its gruesome guises and men who had clung on to comradeship through these organisations. Perhaps it was only in that arena where they felt truly understood; the unspoken shared experiences needing to be clung on to, to balance the lack of understanding in a rapidly changing and seemingly ungrateful world. One of his golfing cronies referred to Edward's death as, 'Doing a Bing', and assured everyone that this would have been just the way Edward would have liked to have gone, after a game of golf, like Bing Crosby.

Isobel sought out Ronnie by the rose garden as the pale sun persevered to bring some light to the chill. 'Dear Ronnie, thank you so much for coming. I know this must be difficult for you.'

His haunted eyes looked down at her and he gave a slight nod. He leaned forward to hold her for a brief moment. 'Thank you, Isobel. I wanted to come and offer my support. I know you will understand if I don't join you for refreshments. I will be available whenever you need to go through things with me.' He shook hands with Tom and Sarah and returned to his car. Annie died a week later.

They got through the socialising afterwards, consisting of a light buffet lunch, provided by the old coaching inn, now a comfortable hotel, in the town. Tom and Sarah had persuaded Isobel not to host this expected repast at her home, pointing out that it could go on for hours there. Isobel was to be eternally grateful for her children's common sense. With a surreal detachment, as if observing herself from somewhere else, she endured the murmured words of condolence and the awkward hugs from strangers; forgotten or never known faces from years gone by; Edward's friends.

By the time the last of the funeral guests had left it was late afternoon. Isobel looked at Sarah, Tom and Alex and smiled gratefully.

'Well, I'm so glad I listened to you about coming here. I think those last two would have stayed all night if we'd been at home!'

Sarah grinned. 'I did have a little word with the hotel and they agreed to come in and start to clear things away at my nod.'

'Well done, darling. Thank you, all of you, for being so wonderful today. I hope it wasn't too much of an ordeal. I saw you, Alex, with that enormous man with all those medals. He could hardly stand straight with the weight of them! Was he asking awkward questions?'

Alex laughed. 'No, no, not at all. I didn't really give him a chance. I said I was a friend of the family and before he could ask me any questions I asked him about his role in the Legion. That was that really. I couldn't stop him!'

Tom put his arm around Alex's shoulder. 'Well done,' he said quietly.

Sarah watched the two men exchange a fond look and felt a sudden envy. They had something which had so far eluded her. The string of failed relationships she had experienced had left her cautious and hardened. Trust her perfect little brother to find such a gorgeous looking man and what was clear to see, at that moment, a pretty strong love. She pushed her bitter thoughts away as she watched Isobel standing by the window, looking lovely in her black suede coat, her dark hair, glossy and soft and the colour of her scarf enhancing her blue eyes. Her mother had refused to buy anything new for the funeral as she had treated herself to the suede coat only a few weeks before and, in any case, had always worn a lot of black. She had a knack of combining colours in her accessories that always looked right. Sarah supposed she was not that different with her own love of black and, apart from their very different eye colour, she and Isobel were not dissimilar, in looks. Well, if she aged as well as Isobel, she would not be displeased.

So, for that day at least, harmony between brother, sister and mother prevailed; united in their loss of one man and, despite the fact that he had played very different roles in each of their lives, standing together as his remaining family.

That evening, they kicked their shoes off and sitting round the kitchen table, drank wine, ate a hearty beef bourguignon, made by Eileen, who had insisted on doing her bit, and shared memories. With each of them determined not to bring old animosities to the table, the conversation flowed. Eileen and Alex listened mostly, knowing how important it was to support without intruding. By ten o'clock they were all exhausted.

Tom hugged his mother. 'Well done, Mum. You were wonderful. I know it was hard for you today. I'll ring you tomorrow.'

Isobel held on to his tall frame for just a moment, tears close by. 'Thank you, darling. You have been such a help. Are you alright?'

Alex embraced her next, saying softly, 'He's fine, Isobel. I'll look after him.'

Tom and Alex hugged Sarah and Eileen in turn and suddenly were gone. The three women stood for a moment in silence. Sarah was the first to speak. 'Well, I'll clear up. You two get off to bed.'

She brushed aside their objections, stating firmly that she needed to move around and in any case she would have a cigarette at the back door when they had gone. After Eileen left, Mother and daughter embraced and said their goodnights, both needing space and solitude. Isobel ran a deep bath, poured in some soothing oil and sank into the fragrant warmth. She closed her eyes and let her mind wander.

Sarah loaded the dishwasher and wiped around the kitchen. It was all so familiar and yet she felt far removed from this place and everything associated with it. She poured herself a glass of wine, lit a cigarette and stood by the back door. In the US she was disciplined to having one cigarette a day – in her own home. She fully intended to stop altogether but not right now, after a trying and demanding day. As she stood, wrapped in a soft cashmere pashmina of palest pink, her small elegant frame leaning against the doorway, she tried to analyse her feelings. It had been a shock to receive her mother's telephone message when she had got in from work.

'Hello Sarah, I'm so sorry not to be able to speak to you directly. I hope you pick this up soon. Darling, I'm afraid I have some very sad and unexpected news. Please can you ring me when you get this message? It doesn't matter what time it is here. I will answer the phone.'

She admitted to herself, as she looked out into the darkness, that she had hurt her father by going to America. She knew she had hurt him before that, by rejecting him whenever he had tried in his clumsy, masculine way to meet her in London. His overbearing, verging on inappropriate, adoration of her, as a small child and even on into her teenage years, had not only exasperated and ultimately embarrassed her, but had often caused her to wonder why such a chauvinistic and old fashioned man was not more taken with his son. She could only now surmise that either Edward had been pathologically jealous of Tom and saw him as a rival for Isobel's affections - mother and son had always been very close, she knew only too well - or maybe Tom being gay had been an insurmountable barrier between them. Had Edward sensed something from when Tom was very young? Surely not; he had never appeared that perceptive and in any case he had rarely taken an interest in Tom's life.

Even through the wool the cold night air made her shiver. Fatigue weighed down on her as she locked up, turned off the lights and made her way upstairs. Isobel's light was on. Should she go in and check her mother was alright? This was another relationship Sarah had not quite managed to fathom. She knocked gently on the door. 'You OK, Mum?'

'Come in Sarah.'

Sarah poked her head around the door, not really wanting to go right in. Isobel looked small in the big bed, her unopened book resting on the quilt. She smiled up at Sarah. 'How are you, darling? Thank you for clearing up. It has been a long day and you're probably still a bit jet-lagged.'

'I'm fine – but ready for a sleep. Can I get you anything?' She couldn't imagine what on earth her mother would want but it seemed the thing to say.

'No, thank you. I'm fine, really. It was nice to sit around and chat over the meal, wasn't it?'

Sarah knew she should stay for a while, or even go across to give her mother a hug, but she held back. She had friends who would have offered to share their mother's bed; to offer physical closeness in their hour of need. The very thought repelled her. 'Yes it was. Well, I'll go to bed and catch up on some sleep now, if you're sure you're OK.'

'Alright, darling. Sleep well. See you in the morning.'

Sarah padded along the landing to her old room. Thankfully, Isobel had changed the colours and furniture in there. Sarah would most certainly have stayed in a local hotel if she had had to sleep in her room as it used to be. Her mother had asked her years ago if she had any objection to the change. Sarah remembered the irritation she had felt at being asked what she considered to be a totally unnecessary question, as she no longer lived at home. She was also honest enough with herself to know that had Isobel not asked she would have felt aggrieved. Now, at the age of thirty five, she still struggled sometimes to understand where in this world she fitted. In Boston, her life was more sorted. Back here, old memories and emotions simmered away just under the surface, always threatening to come to the boil and overflow and make a mess of everything.

At last, after her ritual of cleansing and moisturising, she fell into bed. Isobel's innate artistic flair provided a calm, fresh sleeping place and a sumptuously comfortable bed. The only memento of Sarah's childhood was an array of dolls and teddy bears, propping each other up on a shelf in the alcove to the right of the fireplace. They had a used and homely look about them and their faded colours blended comfortably with the soft, neutral shades of the room. Was her mother hoping for grandchildren one day? The only other colours of note were provided by a vase of anemones. Isobel always placed fresh flowers, usually from her garden, in the bedrooms being used. Sarah snuggled up under the insulating covers and closed her eyes. Without warning, a sob rose up and caught in her throat. She felt like a guest in this family home and, at that moment, completely alone.

Isobel lay wide-eyed in the dark, conscious of her daughter not far away – and yet remote. Her eyes grew accustomed to the gloom but the familiar shadowy shapes of her bedroom seemed different somehow. No, it wasn't the shapes. It was the silence. She reached her arm across the pillows to her right and felt again the empty space. Would she sleep better without Edward's noisy breathing and restless turning? People did – after a time. At that moment it felt as though he had gone on one of his trips abroad – but this time he would not return. I am sixty, she thought. What will life be like without him? She wished Tom and Sarah could find a way to come closer. She had been aware of the effort both of them had made for her sake and that it was unlikely to last. Just as the dawn chorus was reaching its crescendo, she fell into a deep sleep, exhausted from ruminating over the last thirty eight years of her life as Edward's wife.

Sarah flew back home two days after Edward's funeral. She knew that Isobel had hoped she and Tom would find some time to talk but they had not. Even the sporadic conversations that she and her mother had managed had all been taken up with the business of death. On her return to Boston, life continued in much the same way as before. This entailed throwing herself into her work with even more vigilance. She accepted the kind words and transitory support from acquaintances and enjoyed the more reliable and restoring comfort supplied by Hannie, Stella and, in her own unique and often weeping way, Juliana. These women were unquestioning and undemanding, allowing Sarah to speak, or not, of her father, her family. Each of her close friends however, held concerns for Sarah, as they watched her expending ferocious energy and commitment to the cases assigned to her. Financially rewarding and high profile though this work proved to be, they wondered if Sarah would ever stop, take stock and perhaps even find a loving partner. Hannie loved Sarah but had long ago accepted the futility of declaring her feelings. Stella had a strong and passionate relationship with her long term lover, Johnny and Juliana was the matriarch of a large and lively family. Only Sarah seemed unable to form a meaningful attachment.

Edward's ashes were interred next to his brother George's grave, in the churchyard of the looming red brick Victorian church, which also held the remains of their parents. Isobel had no connection with this church but her in-laws had worshipped there. As she and Tom stood, while the vicar recited the ancient words, she knew that her ashes would not join this family. She would ask for hers to be scattered and carried by the winds on the beach in Norfolk where she grew up. She would have her spirit set free. They thanked the gentle vicar, gazed for one last moment at the graves and then turned away to walk down the gravel path to Tom's car. Both knew they would not return.

Over the next few weeks and months Isobel surprised herself at how quickly she adapted to living alone. There were times when she missed Edward and the companionship they had shared but gradually a feeling of freedom crept in. All the time Edward had been away she had managed the home and the children – and herself. She felt guilty to begin with, and disloyal, but as the feelings of loss diminished they were replaced by a new sense of independence, of adventure.

For Christmas Day of the year Edward died, Isobel invited Tom, Alex, Eileen and Ronnie to her home. Tom had suggested Isobel spend the day with him and Alex and stay overnight at their house. He wondered if Christmas would prove to be hard for Isobel without Edward. Isobel had insisted she would like to cook and host the day in her home. She felt compelled to do this, feeling that the more occupied she made herself through these 'firsts' the better. On their wedding anniversary that summer she had spent the day with Eileen, going round one of the many nearby National Trust houses and grounds and later, enjoying a shared supper. Widows, she discovered, did have a deeper understanding, often unspoken, but always steady.

The house looked bright, warm and welcoming. When Tom and Alex arrived early for coffee, before the others, who had been asked to come at midday, the smell of roasting turkey wafted temptingly as Isobel opened the front door.

'Wow, Mum, you look fantastic!'

They embraced and Tom stood back to admire the red dress Isobel had chosen to wear. She looked very beautiful; her dark hair cut in a soft bob and her slim frame elegantly carrying the red cashmere sweater-dress.

'Thank you. I couldn't resist this dress. It was my Christmas present to myself!'

Alex hugged her. 'Isobel, you look wonderful. I've never seen you in red before and it really suits you.'

Thank you, Alex. Actually, Edward never liked me in red and I did feel a bit guilty when I bought this, but I do like it and another woman in the shop said it suited me.'

'Indeed it does. You look stunning!'

She smiled and led them through to the kitchen for coffee. Tom and Alex looked pretty wonderful too and Isobel told them so. She had grown very fond of Alex. Their mutual love for Tom, far from causing any rivalry, bound them together. Isobel would have liked this young Irish man in any case but as she watched her son become content and secure in love, she drew towards Alex even more.

Alex was intrigued by Isobel, so very different from his own mother. In some respects there were similarities, which he felt were largely a generational thing; her absolute loyalty towards, and acceptance of, her husband's chauvinism. But so dissimilar in her independence and spirit, her individuality and her interests outside the home. His mother had never done anything on her own. She had never learned to drive and it seemed to Alex that she had metamorphosed into her husband's persona so that she only ever functioned as part of a couple. He found Isobel attractive and interesting; on the one hand, open, friendly, amusing and yet managing to retain an air of mystery about her.

The day passed in a harmonious and loving cocoon. Sarah telephoned and good wishes were exchanged. She was with Hannie and her family, who, despite being Jewish, always hosted a welcoming and happy meal for friends. She assured her mother that she was fine and wished Tom and Alex a happy Christmas. If, for a fleeting moment, she felt excluded, it passed and she said her goodbyes sounding cheerful.

Edward, Ronnie's Annie and Eileen's late husband Jack, were remembered and toasted. Ronnie struggled at times but felt touched and relieved to be included by such kind people. He had been glad to be able to tell his family that he would be with Isobel this year. After their mother's funeral they had all returned to their far-flung homes and the last thing

Ronnie wanted was an argument about which household he should join for Christmas.

Isobel's life continued without her husband and in many ways became easier to manage. Edward had not left an enormous estate but enough for Isobel to live comfortably and to maintain her home. The following Christmas she went to Tasmania for an extended visit to her old friend, Mary, now a devoted grandmother, and returned to England with renewed energy. Her work at the design shop and her social interests seemed to be enough. Gradually she began to enjoy the periods of solitude, especially in her garden. One thought troubled her. She could not bring herself to tell Tom about his father, particularly as Tom seemed so content and settled with Alex and in his work. Isobel wanted Tom to find peace in his life and genuinely felt that telling him would cause unnecessary anguish. She sometimes wondered if Bill was still alive. It was all so long ago. He had his own life and family in Italy. It was strange to think that his daughter, Caterina, might be a mother herself by now. She wondered if Bill had remarried and thought probably he had. As the years passed the dilemma of whether to tell Tom – or Sarah for that matter – faded and was pushed to the very back of Isobel's mind. She had never believed in going back and concentrated with determination on the present.

13

In 1993 Tom was completing his General Practitioner training, working in a practice situated on a busy road leading to the town centre, when it was announced that a new partner was being taken on. Tom, as the most junior member of the team, had not been involved in the selection process and was as curious as the reception and nursing staff about who would be joining them. On a clear, sunny April morning, which had somehow managed to brighten up the worn and utilitarian decor of the surgery, Alex strode through the entrance of the gloomy red brick building. He was greeted by the senior partner, James Fowler, a man who had worked assiduously for many years as the family doctor to the diverse and ever-changing population of his patch.

'Alex, welcome! Good to see you. Come and meet the team. We're in the back, in what we like to call our staff room, but which is actually a dumping ground.' He gave a wry grin and guided Alex down a cream painted corridor with dull green doors of consulting rooms on either side. At the end was a door marked, 'Staff Only', which he opened, to reveal a large, cluttered but bright room, the sun shining through battered vertical blinds.

'Right, everyone, this is Alex McKee, our new partner. Eight pairs of eyes scrutinised Alex with varying degrees of curiosity. James invited Alex to sit in one of the moulded plastic chairs from the waiting room. The receptionists had set the room out for this meeting and sandwiches and fruit juices were laid out on the table at one end of the room.

'OK, Alex, starting on my left, let me introduce the team. Indicating a small middle aged woman with a kindly face he said, 'This is Eleanor Griffiths, my partner of more years than either of us will admit. I know you have already met at the interviews.'

Eleanor Griffiths shook Alex's hand and beamed a welcoming smile. 'Hello, again Alex. We're delighted you've come to join us. Welcome.'

'Next we have Jason Hardy, who joined us two years ago who you also met at the interviews.'

Alex received a strong handshake from a young man with a shock of ginger hair, a lot of freckles and an engaging smile. 'Hi, Alex, good to have you on board.'

James continued around the loose semi-circle of people, introducing the three receptionists and the two Practice Nurses. Alex noticed that James managed to say something positive about each person without in any way sounding patronising. James was obviously adept at team management from the feel of the room and the responsive people in it. The only other member of the team he had met

144

previously was Eve, the practice manager. This still relatively new post within General Practice was becoming more commonplace, with GP's expected to run efficient and profitable businesses.

About half an hour later, when everyone had eaten and thoughts of the afternoon's work ahead had taken over from polite conversation, the door opened and Tom rushed in. He was slightly out of breath and very apologetic.

'I'm so sorry, James. I just couldn't get away from Mrs Carter!' He looked distraught - until the nurses startled to giggle. Catching their eyes he smiled and James patted him on the back.

'Why do you think I sent you? Good experience - managing to escape the clutches of an extremely lonely and rather demanding woman. Well done, Tom!'

Alex was struck by this gorgeous man. He studied him from the back of the room. He had never seen such brilliant blue eyes in either a man or a woman. James guided Tom over towards Alex.

'Tom, this is Alex, our new partner. Come and say hello.'

The two men looked at each other, shook hands and exchanged welcoming smiles.

'Hi.'

James glanced from one to the other. 'Well, I'll leave you two to get to know each other. I'm off to see my babies. Tom, you're with Eleanor this afternoon. Alex, can you spend some time in the office with Eve? She will fill you in on the latest news and show you your room and so on.'

He moved away to attend to his ante-natal clinic and Tom and Alex looked again at each other. Slate grey eyes scrutinising cornflower blue. Alex spoke first. Smiling, he said, 'So, we're both new boys then?'

Tom caught the musical intonation of Alex's soft Ulster brogue. 'Yes, I guess so. I think you'll be OK here. They are a nice bunch. Well – they have been to me.'

'That's good to hear. How's the training going? I had a God-awful placement – thought I'd never survive – but – here I am - in my first proper job and raring to go!'

He laughed and Tom found himself laughing with him. Sally, the senior practice nurse approached.

'Come on now boys – work to do!' She ushered them out of the room. Alex was taken to Eve's office and Tom joined Eleanor for her packed afternoon surgery. He knew he would get lots of hands-on experience. Eleanor was a gifted doctor and, that rare commodity, a generous and supportive trainer.

At the end of that first day of meeting, Tom and Alex left the surgery for their respective homes. Tom, to a house he shared with Jessie, a primary school teacher and Lloyd, a chef. Alex had found a ground floor flat in the town, opposite a pretty park. The whole of the Edwardian three storey building had been newly decorated and was just a short drive from the surgery. He intended to get a mortgage and move into his own house but wanted to explore the area first.

Each man, in their separate environments, reflected on their day. Alex felt excited and optimistic. It had been a good first few hours. He knew he would enjoy his work with the people at the surgery and he relished the opportunity to gain more experience and to become established as a community doctor. He smiled as he recalled the trainee, Tom and his lack of confidence. He reflected, with amused benefit of hindsight, his own faltering first steps into the world of Primary Care.

Tom, who was slowly gaining confidence with the teaching and support so freely given, pondered over the new addition to the team. He remembered with crystal clarity the modulated voice and accent and those deep grey eyes. He also thought how strong and confident Alex had seemed – like someone who had reached a comfortable place in his life and, he reflected, somewhere in his own, he had yet to find.

Over the next few weeks the new addition to the team made his mark. The patients seemed to like him and his surgeries were always packed. This was partly curiosity and partly Alex's ability as a doctor to treat with dignity and respect the people who consulted him. The partners offered him their advice only when requested and Alex felt he could call on any of them for help if needed. Tom was supervised by James and Eleanor, both GP trainers, and so tended not to see much of Jason or Alex. When they did manage to meet over coffee or occasionally lunch there was rarely time for meaningful conversation. There was little out of work socialising, apart from the receptionists, who shared lunch together occasionally. Once a year, usually in the summer, thereby avoiding the heavy workload of the winter months, a shared evening out was organised as an official social event. This was invariably at a local restaurant, and the partners paid for their staff, as a thank you for their support and hard work.

Tom knew that Jason and Alex had been sailing together. They had discovered this common interest early on and Jason had introduced Alex to his local sailing club. Tom recalled Jason inviting him soon after he had started his training at the practice but he had been completely honest and confessed he had no sea legs at all and had never been able to cope on a boat of any sort. In his mind he recalled his father's disdain and ridicule as he had heaved and wretched over the side of the small dinghy they had used in Cornwall on family holidays. Nevertheless, he felt a pang of envy as he listened to his two colleagues arranging a weekend date to go out in the boat.

It was a Thursday morning in June when surgery had finished and Alex and Tom were off to the local hospital for one of the regular training seminars for local GPs. That day the other partners were not attending, due to holidays and other commitments. James had given up attending any educational opportunities, seeing them as of no practical use so close to his retirement and, although never admitted out loud, was sceptical of the new 'patient-centred' approach and sensitive communication the new doctors were being encouraged to adopt. He was a caring and perceptive man but some of the ingrained arrogance, instilled during his own training, had never quite worn off. Most of his patients were older people and had grown up with the 'doctor knows best' unquestioning acceptance of the medical profession. They continued to place their doctor on a now slightly crumbling pedestal, steadfastly refusing to use first names or to expect anything other than sage advice, the occasional telling-off about smoking, weight and alcohol consumption and a somewhat patriarchal interest in their complaints.

Alex spotted Tom as he was leaving the building. 'Tom! Hop in. I'll give you a lift. You're coming back here later, aren't you?'

Tom approached the battered estate car. 'Yes, I am. Thanks.' He clambered in and Alex zoomed off.

'Should be an interesting one today. Fraser is always good value.'

'Yes, he's my old mentor,' Tom replied.

'Oh, really. Lucky you!'

Tom smiled and glanced at Alex's profile. Both men had loosened their ties; obligatory wear for surgery work. Alex returned the glance with a broad smile in Tom's direction. He had noticed the crisp blue and white shirt and the dark jacket which sat stylishly on Tom's slim frame. His beautiful eyes were impossible to ignore and Alex had been acutely conscious of them each time he had seen Tom.

'So, how are you settling in, Tom? Not too overwhelmed by it all?'

'No, no. I'm really enjoying it. Everyone is very kind and so far I haven't made any enormous blunders ... a few minor ones perhaps but nobody's died through my negligence ... yet!'

'That's grand. Oh, by the way, sorry about this old banger and the mess it's in. You can blame Ruby.'

'Ruby?'

'Yeah, my dog. She sort of came my way when I was in London and I've been stuck with her ever since. I've promised myself a new car when she's gone.'

Tom noticed the rug and bean bag on the flattened seats in the back of the car.

'Is she at home?'

'No, she's at the vets. I'm picking her up on the way back to work. That's if you don't mind having a large, lazy mongrel for company.'

'No, I don't mind at all. I like dogs. We were never allowed one at home. My father didn't think pets were necessary.'

They continued their journey, chatting easily about nothing in particular, but in the process, discovering a little more about each other. Tom was charmed, as others were, by Alex's soft Irish accent. He liked Alex's easy going manner and positive outlook. As they walked into the postgraduate centre Tom felt comfortable beside him and was aware of the charismatic energy Alex gave out. Alex found this gentle man equally enjoyable to be with. He could not recall meeting such a gorgeous looking individual who was so unaware of his looks. Tom appeared not to see the admiring glances aimed at him from the people they passed on their way down the long corridor. They mingled with other doctors over the usual high fat, low fibre buffet. They each had acquaintances amongst the gathering and these lunchtime training sessions were also networking opportunities. In the lecture theatre they quite naturally found seats next to each other. Professor Fraser was his usual entertaining self and soon engaged his audience with his skills as a doctor, researcher and teacher.

Back in the car, Alex and Tom reflected positively on the session and headed for the vet's surgery. Pulling into the small car park at the rear of the building, Alex asked Tom if he wanted to come in with him.

'I'll wait here if you're just picking her up.'

He watched Alex walk off to the front door. He felt a mixture of excitement tempered with his natural caution. There seemed to be an attraction between them. He had observed Alex around and about over the previous few weeks and now he was pretty sure Alex had noticed him too. He was not sure what to do next, except that he knew he wanted to see Alex again, away from work. Ten minutes later Alex came into view carrying a large bundle wrapped in the old rug he had taken from the back of the car. His expression was grim. Tom got out of the car to open the rear door. Alex gently laid the dog on the bean bag, tucked the rug around her and straightened up. With a sigh he closed the door. Before turning on the ignition he looked at Tom with such an expression of sadness in his grey eyes that Tom instinctively put an arm around his shoulder.

'Bad news?' he asked quietly.

'Yeah, 'fraid so.' Alex's voice broke and he swallowed hard. 'Poor old thing. The vet tried to remove the tumour but it's no good. She's riddled with it. I thought that was the case but it's still bloody awful when you hear it.' He gave a weak smile and briefly put his hand on Tom's.

'I'm glad you are here, Tom.'

On their return to the surgery Alex told Tom how Ruby had belonged to the old woman in the flat

151

below his and when she died there had been no-one to care for the dog. Ruby had spent most of her time with him anyway. He had taken her for walks and looked after her when the owner had finally gone into hospital.

'There was no way I could have let Ruby go to a dog's home or be put down, so she's stayed with me in my various homes since my final year of medical school.' Alex parked at the back of the surgery, made sure Ruby had water and left the window open a little.

'She'll be fine. I'll check on her between patients. She's still groggy from the anaesthetic anyway. Thanks, Tom. It really helped having you with me'

'That's OK. I'm sorry it was bad news.'

They each went off to their respective consulting rooms for the next few hours. One of the receptionists offered to keep an eye on Ruby.

Two days later, in the early evening, Tom was reading through some case histories as revision for his next assessment, when the phone rang. He heard Jessie go into the hall to answer it.

'Yes, he's here. Hang on and I'll find him. Tom, it's for you!'

He pushed the papers to one side and opened the sitting room door. Jessie grinned as she handed him the receiver and speaking in a loud stage whisper said, 'Sounds rather nice!'

Tom shooed her away. 'Hello?'

'Hi, Tom, it's Alex.'

Tom smiled. 'Hi, Alex. How are you?' He wondered how Alex had got his number. There was a slight pause.

'I'm fine ... but Ruby's gone.'

Tom knew from other people who had lost pets just how heartbroken they could feel. 'I'm sorry, Alex. Were you there?'

'Yeah. I took her to the vet because she was obviously in distress and he took one look at her and said it was time to put her out of her misery ... so ... he did.'

His voice sounded flat and empty. Tom hesitated. He was pleased that Alex had rung him but now was at a loss as to what to say or do next. Perhaps he should offer to go and see Alex. He was just on the point of speaking when Alex said, 'I don't suppose you fancy a drink do you? I certainly could do with one.'

'Of course, where do you want to meet?'

'Well, you know the area better than I do ... so, any ideas?'

Well, if we want to avoid driving there's a French place, 'Le Papillon', about half way between you and me. It's simple and it just serves a couple of good hot dishes each evening. That's if you're hungry ... and it's licensed.'

Alex wrote down the details and they rang off having agreed to meet in half an hour. Jessie, who had been hovering at the kitchen door, grinned at Tom and said innocently, 'I take it you won't be sharing my cauliflower cheese then?'

Tom smiled back. 'No, 'fraid not. Sorry, Jess. Can I have it tomorrow?'

'Jessie, who had got over her disappointment at never having Tom as her lover, but who still adored him, smiled back benignly. 'Go on then. Make sure you tell me all about him though. He sounds rather gorgeous. Is he Scottish?'

'No, he's from Ireland, actually, but, yes, he's got a great voice, don't you think?'

14

Alex entered the small, dimly lit restaurant, scanned the room and raised a hand in greeting as he spotted Tom sitting at a corner table. He took in the clean white table cloths and crisply folded linen napkins, which stood out against the dark ochre walls. Behind the cluttered bar stood a middle aged, plump woman with a beaming smile. She nodded at Alex as she polished glasses without looking down at them. Candles were lit in wax laden wine bottles at each table, casting bizarre shadows around the room. Large, wooden framed illustrations of exotic looking butterflies hung on one of the walls at the side of the bar. A few other tables were occupied. The wiry, moustachioed host welcomed Alex with a throaty French accent.

'Good evening, monsieur. Welcome to Le Papillon. Do you wish to eat?'

'Thank you, I'm meeting a friend and he's over there.'

The little man led the way to Tom's table and with a flourish, pulled out the chair for Alex. 'Now, messieurs, would you care for an aperitif, or perhaps you would like to have just the wine with your meal?'

Tom looked at Alex. 'Wine? They do a very good house red if you're happy with that.'

The owner took their order and returned swiftly with a carafe of wine.

'Tonight, we have the coq au vin or the lamb cassoulet. Both are very delicious!'

They both ordered the coq au vin. Alex swallowed a large mouthful of wine, smiled faintly and looked at Tom for a moment. 'Thanks, Tom. I hope I haven't spoilt your plans for this evening.'

'No, no, not at all. I'm glad to come away from my revision. Are you OK?'

'Yeah, I am really. It is going to be strange without Ruby, but really, she was suffering and had to go. I'll soon get used to being without her. I never planned to have a dog. I promised myself a new car once she'd gone, so I suppose I've got that to look forward to.'

He did not sound in any way excited or enthusiastic. Over mouth-wateringly delicious food, they talked. Their backgrounds were very different and yet they both sensed a kindred spirit. Replenishing their glasses, Alex said quietly, 'So, your father doesn't know you're gay?'

'Well, if he does, he keeps it to himself. Mum has always felt that it should come from me and I've never wanted her to tell him anyway.'

'Why not?'

156

Tom hesitated as he struggled to find the appropriate words. He had not been expecting to talk about his father to a relative stranger and he knew that once the floodgates opened there would be too much to say. In any case, he did not want to spoil what was turning out to be a really enjoyable evening.

'We have never been that close, I guess. He wouldn't understand. He'd be horrified. I don't think I'm the son he had hoped for ... somehow ... '

Alex saw the darkness of pain in Tom's eyes as his forlorn words dwindled away. He reached across the table and held Tom's hand for a fleeting moment. Tom looked around the room but the other people had gone and the owners were in quiet conversation over their paperwork behind the bar.

They looked at each other in silence for just a moment. Tom drained his glass.

'Hey, I'm supposed to be cheering you up tonight!'

Alex smiled. 'Well, Doctor Gabriel, you have managed that, thank you.'

'Good. Now, it's your turn. Tell me more about you.'

Alex leaned back in his chair.

If they aren't shutting up shop just yet, shall we have a night cap and I'll try not to bore you?'

The proprietor insisted they savour a complimentary glass of his wife's favourite Armagnac, stating that it was very good for their health.

Alex told the story of his upbringing in a small seaside town on the north coast of Northern Ireland.

He had arrived late and unexpectedly in his parents' lives, long after they had given up hope of having children and had sadly accepted that it was God's will. When Muriel had found out she was pregnant she had likened herself to the Biblical Elizabeth, the mother of John the Baptist. Their 'miraculous' baby was born on Christmas Day, 1960. Muriel had wanted to call him John but Jack had overruled her and insisted he be called after his own father, the late and much lamented Alexander William McKee, known to one and all as 'Sandy'. Jack continued working as a bank clerk, a position he had held since leaving school, content never to aspire to a higher position. Muriel gave up her part-time job as an assistant in one of the few remaining milliner's shops along that stretch of beautiful northern coastline. She was a devoted mother to her 'wee Sandy' and would proudly display him in his capacious Silver Cross pram to all around her on their daily walks along the front.

Alex smiled wryly at Tom.

'You really have to have lived there in those days to understand. Even now there are places where it's like stepping back in time. Oh, it's changed for sure, but for me, growing up back then and feeling, 'different', was not a happy time.'

The old Picture House in the town was the only place for entertainment. Alex would go with friends to watch as many films as possible, relishing the escapism. Girls were attracted to him and for a while he went along with the attention in a good-natured and superficial way, but inside he was struggling. In his room at home he lay awake for hours wondering why he felt so sad and so uneasy. His parents' claustrophobic devotion to him was stifling. He began to withdraw from the social activities, limited as they were, and used the excuse of study and revision. Over time, some of his friends fell away and people began to view him as peculiar and not the old Sandy they used to know.

Muriel was concerned but Jack felt proud of his son and had ambitions for him to go to university and maybe enter a profession. Devout, insular, hard-working, Northern Irish Protestants, they had, like so many of their 'Brothers and Sisters in Christ,' never quite managed to follow the teachings of the God they worshipped and the Christ they tried to emulate, when it came to embracing some members of society with compassion and love. Repressed by cultural and religious intolerance, they would have felt that whatever was 'wrong' with their son, was some sort of penance for his, or even their own, sins. In Northern Ireland, sexuality and sexual orientation were not subjects to be discussed. It was as if gay people did not exist and many lives were unimaginably and painfully caught up with guilt and deceit and deep unhappiness.

Meanwhile, the horror of those years in Ireland, with the hunger strikes and the bitter fighting of 'The Troubles', formed the backdrop as Alex grew into manhood. Everyone knew someone who had been affected by violence. Where Alex lived things were relatively quiet, but the constant and horrific deeds of the few affected many, one way or another. He despaired of what he saw as blind faith and bigotry. He made up his mind to study in England. He knew this would distress his parents greatly but he also knew he had to get away. He threw himself into his studies, knowing he wanted a career in medicine. He applied to medical schools in the UK and in 1979, with flying grades, was accepted by Imperial College, London. His by now quite aged parents' joy at his success was tempered with deep sadness. Muriel could hardly bear to think of life without her darling boy. Jack tried to put a brave face on it all, stating unconvincingly that they would try and get over to see their son in London and surely he would manage to come back every now and then to visit.

Alex never found the right moment – whenever that was meant to be - to tell Jack and Muriel McKee that he was gay. Once he knew he was leaving them he was glad he hadn't.

Tom had listened with increasing compassion for the man opposite him across the small table. Here was someone who also had struggled as he grew up and for entirely different reasons had been unable to come out to his parents.

'I guess I'm lucky. At least I was able to tell my mother and she has been great. You must have felt lonely, Alex.'

'Yeah, I did. They were good and kind and so were most people, but they would never have understood. Anyway, in my first year at medical school, they died, suddenly. It was horrible at the time but now I realise it was right that they never knew.'

Tom sipped his Armagnac and sat back to hear the end of Alex's story.

Muriel and Jack were travelling back from a church outing, on a coach, with their fellow church members. They had been on a visit to the Giant's Causeway, taking a picnic and stopping for fish and chips on the way home. This outing was exactly the same as many they had been on, with the same old friends and now a few new, younger families and they still enjoyed the companionship and familiarity of it all. It was less than half an hour's journey but everyone appreciated not having to drive and the chance to chatter. As Alex's mother and father were waiting outside the fish and chip shop, before boarding the coach, a speeding car had mounted the pavement and mown them down. It did not stop and was in the process of being chased by a police car. The pitiful scene of the two bodies strewn across the pavement and the panic and chaos that followed lived on in the minds of the people who witnessed it for the rest of their lives. Muriel had been killed instantly and Jack suffered severe head injuries.

Having consulted the doctors, Alex had refused to allow his mother's funeral to take place until a full assessment of his father's brain damage could be performed. As he and the doctors predicted, his father did not survive and died four days after his wife, with Alex at his bedside, holding his hand.

Soon after the funeral, with the appropriate professionals in control of the estate, such as it was, of Jack and Muriel McKee, Alex paid a solitary visit to the cemetery where his parents had been laid to rest. He looked from the freshly turned earth, the withering wreaths, out over the familiar, hauntingly beautiful landscape and had said goodbye – to his mother and father – to his birthplace - and to 'Sandy'.

'Good Grief, I have talked for far too long! Tom, forgive me. I did say you might get bored. The truth is, I have never told anyone all of that before, not even ... ' He stopped short.

Tom's fascination with Alex's story had shifted inextricably into a wave of disappointment. It was when they had been chatting about their respective training and Alex's London life that Alex had mentioned that he was in a relationship. Tom knew he should not feel aggrieved but his mood had changed. He had felt a real connection with Alex. Now an invisible cloud hung over the evening.

They shared the bill, thanked the owner and his wife and wandered out into a warm, balmy night. A crescent moon shone delicately above them. The street was quiet. Alex turned to Tom.

'Thanks for that, Tom. I really do feel better.'

'I'm glad. See you on Monday then?'

'Right - have a good Sunday. Don't work too hard. You'll sail through this GP stuff. I know a good doctor when I see one!'

Tom laughed. 'Yeah, yeah, flattery will get you nowhere!'

Their embrace seemed as natural as if they had known one another for years, but lasted a fraction longer than either of them had planned. Tom looked closely at Alex, searching his features for any sign of his feelings. Alex appeared to be scrutinising Tom too but both wore careful masks as they stepped away from each other.

'Well, have a good day tomorrow with ... whatever his name is.'

Alex glanced back. 'Thanks. I don't expect it to be easy somehow. I've been trying to disentangle myself from the whole thing for some time now.'

'Oh ... I see. Well ... good luck.'

The cloud lifted.

'Bye then.'

'Bye.'

Alex suddenly called after Tom. 'Here's my phone number if you ever fancy meeting up again.' He scribbled on a scrap of paper found in his wallet and handed it to Tom. They turned again to go their separate ways, each feeling the exhilaration of their time together and the power of their brief physical contact.

Tom walked through the streets on the periphery of the town centre, so quiet, for a Saturday night. Little cameos of life were visible in the rooms of the houses he passed where curtains and blinds had yet to be drawn. He smiled to himself as he recalled how he and Sarah and his mother, on the way back from the park or school, would sometimes play Isobel's game of giving the characters, spied through these windows, names and stories. It had felt a bit intrusive, peering into people's homes, but Isobel made it fascinating and very funny. On a normal evening he would find himself doing the same but tonight he ignored the glow from lamps and televisions as he headed home. He turned over in his mind the evening's conversation. He tried to recall every word, just to gauge Alex's responses and to picture his expressions in his mind. He heard again the rich, lilting voice.

Jessie was curled up on the sofa watching a film when Tom walked in. She immediately turned the sound down and looked up at him with eager curiosity.

'Well? What happened? '

Tom sighed. He was not in the mood for an interrogation. He wanted to go to bed and reflect on the evening all over again. 'It was good. Nice food and wine, you know – just nice.'

Jessie noted his reticence and knew better than to push for more details. She turned the volume up again and smiled. 'Good, glad you had a nice time. See you tomorrow.'

'Yeah, I'm whacked. 'Night.' Tom went through the process of undressing, cleaning his teeth, drinking a large tumbler of water and finally flopping into bed. He switched off the bedside lamp and lay with his hands behind his head. He mulled over the last few hours, yet again. He thought of the few times he and Alex had met and he knew, quite without doubt, that this was the person he had been looking for. The niggling concerns about working in the same practice were pushed to one side and he fell into a deep sleep.

As he walked in the opposite direction, Alex, too, was lost in thought. He had found Tom to be everything he had imagined from observation of him at the surgery on the few occasions when their work coincided. He was undoubtedly the most strikingly attractive man he had met. How come no-one had snapped him up? There was a vulnerability about Tom that touched him and made him feel protective towards him, but over the meal he had sensed a steely determination, especially when he had talked about doing medicine; sounded as though that prat of a father had something to do with all that.

He reached his flat and looked around at the sparse furnishings. This temporary place, until he managed to explore the local area, felt very empty without Ruby. He kicked off his shoes, put on some soothing chamber music and sat to think about Tom. Unwelcome thoughts of the next day intruded. It was something to get through, that was all. Any feelings of love that he had thought were shared between himself and Adam were long gone. The vituperative exchanges between them over the last weeks of their dead relationship had been testament to that and Alex felt only relief to be free. He would get up early, drive to London, collect his possessions and drive straight back. The car should hold everything. He drained his glass and went to bed.

15

Sunday was hot, the moderate June sunshine suddenly overwhelmed by humidity. Setting off early, Alex drove fast on the near-empty roads, with all the windows open and 'Bohemian Rhapsody' emanating from the rickety cassette player. He wanted to get the move out of his previous home over with as quickly as possible. He had no idea if Adam would be there but braced himself just in case.

In the event Adam had decided not to be a part of his ex-partner's exit from their home and his life and had left a cryptic note reminding Alex to leave the keys on the table and not to take anything marked with a blue sticker. Alex spent no time over the task. He could not wait to get out of the flat. Everything about it reminded him of the volatile relationship in which he and Adam had been embroiled. With the advantage of hindsight and taking in the various accoutrements of the ostentatiously decorated rooms, he felt repelled by the place and all the memories associated with it. He squeezed everything into the car, deciding not to reply to Adam's message. He locked the door after him and posted the keys through the letter box. A short way down the road he called at a corner shop and picked up a sandwich and with an exultant feeling of liberation and 'Queen' blasting out, drove away from the steamy, litter-ridden streets of the London suburb.

He remembered how London had fascinated him. The culture change and the freedom he had embraced boldly and adventurously. His fellow students had been a mixed bunch and to begin with he had struck up friendships with anyone and everyone who was available. As time went on and as he grew accustomed to the demands of pursuing a medical career he had become somewhat more discerning. He pruned down his circle of friends and acquaintances and hangers-on. The few lovers he enjoyed brief relationships with were mostly non-medical. It seemed to Alex that within the profession people were not prepared to be open about their sexuality. Juxtaposed to this was the London night life which offered a superfluity of gay bars and clubs. The rising awareness of HIV and AIDS was a hot topic of conversation, not just within medical circles but increasingly amongst the more aware members of the general public. By the time he qualified in 1984, a sense of anxiety had begun to creep in, certainly amongst the medical profession. In the following years, during his house jobs, the world became alarmed. The government's 'Don't Die of Ignorance' campaign caused consternation in some areas; families whose children had read a leaflet which caused them to ask their unprepared parents what 'homosexual' meant, newsreaders and broadcasters using the word 'condom' for the first time to a surprised British public. Ignorance bred fear and prejudice and Alex was aware of the need to inform and educate. He was acutely conscious of the devastating effects of cruelty and ignorance. In his own quiet, but determined way, he tried to pass on the most accurate information he could - to his patients - and to his colleagues.

Now, pushing the past out of his mind and with a lightness of spirit, he indulged in more thoughts of Tom.

The day, for Tom, was quiet. He and Jessie chatted over the newspapers and coffee and Jessie restrained herself from probing too much, even though she was bursting with curiosity. She did ask Tom what Alex looked like. Tom had barely mentioned the new arrival at the surgery in the previous few months, just replying, if Jessie or Lloyd asked, that he seemed pleasant enough but that their paths rarely crossed.

'Come on, Tom. Tell me. Is he good looking?'

'Yes, I guess so.' Tom mumbled from behind the paper.

'Well, what does that mean exactly? I mean, is he tall, short, dark, fair – what?'

Tom knew he would get no peace until he gave her something. Lowering the paper, he grinned across at her. Jessie's open face revealed genuine curiosity.

'Well, since you ask, yes, he is very good looking. He is quite tall; just a bit shorter than me, sort of blonde, sandy hair, good skin ... and nice teeth and ... oh, I don't know ... '

'Well, I know he's got a sexy voice. I heard him on the phone. What colour are his eyes?' Jessie had never met anyone with eyes like Tom's and never tired of looking at them.

Tom closed his eyes and pictured Alex. 'Dark grey ... like a stormy sea.'

Jessie stared, open-mouthed. 'Wow! You're obviously hooked!'

By the time Alex had unloaded the car and cleared the last remnants of dog from the flat he felt tired and unexpectedly dejected. He hated Sunday afternoons; a mental souvenir of his childhood he supposed. Sundays had been made up of the same routine, which never changed, even if he and his parents went on holiday. They never left Ireland, always going to grandparents in Donaghadee. Alex could never understand why they went to another coastal town but the annual visit also included a day in Bangor and a day in Belfast – unless the troubles were particularly violent, when they stayed at home. Whether away, or at home, church took precedence, with attendance at morning and evening services. Sunday lunch never varied from roast meat of some sort with all the traditional trimmings, followed by his mother's fruit crumble or pie, with custard. Little was said over the meal, which always started with the saying of Grace, which he was expected to recite once a month, although his father only ever said the same words.

'Thank you God for this good food and for Mammy who cooked it. Through Jesus Christ our Lord. Amen.'

The oppressive rigidity had warped the love he felt for his parents. Even now, Sunday afternoons haunted him, unless he was preoccupied with something else. Learning to sail had solved the problem, before which, he had spent most Sundays working - an occupational hazard he had embraced. On this Sunday, however, he felt the old melancholy creeping up. Shaking himself, he strode into the bedroom and changed into shorts, T shirt and running shoes. He pounded the pavements for an hour, lifted by the power of a deeply oxygenated system and the release of mood-enhancing hormones.

After a long cool drink and a shower, he felt brighter. The phone rang.

'Tom! Hi. How are you?'

'Fine thanks. I was just wondering how it all went. You seemed a bit apprehensive last night.'

'Yeah, I was a bit. Anyway, it all went OK in the end.'

'Good ... ' Tom hesitated. He had called on impulse and now felt he was intruding. 'Right then ... good ... er ... I ... '

'Thanks for ringing, Tom.'

'That's OK. Glad it went alright. See you tomorrow then.' Tom wished he had not phoned. After all it wasn't his business.

'Tom, if you're not doing anything this evening, do you fancy coming round for supper?'

'Well ... I ... '

'No problem if you're busy.'

'No, I'm not busy.'

'Right then, say about seven?'

Tom glanced at his watch. It was already six o'clock. 'OK. See you then. What's your address?'

He showered and chose his change of clothes carefully, deciding on a cool blue shirt and his new black jeans. It was a warm evening and he decided to walk. He needed time to think. He picked up a bottle of wine from the small communal supply in the kitchen, glad that Jessie and Lloyd were out, so avoiding any questions. The streets were Sunday-quiet. He smiled to himself as he passed Le Papillon, closed and shuttered, and recalled the previous evening. As he approached the row of tall houses, nearly all converted into flats, he felt a rising tension.

Alex plumped up cushions, cleared clutter and put some music on to play quietly in the background. In the small kitchen he prepared the food. He had onions and a selection of mushrooms, enough to make a risotto. The white wine was in the fridge and quite suddenly, he felt a soaring of his spirits. This was a good end to a Sunday. He glanced out of the large window and saw Tom striding along the road, glancing sideways to check the door numbers. He smiled and moved to the intercom as it buzzed.

'Hi, Tom. Come on up.'

The door clicked and pushing it open Tom stepped into the cool, tiled hall. He went up the stairs and there was Alex waiting in the doorway of his flat.

'Come on in.' Alex lead the way.

'I brought this. Nothing special I'm afraid.'

'That's OK. Thanks. I'm doing a mushroom risotto. Hope you eat that?'

'Yeah, great.'

'You know, Tom, when I first came over here and someone asked me to supper, I thought it meant cheese and biscuits and a cup of tea, or maybe even just a bowl of Rice Krispies. That's what supper meant in Ireland, so I had a hot meal to myself and then went to my friends and, lo and behold, they dished up a three course meal. It was a struggle I can tell you!'

Tom laughed, relishing the sound of Alex's voice. Alex laughed too and poured them a drink. Over the next few hours they shared more stories of their lives and found that they had much in common, particularly their love of music. Tom explained how he went to his parent's house whenever possible to play the piano. There was not room for one in the house he shared but when he managed to get a home of his own his mother had promised him the piano. Alex had been a member of a men's choir in London and was looking for one to join locally. Tom told him that Isobel belonged to a community choir and was sure Alex would be welcomed. The risotto was extremely good.

'Do you cook? Alex asked between mouthfuls.

'Actually, I do. I like gardening too, much to my father's horror!'

The easy camaraderie which had begun to grow the previous evening developed through increasingly intimate conversation and laughter. They both knew where they wanted the evening to end and it seemed the most natural thing in the world for Tom to stay.

'This is going to be tricky at the surgery, you know,' Tom said, as they broke from a slow and tender kiss. Alex nodded. 'I know. Let's think about that another time.'

The sound of the radio woke them the next morning at six o'clock. Alex leaned across Tom and switched the radio off. Tom's blue eyes, heavy with sleep, smiled at him in a rush of early morning arousal. Running late, they shared a bracing shower, gulped coffee and toast and Alex drove Tom to his house to change into work clothes. He drove off as Tom sped inside, breathless with the exhilaration of his feelings. All that day, they worked in their respective rooms of the surgery. Alex went off to do a few home visits in the afternoon and Tom joined James for a tutorial.

16

Some weeks later, when Tom was waiting to hear if he had qualified as a GP, James called him and Alex to his consulting room after morning surgery. They had been careful at work not to allow their relationship to show, but it had been difficult at times and the strain was taking its toll on them both. They sat in chairs opposite James, not sure what exactly would ensue but fairly confident that it was not about their clinical competence. The older doctor peered at the two younger men over his half moon glasses, his expression inscrutable.

'Right, I won't beat about the bush. Am I right in thinking that you two are ... how shall I put this ... in a relationship?'

Alex spoke first. 'May I ask why you want to know?

'Yes, you may ask, but I don't intend to tell you because it's not relevant. As senior partner, I need to know, that's all.'

Tom was about to respond when Alex spoke firmly. 'Why's that, James?'

James raised an eyebrow. 'We don't tolerate intimate relationships between members of staff at this surgery – as you well know.'

Everyone at the surgery was aware of James's outward display of benevolent family doctor, adored and trusted by his patients. Some were uncomfortably aware of his narrow and prejudiced views but, over the years, few had plucked up the courage to challenge him. The only person in living memory had been a young trainee and he was dismissed with a cursory reference and no invitation to stay at James's practice. Alex and Tom waited. They had talked about this moment as a possibility and they knew that it would need careful handling. Tom had a desire to hear what possible exception James could have to two doctors working at his surgery who were fulfilling their roles to the utmost of their abilities and who managed to keep their personal lives entirely separate. He leaned forward in his chair.

'Have you received a complaint?'

James did not respond.

Alex stood up. Facing James, he repeated Tom's words, with more urgency.

'James, have you received a complaint?

James leaned back in his olive green, buttoned leather chair, inherited from his father. His repulsion for these two young men bubbled under the smooth surface of his professional demeanour, a performance which had carried him through times of self-doubt and anger and frustration in a profession that was now changing rapidly into a place where he felt like an outsider. He had surmised for himself that Tom and Alex were together and he had found it all profoundly disturbing. No-one had complained and he knew that he was behaving irrationally, but his feelings of repugnance he could not deny. 'Not formally, no.'

Alex leaned on the edge of the mahogany desk, another of James's paternal inheritances, forcing James to meet his gaze.

'And what does, "not formally, no" mean ... exactly?'

James moved the chair back a fraction. He was feeling clammy and trapped. He looked at the two young men opposite him, one glaring at him and the other with an expression he could not decipher. He inhaled deeply and faced Alex. 'It means, young man, that I will not tolerate intimate relationships between members of my staff. That's it. Take it ... or leave.'

'You're just a homophobic, bloody hypocrite!' Alex spat out the words.

Tom stood. 'Look, if I get through, I know that there isn't a place for me here. I've been applying to other practices. So, I don't think there is going to be a problem, do you? James, you have your own reasons for your rules.'

James and Alex looked at him. James knew the practice would be losing an exceptional doctor. Alex knew this was the person he wanted to be with. He wanted to hold Tom right there and then and tell him he loved him.

The silence was tense and uncomfortable for all of them. Alex turned first to leave the room.

'Where do you think you're going?' James rose.

Alex looked at Tom. 'We need fresh air.'

They left the room. James stared at the open door and at their backs as Alex put his arm around Tom's shoulders. He sat heavily. Soon he would be free of all this. He knew changes would be made when he left and no doubt it was a good thing that he would never know what they would be. Since his wife had died five years previously he had visited the house in Provence more and more, aware of the benefits of the temperate climate on his increasingly stiff and painful joints. Stella had never seen the completion of the renovations and so had not left any vestige of herself in the place. James was thankful for that. He had gradually made the old farmhouse his own. There were only a few English people who either lived in the village or spent long holidays there and he had got to know the local people and, over time, had been accepted by them. They treated 'le médecin anglais' with respect and would continue to, he knew, in his retirement. He felt ready to live quietly and to pursue his love of walking, painting and bird-watching. There were dozens of books he wanted to read and the thought of sitting in the evenings, either in his own courtyard garden, breathing in the sweetly fragrant mimosa, or outside one of the restaurants with a glass of the local herby liqueur and maybe some easy company, filled him with a feeling of peace.

He sat for a long while and thought of these comforting prospects. The persona of trusted and kindly family doctor sat uneasily on his shoulders these days, although it had not always been so. For the most part his professional life had been rewarding and fulfilling. He recalled growing up in the big house – this very building – where his father had his consulting and waiting rooms at the front and his mother, who had trained as a nurse, helped with the patients and all the paperwork. Throughout his childhood, James had watched, bemused, as his father had removed his gold watch from his black waistcoat pocket, flipped open the lid and timed his entrance into the waiting room for exactly twenty minutes past nine. The patients were asked to arrive at nine o'clock and the wait was good for them he had asserted. The unquestioning, frightened people never complained. The doctor knew best – even what time to start his surgery.

James found the present day existence of a GP unbearably pressurised. It was all about targets, audits and accountability to Managers. Even the Practice Nurses, he felt, were robbing trainee doctors - and sometimes, it seemed, even himself - of invaluable skills. Patients were becoming unhealthily interested in their conditions and the treatments prescribed. An almost overwhelming lassitude threatened his final days at work. He mused to himself that it must be like the last week in prison after serving a long sentence – surely the hardest time to endure.

He had no doubt that Alex and Tom would go on to become successful doctors. Nowadays, it seemed, any behaviour was acceptable. He despaired at the lack of discipline and the obsession with equal rights which seemed to prevail. With the old values you knew where you stood. As for the deviants, well they were not talked about in decent society and certainly were not free to display their perversions in public. What went on behind closed doors was expected to remain there. Maybe it was just as well that he and Stella had not managed to produce any children. He felt a twinge of guilt at this thought. He knew that Stella had never really come to terms with their childless existence. God knows how they would have turned out. One thing he knew for sure was that he would never have forced his children into any profession they did not want to join. At that moment, he felt weary and rather sad.

At the leaving party for James the staff and partners gathered together in a small private room at one of the better quality hotels in the town. Tom and Alex kept a low profile, mingling quietly amongst their colleagues. No more had been said at work about their confrontation with James, although Tom and Alex had discussed it at length in the privacy of Alex's flat. James had blocked it out of his mind as he was overwhelmed by cards and gifts from his loyal and adoring patients. He said a few words of thanks after being presented with a collection of delicate watercolours of the local countryside. One of his patients, a talented artist, had been approached by Eve, the practice manager, and had agreed to the commission. James was surprisingly touched at such a thoughtful gift and knew exactly where the paintings would go in his cottage in France. He felt a genuine fondness for the leafy, gentle surroundings he had lived in for so long, even at the same time, longing to leave.

Tom completed his GP training and was offered a place in a Practice on the other side of town. He and Alex talked it through in their shared time off. It was a small but modern set up with a good prospect of becoming a training practice. They both felt that they wanted to be together more, when they were not working, so being apart professionally did not present a problem. They spent hours looking for a house – a home of their own.

One evening, just before Christmas, they were sharing a meal with Jessie and Lloyd and Jessie's latest conquest, a surprisingly (for Jessie) mild-mannered, local farmer, whom Jessie had met one parents' evening at the school. Ian was a widower with a seven year old daughter. Lloyd was leaving them later in the evening to join his own family in a nearby town. There, the next day, he would indulge in traditional Jamaican food, cooked by his mother. He would be working at the restaurant on Christmas day, cooking for the usual assortment of lonely, older people and members of angry, dysfunctional families, who needed to escape the collapsing domesticity of their frazzled homes in order to maintain some sort of peace at the season of goodwill. Lloyd was always glad to hide in the kitchen on those occasions and did not envy the frontline staff.

On this night, the large pine table in the high ceilinged kitchen was laden with expertly cooked food, courtesy of the resident chef. It was not often that Lloyd agreed to cook at home, stating firmly that he did enough at work. This particular night was an early Christmas celebration as they were not going to be together on the day. They had all contributed to the cost of the food and Jessie had spent time arranging candles of all shapes, sizes and colours, around the room and on the table. The deep red painted walls glowed seductively in the soft, flickering candlelight and smooth jazz played in the background. Christmas cards adorned the tall black mantelpiece, the old dresser and bookcase, which were decorated with holly, ivy and mistletoe. The food was, unsurprisingly, delicious and the wine far better that their usual plonk.

They were all feeling relaxed and slightly drunk when Tom cleared his throat.

'Alex and I have an announcement to make. We've found a house and the offer we put in has been accepted.'

No-one was surprised, as it had not been kept a secret that they were looking, but there were mixed emotions at that moment. It had been a harmonious and close household and now that was to change for good. Jessie stood, slightly unsteadily, and raised her glass. 'I'd like to propose a toast to Tom and Alex and wish them lots of love, fun and laughter in their new life together.' She burst into tears. The men looked at each other and at the crumpled form of this small, dynamic woman, for whom they all felt varying degrees of affection. Sensing their awkwardness, Jessie looked up from Ian's shoulder, smudged mascara giving her the appearance of a baby panda, and grinned sheepishly. 'Sorry guys. But I'm going to miss you, Tom.'

Tom rose and wrapped his arms around her slender shoulders. 'And I will miss you too, lovely, lovely Jess.' He hugged her and gave her his festive paper napkin and while she blew her nose loudly, gave Lloyd a hug. 'Thanks Lloyd. You've been a great housemate too.'

Lloyd gave his lop-sided grin and raised his glass. 'We're not going to lose touch. Here's to the future - for all of us!'

The house needed some work even though the elderly couple who had lived in it for twenty five years had kept it in good order. The old man had been a quantity surveyor before retiring and so the additions to the once very small Victorian cottage had been meticulously carried out. The local builder, who had been recommended by a patient to Tom and Alex, was also a talented carpenter and specialised in restoring older properties. He was impressed with the use of reclaimed bricks and the sturdy craftsmanship of the woodwork. The garden nurtured traditional English perennials and shrubs. Lavender lined the path to the front door around which grew well established roses and a heavy wisteria. At the back was a long garden, overlooking the river and beyond that, some fields belonging to a local farmer. Noisy sheep and contented cows grazed for most of the year and then, in winter, the emptiness and silence cast calmness over the whole view which became a

Christmas card scene when there was a frost or snow. Tom and Alex knew this was the home they had dreamed of. They craved the peace and privacy afforded by this place. The demands and rigours of their work satisfied their professional needs but they wanted their home together to provide solace and intimacy.

Following Edward's death, despite appearing settled to his mother, Tom experienced turmoil, anxiety even. At the surgery he continued as normal. The work absorbed him and brought great satisfaction. It was at home where his thoughts turned to his childhood and adolescence and his father's attitude towards him. Alex encouraged him to talk about it and this gentle, unofficial counselling gradually eased the burden.

'I think I just need to know why he never liked me. Whenever I have mentioned it to Mum she has said that he did love me but that he wasn't very good at showing his feelings. He didn't seem to have that problem with Sarah ... well ... up until she was in her teens. They fought a lot then, I remember.'

'Perhaps he was jealous. Some men are, aren't they; that closeness between mother and son thing? Edward always seemed to me to be a bit buttoned-up, as if there was something simmering away, under that composed exterior.'

'I know he couldn't face up to me being gay. I guess I should be glad he didn't throw me out. Of course, we never talked about it. If anything was said to him it was by Mum and she knew I didn't want her to talk to him about it. Dad never referred to it. He mumbled behind the newspaper sometimes, about where the world was going and the intrusion into people's lives by the media, that sort of stuff, but there was no way he was going to talk openly about attitudes and prejudices and certainly not about people's sexual orientation! Well, he's gone now, so I shall never know. I'm an adult and I'm still confused about my father. It's pathetic!'

'Well, my Mum used to say that all the traumas of your childhood come back to haunt you between the ages of thirty and fifty!'

'Thanks, Alex, that's really cheered me up. So, I've got twenty years to get through! Where the hell did she get that from anyway? Doesn't sound like your Mum at all.'

Alex laughed. 'No, it doesn't, does it. I think she heard it on the radio!'

Within a few years Tom and Alex made a new start at a purpose built Medical Centre on the edge of the town. The well designed buildings incorporated all the services required by the diverse population of a large housing estate. They were confident that they could work and live together and so it proved to be. At home the old house and garden flourished under their care. Tom, particularly, found gardening rewarding and relaxing. They both enjoyed cooking and their shared love of music. Alex often sang, with Tom accompanying him on the piano, or he would sit reading, while Tom played his favourite pieces. Alex sang in the same community choir as Isobel, his impressive tenor voice proving to be a great asset.

They had a small and loyal group of friends. The choice of people they could trust and with whom they could relax was limited. Lots of their patients would greet them in the shops or out and about but would not consider them, nor be considered, friends. The invisible professional barrier was there for a reason. When people shared some of their most intimate and vulnerable moments, both sides needed protection; not just confidentiality, which went without saying, but a deeper respect; a guarding of the sanctity of their relationship. So, the strength of Tom and Alex's relationship lay in their deep and abiding love for each other and their sheer enjoyment of developing together their home and their workplace. Their practice was known to be welcoming, well-informed and empathetic amongst the gay community and gradually, as sexuality became talked about more openly, amongst the wider population. There were some people who avoided seeing either Tom or Alex, for their own reasons, but they were few. The reputation of excellence spread throughout the area and soon there was a long waiting list to register.

The Centre became a training practice. This was one of the most rewarding aspects of the job. Tom's old alma mater was beginning to turn out a new generation of medics. There were more women than men, the ethnic mix was one of the most diverse in the country and, thanks to an excellent General Practice department, the students who spent time with Tom and Alex were becoming sensitive and empathetic doctors. They not only found time to engage with people, but actively encouraged and practised patient-centred consultations. The results were tangible. Patients and their relatives felt they were being afforded some dignity and that they were being listened to. A mutual respect built up between the practice and the people it served.

At home, two kittens joined Tom and Alex. A dog had been discussed but they had accepted that it would not be fair to leave it alone for such long periods.

17

She felt the warm stickiness of seeping blood, as American Airlines Flight 11, from Boston to Los Angeles, hit the first tower, and felt the haemorrhage down her legs, as United Airlines Flight 175 struck the second.

Hannie saw her blanch and, enveloping Sarah in her big arms, helped her to the women's cloakroom. One hour later Sarah miscarried her 16 week old baby – fifty minutes after his father had died in the World Trade Centre in New York. Hannie stayed with her, rocking her to and fro, rhythmically, saying nothing, feeling everything, for her dear friend. The news had blasted into the office making them question what their eyes told them they were witnessing. The ambulance had arrived miraculously quickly to rush Sarah to hospital. There, the TV screens in every room conveyed the awful truth and, regardless of their condition, the patients were compelled to see the carnage.

Sarah was not consoled by the fact that she was one of so many. She felt insulted that her grief was not acknowledged without reference to the thousands who had also suffered that day. She regretted telling her mother, just a few weeks earlier, that she had met someone. She wished she had not mentioned that he often worked in New York. She recalled only saying that to give the impression that there was nothing serious about the relationship and that she and Michael lived in different cities most of the time. Isobel and Tom telephoned, emailed, made plans to fly out to her, but Sarah forbade them, threatening to move away to an unknown address if they turned up. They were painfully shocked and alarmed in their concern for her. They talked quietly together, instead of being with Sarah, which they both felt was wrong.

For many weeks she went to ground, as an animal, to lick its wounds. Hannie, without whose ministrations she would not have recovered, was the only person Sarah allowed into her apartment. Hannie displayed the strong, sensitive and consistent support that only true friends can offer. She slept in the spare room when Sarah was terrified of being alone. Gradually, as time went by, she gently took Sarah, guiding her out of the apartment, for long, healing walks and allowed her friend to weep, to rage and to mourn. At Thanksgiving, and at Christmas, Hannie cooked delicious non-traditional food. She called in on her parents to share some of the Hanukkah celebrations but did not stay. They understood. Hannie's mother made batches of chicken soup for her daughter to take to her friend.

When Sarah began to talk about what had happened Hannie was there to listen. They would sit by the fire in Sarah's apartment and gradually Sarah found the faltering words to try and articulate her feelings.

'Hannie, what am I going to do? I don't think I can go on. He was the first person I really loved, really wanted to stay with ... and now I've lost him ... and our baby.'

'I know, honey, I know.'

'He loved me, Hannie. He really loved me. I don't know why, but he did. He was so special.

'Yes, he sure was. I mean, I only met him a couple of times, but I could see it. I could see he was a really good guy. They don't come round too often, that's for sure.'

'Did you really see he was special? You're not just saying that to make me feel better?'

Hannie rose and walked over to Sarah. She sat next to her on the sofa. Taking Sarah's hands in her own, she looked into the dark eyes so full of pain.

'Sarah, honey, I would never say anything to you that isn't true. You are my dearest friend and you know I love you very much. Michael was wonderful and, you know what, one day when you are not in so much pain, you will be able to think about the really fabulous relationship you had, even though it was cut short. You will, you will.' She wrapped Sarah's slight frame in her soft, comforting embrace and, as she had done so many times since that day in September, rocked her and allowed Sarah to cry away a small part of her grief.

The following spring, Sarah decided to visit Ground Zero. Hannie's repeated offers to accompany her were gently but firmly refused. She needed to go alone to see where Michael had died. She saw for herself the scale of the massacre and felt very small. She stood anonymously amongst the crowds. She saw the tributes; messages, photographs, items of clothing, heart-rending manifestations of grief and horror. She heard the weeping, the cries of anguish and pain. She knew that Michael's ageing mother lived somewhere in Germany. They had never met. She felt relieved that Michael had not told his mother about her – or about their unborn child. Her own sorrow felt all-consuming. She knew she could not share in his mother's.

As New York picked itself up, so, gradually, Sarah began to do the same. Having made up her mind that she would never again find anyone like Michael and, at the age of forty two, that she would never have a child, she sought refuge in her work, taking on more cases and proving herself to be a talented and much sought after divorce lawyer. She became practised in suppressing the rage that threatened to burst out of her when she was dealing with selfish and greedy clients, who not only had no intention of trying to save their marriages, but who brutally insisted on getting everything they could from each other, in the bitter and damaging death throes of their relationships.

Michael had been the only man with whom she had felt safe, wanted, beautiful and, most importantly of all, needed. As she was growing up that was the one thing she craved; to be needed. Her father did not need her, even though he had overwhelmed her with proprietorial love, when he was at home. It had always seemed to her that Isobel and Tom needed only each other. Men had been transitory figures in her adult life, inevitably failing to comprehend the dichotomy of her strange need to be needed and her fierce independence. Michael had been the first person to look into her eyes and see her for who she really was. They had been on the point of moving in together when he died. Now, Sarah remained in her apartment, her memories and her grief gradually being supplanted by anger and bitterness.

At the time of her father's death, she had felt fleeting sadness, but also a sense of release. She was no longer someone's 'little girl.' She had long-since relinquished that role but Edward had never really accepted her growing up and had taken it as a personal affront when she moved across the Atlantic. He had visited a couple of times when he was over on business and had shared a meal with his daughter but more and more it became obvious that they had nothing to say to each other. The generation gap yawned wider and deeper with every meeting. Sarah found him a reactionary and a snob. He found her out of his reach, both intellectually and emotionally. So, father and daughter gradually drifted apart. Isobel had accompanied Edward on one occasion and, intuitive and perceptive as she was, had known never to go back. She wrote long and colourful letters to Sarah which, over time, became emails. These became less frequent, mostly because Sarah did not respond, or if she did, the content was superficial.

As time passed, Sarah accepted her few very close friends, her clients, with their intensely fraught problems, and her cultural pleasures. She had always enjoyed visiting art galleries and had begun to accumulate a number of prized works. She and Hannie, and occasionally Stella, would enjoy nights out at the theatre or go off to the sun for a few days every now and again. Successful and talented women, they lived their lives comfortably, Hannie and Sarah filling any suppressed loneliness by busying themselves with their work. England seemed almost a distant memory for Sarah and the box in which she had placed memories of her childhood, remained closed, locked carefully and securely.

18

The offices of Fairfax and Lowther nestled in one corner of a leafy square in the small Warwickshire town. Solid, Victorian, red brick buildings overlooked the shady grass and pathways where people sat on benches in warm weather to eat their lunch, or read the paper, or just to gaze at their surroundings. Ronald Fairfax had joined his father's firm immediately after qualifying. He had continued practising after the death of his father and the firm had expanded over the years with the inclusion of Douglas Lowther, a brooding and brilliant Scot. More recently, with Ronnie only working two days a week and soon to stop altogether, Serena Desai had joined them, bringing with her, a much needed balance to the rather drab and decidedly male working environment. Ronnie's room remained much the same as it had been for many years. The overall impression was brown – leather chairs, desk, book shelves. Serena had managed to persuade him to hang a couple of pictures – heavy, oil, landscapes at Ronnie's insistence - and had placed a vivid orchid on the window sill, which he didn't seem to notice and which was religiously fed and watered by Diana Pugh, the long-standing and devoted receptionist.

Ronnie's wife, Annie, had been a beautiful and talented music teacher who filled their home with her piano playing. She was French and considered somewhat of an exotic flower for the gentle, rather shy Ronnie. But theirs had been a strong and passionate relationship, producing two children in swift succession and an enduring love, until she died quite horribly from Alzheimer's disease, which had robbed her of her sparkle and joie de vivre, in a cruel and distressing final journey.

Isobel and Ronnie had continued to meet as client and lawyer and had sometimes shared trips to the theatre, to concerts, or to the occasional flower show. Their relationship had never stepped over the boundaries of warm and affectionate friendship, but both had valued it deeply, and so it was with a heavy heart that Ronnie had gone through all the legalities of Isobel's estate. It was a month since his dear friend had died. He still felt sad and bereft of the vibrant and beautiful woman he had grown to love over the years of their friendship. Isobel's will had been straight forward enough. She had trusted Ronnie as her confidant and he knew that the letter he handed over was going to change Tom's life forever.

Ronnie had telephoned Tom at home and had merely stated that he had another document for him to read. Would Tom be kind enough to make an appointment whenever was convenient? It was not urgent. Now, while Tom read the letter, Ronnie waited in the little room across the landing.

Tom turned to the last page.

' ... *and so, you have a half sister called Caterina. She will be a grown woman now, of course - perhaps with a family of her own. I don't know if Bill is still alive. I don't know where he is living – maybe still in Italy. When we met in 1963 he was teaching at the University in Florence but that was so long ago. He may even have come back to Norfolk. If you decide to look for them I hope they bring you the love and joy you so richly deserve. If you choose not to, please remember that Bill and I loved each other very much and had he known of your existence, he would have loved you too.*

Forgive me, Tom. I hope this is not too great a burden for you to bear. I feel you are strong enough to make your own decisions after reading this and to choose the right path to take.

Goodbye, my darling Tom.'

The light outside was fading when Tom laid down the papers. He took a deep breath in and then, slowly, steadily, blew the air out of his lungs. His gaze was aimed somewhere on the carpet. For a few moments he remained absolutely still. There were so many clamouring thoughts in his head that he knew he had to focus and try to absorb what he had just read, in a methodical fashion, in order to make sense of it. The clock on the mantelpiece struck the half hour. Tom glanced up and realised he would have to leave in order to get to the surgery on time. His legs felt weak as he rose from the chair and he took a moment to breathe deeply once more. It was as if he had been holding his breath all the way through reading his mother's words. He gulped more water, and gathering up the papers and the envelope, made his way to the door. He knocked on the door across the landing and Ronnie opened it. The old man looked pale and tired. Tom took him by the arm and looked into his wary eyes.

'Thank you, Ronnie. I've finished reading it.'

'How are you, Tom?'

'I'm fine. Somehow, I'm not that surprised really.'

Ronnie nodded slowly.

'I have to go. I have a surgery in about half an hour. I'm sorry to rush away.'

Ronnie looked concerned. 'I know how busy you are but couldn't someone stand in for you ... just this afternoon?'

'No, I'm afraid not. Actually, I think I need to do something normal that will make me concentrate on other things. I'll go through all this with Alex tonight. I need to tell him. Thank you, again, Ronnie. I know how much you've done for Mum over the years ... and how much she thought of you. I'll be in touch soon.'

With that, Tom turned and walked briskly down the stairs, said a brief goodbye to Mrs Pugh and stepped out into the cold March air. It was as if he embalmed his thoughts and emotions for the following three hours. He concentrated on the road and then on a busy surgery, consisting of children with middle ear infections, adults with colds that they were convinced were flu, a handful of regular checks on people with chronic diseases and a couple of desperately ill patients who needed to face the final months of their lives and to think about where they wished to be to die.

It was Alex's day off and he had gone sailing. He belonged to a club that used a large stretch of water about ten miles away. When Tom arrived home a mouth-watering aroma wafted to the front door from the slow cooker in the kitchen. The house was silent. He hung his coat up and made himself a coffee. Taking it and his mother's writings into the sitting room, he put on the lamps, lit the fire, closed the curtains and collapsed into the big armchair. He drank the coffee and tried to think clearly. Tiredness washed over him and leaning back against the cushions, he closed his eyes. His thoughts were flashbacks; back to being a little boy, frightened of Edward; growing into adolescence and not knowing how to have a conversation with his own father; coming out to Isobel, at the age of nineteen and being amazed and relieved that she seemed to have known anyway, and Sarah's withering comment that it explained a lot about him and why he was such 'a Mummy's boy.' With a start, he jerked out of these reveries. He had a biological father somewhere – and a half-sister. He opened the envelope and re-read the passage about Bill.

Alex found his partner at the computer when he arrived home. Wrapping his arms around Tom's shoulders he peered over to the screen.

'Hi, what are you looking at?'

Tom clicked off and turned to face Alex. 'Come through and I'll get us a drink and then I'll tell you.'

Alex gave Tom a hug and smiled at him. 'Must be serious if we need a drink first,' he laughed.

'Well, I guess it is.'

Alex looked at Tom as he poured the wine. Something was wrong. They looked at each other across the fireplace, seated in the chairs where most of their conversations took place, at least in the winter months. Tom, choosing his words carefully so as to précis the story, told Alex about the contents of Isobel's letter. Alex listened, not once interrupting but feeling increasing compassion for Tom, as the truth unfolded.

' ... So, it would seem I have an unknown biological father somewhere ... and a half sister!'

Alex smiled gently. 'At the risk of sounding like a therapist, 'how does that make you feel?'

'I've been trying to decide myself,' Tom replied, momentarily returning a thin smile. 'I think I am shocked but not really surprised. I feel as though I sort of knew. It certainly explains a lot about my relationship with my father. Mum says they had an unspoken agreement never to discuss it ... but he must have known. Can you imagine living together for as long as they did without ever talking about something as important and fundamental as who the father of their son was? D'you know, Alex, I think that surprises me more than finding out my father was not actually my father ... the fact that it was never talked about. What does that say about their relationship for, God's sake!'

'Well, I guess they were of a different generation. I mean, we know quite a few people who went through what we consider to be strange relationships, particularly during and just after the war, don't we? Even in your family there were irreparable damages done and there were two generations of troubled men. Your grandfather was in France, wasn't he; the Somme or somewhere equally horrific? Your father was a fighter pilot. God knows, they went through pretty rough stuff. His older brother was killed in action! Surely that must have affected his ability to relate to other people. I wonder how unhappy he really was. No wonder he fell for someone as lovely and caring as Isobel.'

'Yeah, I know, and I've spent my whole life trying to reason why he was the way he was towards me. I suppose, in a funny sort of way, this gives me an answer. But, Alex, how the hell did Mum carry on living with him ... living a lie? God, she must have been deeply unhappy and yet, she never showed that, not to any of us.'

They continued to talk through all the facts Isobel had presented to Tom and to fill in the gaps, wherever they could, with speculation and incredulity in equal measure. Eventually, after midnight, they went to bed and with the firm conviction to try and find out more about William Harvey – together if possible – they fell asleep. Tom dreamed about his childhood, which he had not done for a long time. In these restless dreams, he saw his father fleetingly and barely recognisable but just the awareness of the shadowy figure was enough for him to feel the fear. In the early morning he awoke, glad to put the dream away but startled by the realisation that the presence in his dreams was not in fact his father. Alex slept deeply beside him. Tom eased his legs over the side of the bed and silently left the room.

It was six o'clock. He had slept longer than he thought he would. Outside the sky was dark and a strong breeze whistled through the trees. Grabbing a heavy coat, warm scarf and gloves and pulling on his boots, he unlocked the back door and stepped out into the cold, fresh air. He walked out to the road and turned towards the open countryside. The walk was so familiar he did not need a light and was free to let his thoughts take him wherever they wished. The sun rose and colours appeared in shades of olive and pewter and copper. A flimsy veil of mist hovered over the fields. Tom reflected, with sadness, as he had so often in his life, on the possibilities of mutual love that were lost forever, between himself and the man he had known as his father. Tramping along the damp roadside he also felt a rising sense of excitement at the prospect of finding the man his mother had once loved and who was his real father. He recalled Isobel's words about not wanting to inflict on him this news about Bill. She had felt that he had had enough of a struggle coming to terms with being gay, particularly without paternal support, that she could not impose more anguish on him. Even when he and Alex had demonstrated their commitment to each other and settled into their life together, Isobel had felt she could not burst that bubble with such news. Tom wondered why his Mother had held back, even after Edward had died.

He knew she had loved him and so he had to believe her words. He also knew that he would not have a satisfactory answer to this particular question because a part of him was angry with her for not having had the courage to tell him face to face. She had asked for his forgiveness for this decision and he knew he would give it – but not yet.

Turning back towards home, his thoughts turned to Sarah. Here he was presented with heavy foreboding. All he knew, right at that moment, was that he could not tell her yet. He was mature and experienced enough to acknowledge that he needed time; time to sift through his own emotions, to plan how to proceed, if he was going to track down William - Bill his mother had called him - and time to go back to the places Isobel had described in her letter. He might find some clues to the whereabouts of his real father. Perhaps, somehow, he would find his half sister, Caterina.

He was glad it was a Saturday and neither he nor Alex was on duty. As he approached the house he became aware of the damp chill creeping into his body, despite his coat. He felt a deep sense of gratitude that he had Alex, who would support him and help to find the man he knew, with sudden, absolute conviction, he wanted to meet. He took a hot shower and dressed in his old comfortable cords and sweater.

Alex awoke to the smell of fresh coffee and toast and bacon. He smiled lazily to himself and then remembered the news of last night. What lay ahead, he wondered, as he padded into the bathroom? Would finding Tom's father change their lives for the better or not? How would they be affected? He knew for sure that things were not going to be the same.

Over breakfast they talked through all the bits of the story as they had the previous evening but this time they were more focused and eager to make plans.

'Where do you start,' asked Alex, through a mouthful of toast and honey.

'I'm not sure, but I guess, Norfolk.'

'Yeah, that's what I thought. The trouble is, when? I mean, you've no leave until May and aren't we supposed to be booking our "last minute-somewhere hot and exotic" holiday for then?'

'Yep, I know, but, Alex, I really have to make a start. Apparently North Norfolk is lovely in May – or so Mum used to tell us. Mind you, she used to say it was lovely whatever time of year it was! And there's terrific sailing there, I gather!'

Alex burst out laughing. 'You're so subtle, Dr Gabriel. I suppose you've got it all worked out, have you?'

'Well ... not exactly ... but we could look up a few places and names and so on and go on from there.'

Alex knew this was the start of something so important to his partner that he would have to embrace it with enthusiasm and indeed, he was beginning to think of it as a bit of an adventure, to be shared – and for him to pick up the pieces should things go wrong – which they might well.

They spent the rest of the day on their computers, searching for 'William Harvey,' or 'Bill Harvey.' They added 'artist' or 'painter', the UK and Italy.

The University of Florence website had no record of anyone with that name. It seemed that he had existed and worked there long before everyone had online details.

'How about trying Caterina's name?' Alex suggested as he brought mugs of tea into the study.

I have.' Tom replied wearily. 'Nothing doing. Anyway, she probably got married so her name would have changed.' He slumped back in the large swivel chair by his desk at the window and gazed wearily out towards the garden. The light was changing as the day drew to an end. The early daffodil and crocus bulbs were just beginning to sprout under the gnarled old apple tree and the fields rose gently into the distance and blended into the dreamy twilight. Tom felt, quite suddenly, very sad and somewhat disturbed. He turned to Alex, who was sipping tea and seated in his own comfy chair by his desk on the other side of the room. They had had no trouble deciding who should have the window slot for their desk. Alex found the view out of the window distracting and preferred to work by artificial light, in the darkest corner of the room, usually ear-plugged into his I-Pod. Each of them had their own clutter around their desks and the rest of the study was lined with books; many medical textbooks and journals but interspersed with books on boats and sailing, gardening, sport and travel, art, the theatre and music.

Tom looked at his partner and struggled to find the words to describe his mood. Alex turned and saw Tom's expression. He put his mug down and said gently, 'I guess this is all making you feel a bit unsettled isn't it?'

Tom nodded but remained silent. Alex came across the room and squatted by Tom's knees. 'It's OK to feel unsure and troubled by all this, Tom. You wouldn't be human if you didn't. We will get there you know. The world is very small. We'll start with Norfolk and then if nothing comes of that we'll whizz over to Florence and do some searching there. To be honest, I rather hope we don't find him in Norfolk. I quite fancy a stay in Florence!' He grinned, his infectious smile lifting Tom, as it always had. Tom smiled back and touched Alex's face.

'I don't know what I'd do without you.'

Alex covered Tom's hand with his own. 'I know. The feeling's mutual. I don't need to tell you that.' He rose and moved to switch off his computer. 'Come on; let's pack up for today and go to the pub. I'm famished!'

Tom switched everything off and drew the curtains. He could hear Alex whistling his latest piece for the choir. Not for the first time he thanked whatever fate had caused their paths to converge all those years ago.

19

'He may even have come back to Norfolk.'

Tom glanced up from the holiday cottages website. A sudden hail storm was clattering against the windows and pounding the spring flowers in the garden. Looking at the screen he felt pleased with his find. He had no idea if the place would be close to where Isobel had grown up. He could not remember all the names of the villages she had occasionally mentioned. But he knew they must be roughly in the right area and he and Alex were rather looking forward to exploring. He clicked off and leaned back to watch the weather. In seconds the hail stopped and a brilliant ray of late afternoon sunlight broke through the charcoal clouds and cast its warmth on the struggling flowers. The familiar mist shrouded the field beyond the river and the plaintive bleats from the new lambs echoed from somewhere out of view. Tom mused on the journey that lay ahead. In less than a month he and Alex would be off on their search. They had considered going to Florence and searching through university archives but neither of them spoke Italian and they had no idea if Bill or his daughter still lived there, or what her second name would be. Isobel seemed to have pointed them in the direction of Norfolk. Was that why she had wanted her ashes taken there? Would someone remember William Harvey?

He rose, and with a feeling of adventure and almost childlike excitement, moved to the piano. Was he foolish to feel like this? He could be heading for disappointment, heartache even. He lost himself as he always did as his fingers touched the keys and the mellifluous notes from his mother's piano filled the room. So lost was he in getting to grips with a new piece, that, at first, he failed to hear the telephone. Its persistent ring eventually punctured the music.

'Hello, Tom Gabriel here.'

The doorbell rang.

The steady male voice at the other end of the line spoke carefully, unhurriedly.

'Tom, David Okolo here.'

Oh, hi, David. Hold on, can you? The doorbell has just gone. I won't be a moment.' Tom knew the neurosurgeon and guessed that he wanted to discuss one of his patients.

He went to the front door and, as he opened it and was about to say he was on the phone, he saw a policewoman and a policeman standing on his doorstep.

Fear grabbed him by the throat.

'Dr Gabriel?' said the policewoman.

Tom held his breath and gave a brief nod of his head.

'Can we come in for a moment? Perhaps we could find somewhere to sit?'

Tom struggled to move. The two visitors took control and led him towards the sitting room.

He stopped abruptly and turning to the policewoman, said in a voice which sounded far away to his ears, 'It's Alex, isn't it?' She nodded and a voice came from the telephone receiver.

'Tom, are you there?'

'Do you want me to take that, Dr Gabriel? Perhaps whoever it is could ring back?'

The ghastly realisation dawned on him that the telephone call and the visit from the police were connected. He picked up the receiver with shaking hands. 'David?'

'Tom, we have Alex here right now.'

It was something in his gentle tone. Cold dread struck. His mouth was dry and no sound came from his constricted throat.

'Are you there, Tom? Look, there has been an accident. Alex is in ICU. I've operated; subdural haematoma. He's got multiple fractures and a pneumothorax, but they will heal. His head's in a bad way, Tom. It took them some time to find any ID, so he's been with us for a while. The police will be calling at your place but I thought you would want to hear it from me. I'm sorry to break such news to you ... Tom ... are you there?'

Tom had listened, had sunk to the floor and was gulping for air.

'Tom, are you OK? Is there someone who can bring you in? You perhaps shouldn't drive yourself.'

His throat tightened even more and he found it hard to swallow but he forced the words out.

'I'm coming to you now. Hang on to him, David. Don't let him go. Hang on to him ... please.' Tears streamed down his face as he struggled to push away the agonizing thoughts that were pressing themselves into his head – that he might be about to lose Alex. No, no. 'Just hold on to him, David. I'll be there. Hold ... him ... '

The policeman took the receiver and spoke calmly to the doctor on the other end. In a few seconds they had agreed that they would deliver Tom to the hospital.

David Okolo felt a lump in his throat. Tom, dependable Tom, for whom he had the greatest respect, had sounded so desperate. He replaced the receiver and walked out of the glass walled office, back to the bed nearest to the central station, where the unrecognisable Alex McKee lay prone and entirely dependent on the surrounding technology and the skilled dedication of the ICU staff. He had come in barely alive and only hanging on because of the ministrations of the frontline staff.

In all his years, tending to the pulped heads and torn spines of so many people, David still found the shock, anguish and disbelief of the relatives hard to cope with. They touched him every time. Their lives completely upturned in an instant; often never to be the same again. A skilled and revered surgeon, he always endeavoured to imbue in his students the need to try and feel what the distraught relative would be going through. The long and tortuous recovery from severe head injuries was an area he found particularly fascinating and he was an acclaimed author of many papers and a couple of books on the subject. Alex could not have been in better hands. And yet, gifted and dedicated as he surely was, David Okolo could not perform miracles.

Tom could not stem the trembling of his limbs, the rapid pulse and the waves of nausea, all of which threatened his ability to think straight. He knew he had to get to the hospital as quickly as possible and the police would be able to get him there more efficiently than anyone else. He could hear them telling him about the accident but he could not absorb what they were saying. The policewoman sat in the back of the car with him and at one point took his shaking hands in hers. She looked directly into his eyes and tried to get him to concentrate. The traffic was heavy in the town. He made himself concentrate on the fact that with every minute he was actually getting closer. He was never to recall that journey.

The harsh sound of the buzzer he pressed at the entrance to ICU sounded intrusively loud in such hushed quarters. A nurse opened the door. She looked kindly at the tall, pale man.

'Hello, can I help you?'

The policewoman handed Tom over. 'This is Dr Gabriel.'

Tom felt his chin tremble and struggled to get the words out. 'Alex McKee. I'm here to ... '

He looked helplessly at the nurse who immediately took control. This poor man was about to get another big shock. The staff had all been informed that Alex and his partner were doctors. The National Health Service always took particular care of its own. She took Tom's arm.

'You're Tom, aren't you?'

He nodded.

'My name's Kelly. Come on. I'll take you to him. Have you been told anything?'

'Yes, Mr Okolo phoned me.'

They went through a short corridor, off which were some offices and store rooms and a private room where Tom knew the bad news was delivered to people ... like him ... today.

The steady, rhythmic click and sigh of the ventilators and the beeps of the monitors greeted them. The six beds, spaced well apart, each with its central console for charts and notes, held people in varying stages of consciousness and brokenness. Tom inhaled deeply, gathering his courage, as they approached the first bay, which was hidden from their view by rigid, grey, portable screens. No more unhygienic curtains of old, his mind registered, bizarrely.

'Wait here just one moment please.' She disappeared behind the screen.

Tom waited, nausea rising bitterly at the back of his throat. A grey haired male nurse came out to greet Tom. He looked very solemn.

'Hello. You're Tom, I gather. I'm Peter and I'm looking after Alex on this shift. Kelly is helping too.

You do know that Alex has sustained some very severe injuries?'

'Yes.' Tom quite inexplicably wanted to run out of this place and never see Alex with, 'some very severe injuries.' Perhaps if he left it would all turn out to be a dream. He would go home and Alex would be there, laughing and joking and sharing with him again. But the screen was moved back to reveal the shocking and horrific scene. Tom had enjoyed his training in ICU. He had loved the drama of it and the precision and discipline of the care given. Now, he saw the person he loved, wired up and bound up and surrounded by all the bewildering trappings of modern intensive care – life support. Alex's face was swollen, his eyes invisible in the vivid blood-filled cushions of his soft tissues. His mouth hung, distorted by the tubing, which inflated his lungs with automated breaths, in and out, in and out. His head was bandaged, with a ridiculous tuft of hair sticking out of one side. Drains, containing blood-stained fluid hung at either side of the bed. He was catheterised. One leg, an arm and his pelvis were held in place with assorted metal fixators and the other arm and his hands, lacerated and swollen, lay limply on the sheet. But it was his distorted head that Tom stared at.

'My poor love.' He gradually dragged his eyes from Alex and his professional self absorbed the readings on the monitors. Peter lifted a chair nearer. 'Here, sit down. I'll see about a cup of tea and maybe we can have a chat in the office in a while? Mr Okolo was called away but he is hoping to pop back later.'

The only unscathed part of Alex's body he could touch was his left shoulder. Tom laid his hand gently on the flesh he so loved and whispered to Alex that he was there with him. Hours passed. Nurses came and went, quietly performing their vital tasks. Tom tried to sit out of their way and they cast kindly glances at him. Some time later; Tom had no idea how long, David appeared. The big burly man looked carefully at Tom.

'Can you come to the office for a moment and I'll fill you in on what we've done?'

They went to the doctors' office, not the private room and somehow, Tom took comfort from that. He had dreaded being taken to that room. In fact, there was a grieving family in it, to whom David had just delivered the news they had been dreading. Patiently and with his innate, calm professionalism, David explained all that had been done from a medical point of view. He was also able to repeat what he had heard about the accident though he warned Tom that he would need the police to explain the details.

'Tom, at this point, no-one can tell what sort of recovery Alex will make. His wounds and fractures will heal and, provided no infections set in, his chest will also get better. The subdural haematoma was severe but I've done the best I can.'

David was not prepared to speculate on Alex's recovery. Tom understood. 'Thanks for being straight with me, David. I know you can't say more. I guess we'll just have to wait.' The calm and rational words belied the dread he felt inside.

From what David had heard, an articulated lorry travelling in the opposite direction had veered across the winding road and ploughed straight into Alex's car. The current theory was that the lorry driver had fallen asleep at the wheel. Alex had been driven off the road and down a steep ravine, pounding into rocks and trees as he fell and finally coming to a halt at the bottom with the car completely smashed and stuck in small stream. The lorry driver had braked, desperately trying to remain on the road, but had crashed into a tree on the opposite side of the road, which by then was completely blocked by his massive vehicle. He was shocked but had escaped with minor injuries.

David explained his understanding of the rescue as clearly and simply as he could, just as he would have done to a non-medical person. He knew from experience that much of what he said would not be absorbed by Tom.

'By the time they reached Alex he was unconscious and bleeding heavily. A straight stretch of the road was closed off so the air ambulance could land. The paramedics and the doctor on the scene carried out life-saving procedures, resuscitating Alex when his heart stopped. The journey to the hospital took only minutes and the emergency team were on hand ready to take over. But, Tom, you must understand, Alex was down there for a while before they got to him.'

Tom listened, picturing in his mind the scene and wondering how Alex had felt, what terror must have taken hold as his car went off the road. It was at that moment that he remembered the cats would probably have been in the car too. Of course David would have no idea but he found himself asking all the same.

'Did anyone mention our cats? We'd been away for a couple of days, you see, and Alex was going to the supermarket near the cattery and then he was going to pick them up and bring them home ... '

David was not able to help. No-one had mentioned any animals being involved, but he knew how everyday, mundane details came into people's minds when they were in shock.

'I expect the police will be able to tell you. Now, Tom, there is nothing you can do here for Alex and I think you should go home and try and get some rest. You know we will call you if there is any change.'

Tom knew he was right. Alex was in a place he could not reach. He felt suddenly full of despair and very tired. 'Can I just go and say goodbye to him?'

David nodded, walked a short way with Tom and watched his friend walk slowly towards the bed. The screens had been removed giving the staff full view and immediate access to Alex. Tom leaned over and tenderly placed a kiss on the bandaged, swollen head of his partner.

'Hang on in there, Alex. You can make it. I love you ... and we have things to do together, remember?'

Outside, the night had settled and the eerie emptiness of the dark hospital grounds contrasted with the bright lights just inside the automatic doors. Tom breathed deeply and stared up at the starless sky. One of the night staff had called a taxi for him and as he stood and waited he thought of the people he would need to tell. The taxi driver, thankfully, was not particularly chatty. Tom gave his home address, did not care what it would cost and leaned back to close his eyes. His mind wandered from the present to the past and he relived moments in their lives that he and Alex had shared and which had brought them such happiness. Despite his anxiety he must have dozed for a few minutes as he started jerkily when the driver spoke.

'Down here, is it?' he asked.

Tom shook himself and shivered. 'Yes, here will do, thanks.' He paid and watched the rear lights disappear. The house felt quiet. No Alex to hug, no cats nuzzling up to his legs, wanting food. No lights on. No smell of cooking from the kitchen. No warmth. No life - except the beating of his own heart.

He turned on the heating, some lamps, poured a glass of brandy, picked up the phone and took it into the kitchen. Who was he to ring? Glancing at his watch he saw it was three o'clock in the morning. He felt alone. Isobel came into his mind and he missed her comfort and common sense. There was nothing he could do but wait a few hours and then ring his colleagues before morning surgery started. He closed his eyes as the warmth of the brandy filtered down through his system. He would ring the police. The call was picked up by a bored sounding man. When Tom said who he was the man said he would have to make some enquiries as he wasn't sure who was dealing with the case and maybe, as it was night time, Tom should ring back at nine o'clock? He went upstairs, into the bedroom and lay on their bed.

'I know I don't pray. I don't know who I'd pray to, anyway, but whatever is out there that's more powerful than us, can you please bring him back to me? Please?'

Sleep took over. Troubled dreams invaded his mind. He woke up two hours later with a stale, dry mouth and a thumping head. Reaching over, he picked up the phone and rang ICU. No change. Yes, they would see him later. Goodbye.

The shower was stingingly hot and the rumbling in his stomach reminded him that he had not eaten since lunchtime the previous day. He made himself eat some toast and drink strong tea. He rang the surgery. They were all shocked, of course, but also kind and supportive and no, no, he was not to worry, even though he and Alex had been due to do two morning surgeries. He was not to think of it. They would manage. Their locum would cover.

PC Donaldson suggested that Tom should come along to the Station and he would fill him in. He would not comment on anything until they met face to face. Sitting in a sparsely furnished interview room, the young policeman was almost comical in his attempts to sound authoritative, when he was clearly finding it difficult to talk about such emotional issues.

'I'm afraid the car is a write-off, sir. Er ... yes, the officers on the scene did, in fact, spot the remains of a cat carrier and, yes ... er ... after the fire service freed Dr McKee from the wreckage, they did, on closer inspection, find the ... er ... dead animals, sir. There was no way anyone could have saved them. I'm quite sure they would not have suffered. They must have died instantly.'

The well-worn platitudes fell more easily from his lips. He took Tom to the pound to see for himself the remains of Alex's prized MX-5 - what remained of it. Tom thought he might vomit, but gasped for air and steadied himself. He thanked the young policeman, who told him there would be an inquest and he would be informed.

His eyes burned and his head ached. When he got home he rang Eileen and Ronnie, Isobel's closest friends, but good friends of his too. Eileen immediately insisted he go to her for a meal after being at the hospital. It made sense as she was nearer and Tom gleaned some homely comfort from her. In the end he stayed a couple of nights. Eileen had made the bed up in her pretty spare room and made her home his for as long as he needed. Ronnie called round when Tom was there and the three of them talked quietly about the whole horrible business and tried not to think of how Alex might be, should he get through it all. They were kind in their response to the cats' fate too. 'Poor wee creatures,' Eileen whispered, wiping her eyes with a tissue.

Tom was plagued with anxiety about not wondering where Alex had got to that day.

'I didn't think about it. Alex was going to the sailing club in the morning, then the shopping and then the cats. I suppose if he had been much longer I would have begun to worry ... and all that time he was ... '

Eileen and Ronnie listened.

'It meant I could sort out our trip to Norfolk ... a place to stay ... for when we go looking for ... '

Eileen sat next to him and held his hands.

'You must stop thinking over all that. You are not to blame. Just you concentrate on that man of yours and getting him through this. He needs you to be strong.'

Tom contacted their close friends over the next few days. The news had spread rapidly amongst the patients and further afield to work colleagues in other practices and the local hospitals. He sat for hours at a time with Alex, waiting, watching. He talked to him, played his favourite arias, gently placing the earphone in the one ear that was visible beneath his bandaged head. Each time he returned home there was a pile of cards and letters for Alex. The answer phone was full with messages of concern and support. Tom felt touched but knew he could not begin to call them all back. He made a note of the callers and opened the mail which he stored carefully to show Alex when he came round. He did not allow himself to think that Alex may not return to him or that he might be permanently damaged.

He had phoned Sarah the day after the accident. He was not sure why, except that she was his sister. Unusually, she had answered her phone, her voice husky and with rasping breaths.

'Oh, Tom, are you OK?' She coughed painfully.

'Well, I am, but you don't sound very good.'

'Oh, it's just a throat infection. I'll be fine in a day or two. What's up?' She sounded guarded, the way she always sounded on the rare occasions when they spoke on the phone. Tom told her. She said she was sorry and to keep her informed and she wouldn't stay on the line as her throat hurt when she talked.

A few days later, desperate for some distraction, Tom resumed his duties at the surgery, on the understanding that he was free to go if the hospital called. He once again experienced the balm of his work. For short stretches of time he was able to push to the back of his mind the sight of Alex - still unconscious, though lighter and in expert hands - and concentrate on other people's problems. Just as his own patients had faith in him, so he entrusted Alex to David Okolo and his team.

20

Tom gave a last glance around the house before locking the front door. His legs brushed the lavender on either side of the path, the fresh fragrance wafting up, as he carried the box of food to the car.

'Right, that's it. Let's go.' He climbed into the driver's seat next to Alex and turned on the ignition.

Alex smiled 'This is it then!'

'Yeah, this is it!'

They drove off in the roomy estate car, which they had bought when Alex's wheelchair needed to be accommodated.

'I'm not sure if I feel excited or terrified. We would have been doing this a year ago when I'd not long found out and now I guess I've had more time to think about it all. I still don't know if we will find him, you know – quite probably not. I mean, why should he come back to Norfolk, when he lived and worked in Italy?'

Alex knew Tom was anxious about the possibility of meeting the man who was his biological father.

They had shared many conversations about all this as he had recovered from his injuries and gradually returned to work. After regaining consciousness two weeks after the accident, he had endured a long and painful process, but now, with the occasional aid of a walking stick, he was pretty much back to how he had been. The scars had healed well, the bones aligned and mercifully his head injuries had not left any permanent damage. He experienced low back and leg pain sometimes and sudden fatigue - but overall an impressive recovery. Tom had nursed him and helped him through the labours of physiotherapy and the troughs of depression which had accompanied rehabilitation. Alex knew that Tom had put on hold his desire to find Bill Harvey but now, having both secured a holiday, they were at last on this stage of the quest.

'Well, he was brought up there and he's an old man now. Sometimes people retire to old familiar places.'

'I suppose so. He must be in his late seventies at least. Mum mentioned in her letter that he was 'a bit older than her.' That could mean anything. He might be dead.'

'Well, if he is, we might just be able to find someone who knew him, or his family, and tell us a bit more about him.'

'I keep thinking, Alex, about that time you and I were on holiday in Italy and we spent a couple of days in Florence. Do you remember we went into one of the university buildings – natural history, I think? We paid to look around that amazing anatomical exhibition. I can remember the courtyard, the honey-coloured walls and shady cloisters because it was cool in there. Now, I wonder if my father ever worked there. I know he was an artist but I can't imagine he never went into other parts of the university. There were artists there that day, sketching, I remember now. And all the famous sight-seeing places; he must have gazed at Fra Angelico's frescoes and those wonders in the Uffizi just like we did. He might have sat in the same cafes, strolled down the same streets. Who knows? I wonder if we'll ever find out.'

'We'll find something, Tom. There must be someone who remembers him. If we need to go Italy, we will. His daughter may still be in Florence. The university arts faculty must have archives.'

The container of Isobel's ashes, long overdue for scattering, was tucked into a corner of the boot, held securely by their luggage. They would respect her wishes and scatter them on the beach. The house they were renting for the next two weeks was just a few miles outside the small town where his mother grew up and near her favourite beach. It was Eileen who had remembered the names of the places Isobel had told her about and she and Tom had looked them up. A traditional Norfolk flint and brick cottage, it promised a spectacular view across the marsh to the sea, and was within walking distance of the sailing club. Alex, though not able to sail on his own any more, had heard from their old colleague, Jason Hardy, who was now retired. He lived a mile or two inland but kept a small boat at the club. Tom had been determined to book somewhere that allowed

Alex to go sailing with Jason. He hoped it would be therapeutic as well as enjoyable.

They watched the landscape change as they continued into East Anglia; driving on long straight roads, dividing the vast, flat fields and then on to the gentle, undulating countryside, as they drew nearer the coast.

'Why does everyone say Norfolk is flat? This is not at all,' Alex remarked.

'Because they don't know this part in the North – thank goodness. Mum said it was beautiful and unspoilt, but now it's featured in the Sunday papers as, 'Chelsea by the Sea'. We'll see for ourselves, I guess. I can't imagine commuting to London from here, but I think it's the second home thing. You know, holiday homes and all that.'

The road swept down a gradual slope towards the sea. They could just glimpse it far out beyond the marshes and the golf course. Joining the coastal road they passed pretty houses and cottages, small hotels and pubs and just one shop – a general stores advertising freshly baked bread and local produce. There appeared to be empty premises along the way, some with faded signs indicating their original function: post office and village stores, crafts and gifts, a butcher. Just out of this small smattering of buildings, which included a church and a rather scruffy hotel in the process of being refurbished, they spotted a fresh fish shop. A large blackboard listed the many varieties of fish, crabs, whelks, lobster and other delicacies. A couple of miles on, with open countryside, fields of wheat stretching for miles on their right and the sea on their left, not visible through the trees, they approached the Staithe. Here there was more activity, a large shop with all things nautical, brightly coloured clothes and equipment, displayed to tempt holiday makers in. To their left, just off the road, was the sailing club. Boats of all shapes and sizes squatted at quirky angles, waiting for the tide to come in and restore grace to their curvy carcasses. Alex looked longingly at the scene. He was desperate to get out on a boat. Tom saw his expression and grinned. 'Not long now. Jason said he'd call us later.'

Not far down the road they spied the rental cottage. The doors and window frames were freshly painted in a soft sage green and the walls were strewn with old roses. As the website pictures had promised, pretty, English cottage garden flowers filled the small front garden. The owner had left the key under a plant pot and on the kitchen table, a welcoming home-baked loaf of bread and a jar of Norfolk honey. Milk and butter were in the fridge. By early evening they had unpacked, explored the charming rooms and wandered out to the back garden with a glass of wine to sit and admire the view. Alex absorbed the towering sky, the stretch of marsh below a wooden fence at the end of the garden and beyond, the sea and the early evening sun, illuminating the colours and textures of the tranquil scene.

Tom watched Alex. How many times in the last year had he been reminded that he had almost lost this precious man? He saw the effects of the ordeal Alex had survived, in the thinner body and lined

227

face. He was still immensely attractive but seemed to have aged before his time. They had spent many hours, during Alex's recovery, talking about the accident, the conviction of the lorry driver and the astounding ability of human bodies to repair and recover. Recently, Alex had decided that he had talked enough about it all. Physically he was getting stronger but Tom wondered if the mental anguish, so apparent in the early weeks, sometimes still prevailed. They had talked about how people, when hearing of someone surviving a near-death experience, invariably asked how it had affected that person's life. Profound self-realisations were the unspoken expectation. Alex had struggled to satisfy this need in others, often disappointing, by stating, quite honestly, that he had no deep and meaningful words to offer. He was just glad to be alive and able to use his traumatised brain once again. But Tom knew that certain aspects of the accident still haunted him. Alex accepted that the lorry driver was at fault but he sometimes said to Tom that if he had not been selfish about owning a convertible and had been in a sturdier vehicle, not only might his injuries have been less, but the cats may well have survived. Sometimes it felt to Tom that Alex was more distraught about the cats than any other aspect of the event.

He had tentatively suggested counselling and Alex had cast him a look of such derision that he had not pursued the idea. Tom knew that work at the surgery was a mixed blessing for Alex; demanding and fulfilling but also exhausting. He recalled his mother's words when he had found things difficult or upsetting. She used to listen to him and then say, 'Nothing stays the same. It will come and it will go and you will look back on that time, having got through it and it won't feel so bad.'

Looking at his partner now, Tom saw a smiling and relaxed man. Whatever else happens on this holiday, he thought, it will do Alex good. He stopped short of thinking that nothing else would come out of their stay and decided that at the very least he would find someone who had known his father.

Alex turned to look at Tom. 'Wow, I can see why someone would want to paint here. This is beautiful, isn't it?'

'It is. I can see why Mum loved it so much.'

They walked down the road to a bustling pub, which proudly stated how ancient it was, but had been done up as a stylish gastro pub by new owners. They managed to get some food but not until they had waited an hour while young families and a few older people ate their earlier meals. The food was fresh and delicious and by the time they wandered back, slightly unsteadily, Alex leaning on his stick and on Tom, it was nearly midnight. They slept deeply and awoke to the sound of the birds which, apart from the sea gulls, called and sang with sounds new to their ears.

The plan was for Alex and Jason to go out later in the day when the tide was right. This gave Tom and Alex time to start their search. In the pub, the previous evening, they had made a few enquiries but none of the locals were in and the owners seemed not to know any history of the area except the age of their pub. One man who had overheard them suggested the pub at the other end of the village where most of the locals went. The old fishing families still went in there as they always had done. He was sure they would be the best people to help. They decided to go to the fish shop first and then visit the pub at lunchtime. The cheery woman in the fish shop reiterated what the man the night before had suggested.

'Oh yes, The Anchor, that's right. You're bound to meet a Shilling in there.'

'A shilling?' Tom queried.

'That's right, my dear. The Shillings; that family's been fishing round here forever. What they don't know about folk here, nobody knows.' She wrapped their bass in paper. 'There you are. Enjoy them.'

After returning to the house, which was just about a long enough walk for Alex, they drove to The Anchor. Situated on the edge of the village and down a narrow road towards the marshes, the old seventeenth century building nestled behind trees and most likely would never be visited without prior knowledge of its existence. Stooping to enter through the open doorway, they found a dim, plainly furnished room. The inglenook fireplace to the right and the bar straight ahead were of blackened wood. Even though it was warm outside a fire had been lit and appeared to be the only source of heat. The ceiling retained the brown and yellow stains from many years of smoking customers. At the bar stood an elderly man talking to the even older and stooped barman. By a window a group of men were seated at a table, playing cards. Other than that the place was empty. As they approached the bar the two men stopped talking and stared, sizing them up, as they did all new-comers. Tom and Alex smiled and said hello.

'Afternoon,' replied the bar man cautiously.

'So, what do you fancy, Tom?' Alex asked, suppressing a grin.

'Oh, I'll have a half of the local bitter please, replied Tom, avoiding Alex's eyes.

'Right, two halves of bitter please.'

Feeling the scrutinising eyes of all the occupants of the pub, they paid for their drinks and walked over to sit at another table by a second window which looked out on to a scruffy yard full of old barrels and bits of what looked like old farm machinery. Neither of them felt comfortable enough to start up a conversation about looking for Tom's father, but Alex looked around the room and smiling, said loudly, 'Well, it's a grand day isn't it?'

The eyes studied him.

'That it is,' said one of the men at the window. 'Wind's getting up though. Not going to last today.' The other men nodded in agreement. After a few moments Alex spoke up again. 'Might be alright for a bit of sailing then, do you think?'

'That why you're 'ere then?' asked the man behind the bar, 'for sailing?'

'Well, I hope so.'

The atmosphere chilled. No-one spoke. Tom gave a nervous cough and decided to brave it out.

'Actually, we're hoping to find out about someone who used to live around here.'

The eyes focused on him, the game of cards halted, the customer at the bar perched on one of the high stools and the barman put down his tea towel. One of the group of men, stout and ruddy-faced asked, 'And who might that be then?'

'His name is William Harvey. He was an artist and he lived in this area some time ago.'

The listening men seemed to give this some thought and began to talk amongst themselves.

'Wasn't it the Harveys who ran The Crown years ago? Didn't they have a boy?'

'Aargh, that's right. Back in the sixties weren't it?'

'Lord knows where he might be now. Must be gettin' on – if he's still alive.'

'Michael Shilling'll know, I'll bet.'

Tom and Alex heard the name for the second time that day.

'That's right, Tom said, 'Shilling. Did you say Michael Shilling? Only, the lady in the fish shop mentioned the Shillings and said they might know.'

The bar man took up the conversation. 'Well, Michael's getting on himself now of course, but he knows what's what, that's for sure. He'd be your best bet, no doubt about that.'

Tom approached the bar. 'Does he come in here? I mean, do you think I could meet him here and ... you know ... ask him?'

'Not before six you can't.'

'Right.'

'And not today, neither.'

'Oh, I see. Can I ask why?'

'He don't come in 'ere on Mondays.'

With that, the bar man took up the polishing of his glasses and turned towards the shelves behind. Alex joined Tom and asked if there was any food served. It seemed a long time since breakfast. Once again they were studied.

'Crisps or nuts,' came the reply.

Tom persisted in trying to engage the man. 'If I want to catch Michael Shilling tomorrow, when would be the best time?'

One of the seated men shouted across,' He'll be in by 'alf past six.'

'Thank you,' said Tom. 'I'll come here and wait ... if that's alright.'

He and Alex made for the door, eager for sunlight and food. Something made Tom turn and say, 'I don't suppose any of you remember Thomas Armstrong, do you?'

A few nods were exchanged.

'Used to have the chemist shop in the town years ago.'

The most decrepit of the group had spoken.

'Long gone though. Aint no proper chemist shop now.'

Tom couldn't resist asking. 'Do you remember his daughter, Isobel, by any chance?'

The old man pondered for a moment. 'Aargh, I do. Used to help out in the shop. Where's she now I wonder? All gone, all gone ... ' His voice faded into a faint croak and he picked up his glass with a trembling hand and became silent once more.

Out in the air they exchanged wry grins.

'What a funny old place. I didn't think they still existed,' Tom commented, as he looked at the ramshackle old building and the faded sign, swinging stiffly in the sea breeze.

Alex was reading a notice pinned to a wooden post on the edge of the field opposite. 'So, this old place is to be refurbished under new management; rebuilt more like! And a caravan site in this field.'

'Perhaps that's why they seemed so miserable. They looked as though this was their home from home, and for years, I should think.'

'Yeah, probably. Anyway, I'm starving!' Alex shouted over his shoulder as he walked to the car. 'Let's go and find some food!'

They picked up some basic provisions from the store on the way home and tucked into a cold meal of local bread, cheese and ham. Jason knocked on the door as they were finishing. He filled the small kitchen with his size and his exuberance. Always thumpingly loud and enthusiastic, he had not changed much in the ten years or so since they had seen each other, apart from some extra bulk around his middle. He was, however, sensitive and gentle in his questions to Alex, about the accident. Tom watched them climb into Jason's battered old land rover to drive the short distance to the sailing club. The sea bass was promised for their supper.

Tom decided to explore some of the nearby villages and, in particular, to look inside any art galleries. He knew the likelihood of finding any of William Harvey's paintings was remote but still felt compelled to go and look. By mid afternoon he found himself in the village where his maternal grandparents were buried. Isobel had told him the name, in her stories of Norfolk, but it had only resonated with him when he had checked the map of the area. He pulled up by the church and walked into the graveyard. It took a while to find them. The simple headstone was engraved just with their names and their dates of birth and death. Tom had never met them but the sense of history – of passing time – touched him. 'Nothing stays the same,' he murmured to himself as he walked through the lytch gate.

Across the road from the church was an art gallery with the inevitable craft shop attached. He walked through the scent of Norfolk lavender, emanating from the array of soaps, room sprays, candles and multifarious 'gifts for the home' and through to the small space at the back. Here were many landscape paintings of the area. Some were spectacularly bad but a few caught the eye and had obviously been painted by skilled artists. He examined the signatures. None of the pictures bore the name Harvey. A young woman with an unruly mop of red curls approached him. Her voice was deep and gentle.

'Can I help at all? Were you looking for anything in particular?'

'Not really ... well ... yes ... I suppose I am.

She smiled up at him, waiting and caught by his startlingly blue eyes.

'Have you ever heard of an artist called William Harvey?'

She repeated the name slowly to herself and then shook her head. 'No, I'm sorry, I haven't. Is he local?'

'Well, he was, but a long time ago. I don't even know if he is in this country anymore. He lived in Italy years ago.'

The woman looked up. 'How old would he be now?'

'Oh, late seventies I should think. Why?' Tom's pulse rate increased.

'Well, it may not be him but it seems almost too much of a coincidence if not.' She was moving towards two small wooden framed watercolours in the corner of the room. Tom watched, hardly daring to hope. He followed her.

'You see the signature is indistinct but I think it reads 'B.H'. Have a look.

Tom had seen the pictures but had not spotted the unobtrusive initials and presumed they were unsigned. He put his glasses on and peered into the corner. There, mingled with the mauvy-brown of the marsh at sunset, he saw 'B.H. '07'.

The woman watched this tall, attractive man as he studied the pictures.

'Could he have called himself 'Bill Harvey'? If so, these might be his,' she proffered.

Tom turned to look into her enquiring face. 'Yes, my mother referred to him as 'Bill.'

'Oh, he's a friend of your mother's?'

'Yes, sort of ... he was ... a long time ago.' He turned back to the paintings. '2007. They're recent then?'

'Yes, it would seem so.'

'So, do you know him? I mean, have you met him?'

She hesitated. Somehow, she felt she wanted to help. It was obvious that finding William, or Bill Harvey, was important to this person and she knew she was about to disappoint. 'I'm afraid not, no.'

His face fell.

'You see, I only took over here last year and I haven't taken in any new stock of paintings just yet.'

'I see. I don't suppose you recall this man perhaps calling in to offer more pictures. I mean ... '

She interrupted him. 'No, I'm so sorry. I will ask around though, if you like. If you leave me your number, I'll certainly contact you if I hear anything about him. Tom wrote his mobile number on a card at the till. He looked into the face of the young woman. She had freckles and smiling green eyes he noticed. He felt her concern and was warmed by it.

'Thank you for your help.'

'Not at all. I hope you find him – if he is the William Harvey you're looking for. He might not be, of course,' she warned.

'No, he might not be.' Tom replied and said goodbye. He sat in the car thinking. The date said '07 and the girl had assured him none of their paintings went back as far as 1907. That means he could be here - if it is him. For the first time, he allowed himself to believe that his father could be living nearby. Michael Shilling – tomorrow night. Would he be the one to tell him?

The gallery Tom called into on the way home was full of large modern paintings, some of which captured the scenery in dramatic strokes of striking colours, so as to overshadow the gentler, subtle tones of the more traditional styles. Tom felt these 'corporate' paintings, clever and vibrant as they were, seemed to be of another place, not here. Already the light and the clean air were captivating him. He admitted to himself that he was not very knowledgeable about art but he knew what he liked. Perhaps William Harvey painted in different styles. Maybe some of his pictures were large sweeping canvasses of bold colours.

He concentrated on preparing the food when he got back to the house. Alex and Jason returned in the early evening, glowing and windswept and hungry. Tom saw, with relief and pleasure, Alex's tired satisfaction and enthusiasm for the sailing they had enjoyed. Jason was good company and they reminisced over the old days, the ever-changing world of medicine and Jason's idyllic-sounding retired life. They did not discuss Tom's quest. Tom, conscious of a potentially futile mission, needed to hold it close for the time being. Later, in bed, with a mild breeze from the sea whispering at the open window, Alex fell immediately into a deep and restorative sleep. Tom lay beside him and wondered, yet again, if he should continue his search. If, tomorrow, Michael Shilling did indeed tell him of Bill's whereabouts, would he be able to go and seek Bill out; to barge into the life of an old man whom he did not know and then to announce that he, Tom, was his son? He thought of Edward, the father he had grown up with. Many times he had made excuses for Edward's behaviour towards him. He must have known Tom was not his, but for how long? Isobel had said in her letter that it was something never verbally acknowledged between them. How the hell did they live together with such a massive, bloody great elephant in the room? God knows how they maintained their relationship. He knew from his work and from odd comments his mother had made about her contemporaries that many marriages of that generation had survived only because of convention and pride. How very sad. As the night sky began to lighten he laid his arm across Alex's sleeping form and closed his eyes.

In the morning Alex left Tom sleeping and drove off to buy a newspaper and some more bread. As he drove he wondered how Tom would take it if he did not find William Harvey, or, and perhaps worse, he did and the old man had no desire to know that he had a son, from out of the blue, and from a brief liaison forty five years ago. Alex knew how much this meant to Tom. He felt guilty for the delay caused by the accident. Well, he decided, they would cope with whatever came their way. He could not share quite the same optimism as Tom but he would support him.

Tom awoke to the sound of Alex singing and clattering about in the kitchen. He lay, in the spacious light of morning, looking out at the sky. Did this place hold anything for him? If he met Michael Shilling this evening and if he knew of William's whereabouts – what then?

21

For a time, Tom had held back from telling his sister – his half sister! A part of him had not wanted to include her. After all, they were hardly confidants. He recalled Sarah's response when one day he had finally plucked up the courage to tell her. She had maintained her distance all these years and Tom had grown to accept that they would never be close. He had thought of ringing her and immediately rejected the idea. She rarely answered anyway. Telling your sister that the father you thought you both shared was the biological father of only one of you was not the sort of message to leave on a telephone. He had considered writing a letter but knew the moment would pass if he did not act swiftly. So, an email it had been, one evening when Alex was recuperating and had gone to bed early. He had told Sarah of the visit to Ronnie Fairfax and of Isobel's letter. He had described, as best he could, the shock and confusion he had felt. Finally, he had needed to explain why he had not told her sooner. In this, he was honest about not knowing how or when to broach the subject; of his anxiety about her reaction; of his own uncertainty. The accident had delayed telling her even more. It was not that it had all been pushed out of his mind – not at all – but Alex's well-being had been paramount and so time had passed.

Tom recalled the moment, when his finger had hovered over the mouse and the cursor over 'send'; the fleeting hesitation when you know that, once you click, it is out of your hands and cannot be reclaimed. He had left the email unsent while he checked that Alex was asleep and poured himself a beer. Then he had sat down once more and stared at the words he had typed. One more gulp and, 'click,' it had gone.

Sarah had arrived back at her apartment just before midnight. It had been a good day; long but successful. The case had gone well. She was confident of positive reports in the press the next day. Her client, a high profile politician's wife, had won a substantial amount of money from her cheating ex-husband and he had been publicly humiliated. Sarah and her team had ended the day by dining at their favourite restaurant and drinking more than usual. There were two messages on her phone; one from her friend, Merle, inviting her to supper and the other from a colleague offering congratulations on the case. News travelled fast in the firm. Too tired to check emails, she fell into bed to sleep soundly. The following morning she awoke late but feeling remarkably fresh considering the night before. She was taking a day off, a habit she had formed some years earlier, as a reward for completion of a successful case, or as a consolation if things had gone badly.

This particular morning, she went for a jog around the block, picked up some newspapers on the way back and after showering and making coffee, read the accounts of the case. She smiled at the descriptions of her as one of Boston's most successful divorce lawyers. She had worked hard to get where she was in a competitive, still male-dominated profession. There were emails from colleagues, mostly congratulatory, some generic office ones and one from Tom. She and her brother only exchanged emails when something important happened. After Isobel's death there were a few regarding her estate and then, after Alex's accident, some progress reports on his recovery, which Sarah had not requested but which she had occasionally responded to. So, with some curiosity, Sarah read Tom's words.

'Well, well, so Tommy is my half brother!' she stated out loud as she leaned back in the chair and absorbed Tom's news. She was not sure what she felt. On one level it made no difference to her. On another, she thought it helped to make sense of her feelings towards Tom; feelings she had not tried to analyse because of the unease they engendered in her, the discomfort ... the guilt. Had she, in a child's intuitive way, sensed something different about her brother ... no ... impossible, surely. And yet, there had always been a barrier between them. She knew she could have broken this down and that it was she who maintained it. How on earth had Isobel and Edward stayed together? Had her father known? Was that part of the reason he poured all his attention on to her? And Tom – how was he feeling now? He had stated in the email that as soon as Alex was well enough they were going to Norfolk to see if they could trace this William Harvey. Sarah was irritated not to have been told this news earlier and surprised to feel genuine concern for her brother. It must be hard for anyone to find this out about their parents, but Edward had treated Tom so unfairly, she wondered if it was a relief for him to know that Edward had never been his real father - his biological father.

On impulse, she picked up the phone and made the call to England. She had no idea what she would say but felt instinctively that an email response from her was not appropriate. After a few rings it was Tom who answered. 'Hello, Tom Gabriel here.'

'Hi Tom it's Sarah.'

There was a short pause.

'Sarah! Hi. Are you OK?'

'I'm fine. I just read your email, Tom.'

'Right. I was going to ring you but ... '

'I know. I'm never in. You don't need to explain. I just thought I'd call and see how you are. Yeah, I know, doesn't sound like me, does it!'

'Well ... '

'So ... how are you, Tom?'

'Well, I'm OK, really. I've had some time to get my head round it, I suppose. Alex's accident and all that has sort of taken over a bit.'

'Sure.'

'How about you, Sarah? I hope it wasn't too much of a shock. I tried to put it sensitively in the email, but you know feelings don't come over very well electronically, do they?'

'Look, Tom, I'm OK about it. I mean, I'm sort of processing it a bit and no doubt there will be some moments when it hits me, but, in a strange way, I sort of wonder if this is why we have never got on. Is there something subliminal that makes a difference between siblings and half siblings? I don't know, do you?'

Tom remembered the jealousy and friction between them. He was so surprised and touched at Sarah calling that he felt nervous of treading into speculations about their relationship. 'No, I'm not a psychologist, I'm afraid.' He paused for just a moment and then added, 'What I do know, Sarah, is that it makes no difference to how much I care for you. I know we don't talk about our feelings for each other ... and I don't expect you to start now ... but I love you as my sister and I always will.'

To Sarah's surprise – and alarm – tears came to her eyes. She swallowed hard and took a deep breath. 'I know you do, Tom.' She cleared her throat and moved on. 'Aren't you amazed that Mum and Dad stayed together all those years? He must have known, don't you think?'

'Yes. I can't quite get my head round that. I don't know whether to feel sad or angry ... at both of them ... for different reasons. I even find myself sometimes feeling a bit sorry for Dad ... and then I think how unhappy Mum must have been. Marriages of that generation hung on through thick and thin, I think. Divorce was such a shameful thing to go through back then.'

'Unlike today! And I should know. It keeps me employed!'

They laughed. Tom felt a warm surge of affection for his sister. He had no idea what she was feeling - but she had phoned.

'I must go, Tom. How's Alex?' her voice had returned to its normal brusqueness.

'He's mending, thank you. Thanks for ringing, Sarah. It is good to hear your voice.'

'OK. Well, keep me posted when you go to Norfolk. I wonder what the artist William Harvey will be like ... if you ever find him. Bye Tom.'

'Bye.' The line went dead. Tom replaced the receiver and stood still for a moment. The relief he felt, now that Sarah finally knew, was immense. He had no idea how she would feel as time went on and she had more time to consider. He just hoped she would stay in touch. Maybe it would get better; maybe not. It could not be a lot worse than it had been up until now. It really was quite something for her to call him. It was probably best just to be thankful for that.

He walked slowly back to the kitchen where Alex was hobbling about keeping an eye on the cooking. He had been as surprised as Tom at the call from Sarah. Now, he scrutinised his partner's expression. Tom was smiling – all be it in a slightly bemused way – but calm – not the usual reaction to a call from his sister.

Alex moved the sauce off the heat and sat stiffly at the table. 'OK?' he asked carefully.

'Yeah, I think so.' Tom ran his fingers through his hair. 'I think so.'

'Sounded like a sort of normal conversation to me.'

'Well, I suppose it was. She was really quite sensitive about it all and it must have been a big shock to her.'

Over supper they had talked more about this unexpected reaction of Sarah's. Naturally cautious, after all the years of hostility, their overriding feelings were of relief. Who knew how she would be from now on but that particular communication had gone better than expected.

Sarah had come off the phone and spent some time thinking back over the years. After Isobel's death, she had experienced some complex feelings. Isobel was old and so there was less a sense of shock, more a sense of inevitability about it all. It was only when Sarah returned to her apartment after the funeral that she had given herself the time to think about her mother. She admitted to herself that Isobel had been a caring mother, always there at the beginning and the end of the school day, enthusiastically involved in school activities; supportive, wise and reliable. And yet, Sarah had still felt the less special child. Tom was the one who she saw laughing and playing with their mother. Tom could make Isobel laugh so often. Sarah could never quite manage that. She knew that often she had pushed her mother away. Now, with her death, inevitably, she was reminded of other deaths. Why did life rub salt in healing wounds? Yes, some wounds were still raw, but they were healing and then along would come another death, with all the trappings, all the platitudes, all the conventions, to inflict pain and to reverse the healing process for a while, leaving a deeper scar. Sarah spared a thought for her brother. The uninvited pang of guilt that had intruded occasionally, over the years, rose up once more into her thoughts. The box, so carefully sealed, had opened and Tom presented himself to her as clearly as if he was there in the room.

Nothing could change what had gone before and yet everything she recalled now had a different slant to it. Well, it would certainly give her therapist something to chew over, she had thought, wryly.

22

Tom and Alex's eyes adjusted as they stepped from bright, early evening light into the gloom. Just as before there was a group of men at a table, playing cards, the same man at the bar chatting and in the far corner by the window, another man. He seemed to be in conversation with everybody there, on and off, but sat separately with a watchful black Labrador at his feet. Tom tried not to stare. Was that Michael Shilling, he wondered. Alex spoke in a friendly voice.

'Hello, again. We were in the other day if you remember and ... '

'I remember,' replied the man behind the bar casting a belligerent glance at them as he wiped the counter. 'What can I get you?'

'Two pints of that excellent local beer we tried the other night please,' Alex replied in what sounded to Tom's ears to be rather over-the-top affability. They waited while the beer was pumped out. A voice from the card table gathering called out. 'You were looking for Michael Shilling weren't you?'

Tom turned. 'Yes, that's right.'

'Well, you don't 'ave far to look. He's there by the window.' The man returned to his card game and the indecipherable mutterings of his friends. Tom and Alex looked at each other, paid for the beers and walked across to the old man with his dog.

'Excuse me,' Tom said gently. There was no response. The old man had his eyes closed and had not appeared to hear him.

'You'll 'ave to speak up. He's a bit deaf,' shouted one of the card players.

'Thanks,' said Tom. Leaning forward a little he spoke loudly. 'Excuse me, but are you Michael Shilling?'

'Bloody stupid question, if you ask me,' muttered one of the group. 'I just told 'im who 'e is!'

The man opened unseeing eyes and turned towards Tom and Alex. Tom did not know why, but he was shocked to see that Michael Shilling was blind. The dog studied them and Alex reached forward to stroke him gently.

'That's me,' replied Michael. 'Who wants to know?'

They pulled chairs up to the low table. 'My name is Tom Gabriel and I'm looking for someone called William Harvey. He was an artist and used to live around here a long time ago.'

'Are you now? And why might you be looking for him, may I ask?'

'Well, he was a friend of my mother and ... as we are on holiday here we thought it might be nice to see him.' Even to Tom's ears this sounded a somewhat fabricated reason.

Alex chipped in. 'Tom's mother has passed away, you see, and we are here to scatter her ashes. We'd be interested in meeting anyone who knew her, as she grew up here too.'

'And who are you?'

Tom and Alex exchanged glances.

'This is my good friend, Alex. He's ... here for some sailing.'

It's the twenty first century and I'm stumbling over saying Alex is my partner, thought Tom and he looked for understanding from Alex. He got it. They both knew it was better not to complicate things any more than they seemed already. These men may or may not have understood but it was easier not to try and find out.

'Aargh, now I'm getting it. So who was your mother, Tom Gabriel?'

'Her name was Isobel Armstrong and her father owned the chemist shop in the town.'

Michael ruminated quietly for a moment. He drained his glass and Alex immediately stood up and offered him another.

'Won't say no ... if you're offering.' He straightened up his arthritic, old body and turned his weather-beaten, leathery face towards Tom. 'I remember your mother ... went off to be a nurse. She was a beauty, right enough. My brothers and me ... we all fell for Isobel Armstrong in them days.'

Tom smiled. The old man was quiet and Tom wondered whether to prompt him about William. Alex moved the replenished glass towards Michael's hands and said gently and clearly, 'She remained a beauty all her life, Michael. Now, what about William Harvey?'

'Yes, I know, I know. I'm just remembering when I last saw Isobel Armstrong. Aargh, yes, it was when she bought some mackerel off me, one evening when I'd just got in with the littlest boat.'

'And William Harvey?' Tom prompted.

Michael took a long swallow of beer and wiped his hand across his top lip. 'Bill Harvey. He's back. Gettin' on a bit 'imself now. 'e went to Italy or somewhere. Any road up, 'e's back.'

Tom's pulse quickened.

'What did you want to know again?' Michael asked vaguely.

Tom leaned forward and tried to keep the frustration out of his voice. 'You say he's back, Michael. Bill Harvey is back. Does that mean here? Is he living around here?'

'That's what I've 'eard. Over at the Staithe. I suppose if 'e's still painting that's as good a view as you'll ever get. Oh yes, a good view right enough.'

'Could you tell me where this place is, d'you think?'

'Oh, it's about a couple of miles from here, right on the Staithe, but tucked away round the back. You can't see it from the road. Very hidden, right on the water when the tide's up. 'Little Tern' is the name. Don't know why they have to give it such a daft name. Bloody millions of birds around 'ere. That one aint nothin' special.' He took a slurp of his beer and settled his chin into his chest as if to indicate the conversation was over.

'Thank you for the information,' Tom said, wondering if he should offer the old man another drink. Alex, who wasn't driving, had already decided he liked the beer and stood up.

'Can I get you another?' He spoke clearly to Michael, who immediately looked up from his chest.

'Well, if you're having one, I won't say no.'

Tom indicated that he was happy with his one drink. Over the next half an hour or so Michael told them about his family of fishermen. Only the youngest son continued to go out now, but for many years Michael and his father and two other brothers had eked out a living from the North Sea. Now even the old whelk sheds were empty and other, bigger and more commercially viable organisations had taken over. Just as the old pub was crumbling irretrievably into the past, so it seemed were Michael and others like him. He told them about his sight going and how it had darkened his once wide, exhilarating, sea-sprayed world into a life which consisted of a slow walk from his cottage to the pub, with his faithful dog, Clipper, and back again, to listen to the radio on his own. It was hard not to be moved by the old man's tale. Tom plucked up the courage to ask when he had lost his sight, although, out of habit, he and Alex had already mentally diagnosed possible causes.

'Just went gradually, over time. They told me I'd got that diabetes and some other thing what affects your eyes. I don't trust any of them. Wouldn't have gone near them 'cept for my wife nagging. She's gone now, of course ... but she made me go to them in the end. Too late to do owt about it, though, by then.'

This time he settled his head down even more and appeared to be nodding off.

'You won't get no more from 'im tonight,' shouted over one of the card players. That's more than I've 'eard 'im say in a long time.'

They thanked the barman, said good night to the others and stepped out into the cool evening. The sinking sun cast a peach-pink glow over the marshes to their left. The field opposite, the site for the new caravan park, appeared empty, but small insect and bird sounds emanated from within the unkempt grasses; the only sounds. Everywhere was held in stillness; peaceful and undisturbed. The engine of the car starting up seemed a violation of this tranquillity as they eased away up towards the road.

'Well, now we know where he is, what do you want to do? Alex asked, searching Tom's profile. Tom concentrated on the road ahead. After a moment he said quietly, 'I really don't know, Alex. I'm excited on one level and on another, I feel like I'm going to barge into this man's life; someone who sounds as though he has come back to this place for its beauty and its peace ... and cause him ... who knows what damage. I don't think we can go to his home now ... this evening, do you?'

'No. In any case we need to eat. But, I tell you what, let's park by the big beach and go for a walk. You need some space to think and maybe we should sleep on it. In the morning you will know what you need to do.'

Tom smiled at him. 'That's one of the things I love about you, Alex, your confidence about things turning out OK. You really believe that in the morning I will feel surer of what to do, don't you?'

Alex laughed. 'No ... I don't *believe* that. I know it!'

They parked on the rough, sandy ground of the beach car park, where there were just two other cars. The early season holiday makers had gone back to their rented houses, or to their own properties, perhaps due to be let for the busy season. So there was no charge for the car park, as in the day. The little green wooden hut was shut up for the night, as was the small cabin beach shop.

They walked over the dunes to the wide expanse of beach. The tide was just beginning to go out. The sea reflected a sky which had changed from daylight turquoises, blues and greys, to rose and gold and amber and above, the dark of the approaching night. They linked arms and sloshed along at the water's edge, carrying their shoes and feeling the slight pull of the shallow waves on the cool, wet sand beneath their feet. They were silent for a long time, close and at ease in their companionable isolation. It was as if the rest of the world had disappeared and only they remained, with the elements of air and water enfolding them. Tom spoke first.

'You know, right now, I could just stay here and pretend that nothing else exists. I wouldn't have any decisions to make and life would not get any more complicated.'

Alex remained silent.

'It's a funny thing, Alex, but one of the reasons I think I can go and see William, is because of Sarah's reaction.'

'In what way?'

'This morning, when I woke up, she came into my mind ... the time I told her about William Harvey. Well, I think I must have been expecting her to use me being only her half brother to distance herself even more. But she hasn't, has she?'

'No, she hasn't,' agreed Alex, holding back from warning Tom not to expect a significant change of heart from his sister after all these years. 'But Tom, you must do this for you and you alone. It really isn't anyone else's business. You're the one who will live with the outcome ... whatever that proves to be.'

'I know, but what about us? I mean, how do you feel?'

'I love you and I want what's best for you. If you want me to stick my neck out and tell you what I really feel, then, I think if you don't go and see him, you'll never rest. Isobel must have wanted you to try, or she surely wouldn't have told you.'

Tom hugged him and held him close. 'I love you Alexander McKee.'

'And I love you, Thomas Gabriel.'

They held each other, each giving and gaining strength and support from the other, as they had done for so long. Turning back, their footprints invisible, as the sea washed them away, they remained silent, both contemplating the next day.

They talked later over supper. Jason had phoned. He was taking the boat out the next day. Alex, who felt strongly that Tom should go to see William

Harvey on his own, was relieved to have a genuine reason to be out of sight.

'We'll be out in the morning. You can tell me how it went when we get back.'

Tom was less certain about going alone, but realistic enough to acknowledge that he was nervous about this possible meeting, with or without Alex's physical presence. The sea air had caught up with them and they both slept well.

Tom awoke with a start and looked out on a fine warm day. He and Alex walked down to the sailing club. Alex turned to him and held both of Tom's shoulders in a firm and confident grip. 'It'll be fine. Just be yourself. Be honest. That's all you can do. How he takes it is up to him.'

Tom grinned weakly. 'I know, I know. Right. See you later. I'll see you back at the house. Don't rush. Have a drink with Jason. I don't want him to sense anything strange.'

Alex patted his shoulder. 'OK. Good luck. See you later.' He turned and walked towards the sailing club. Tom watched his figure become lost in the busy, lively groups of amateur sailors, all keen to get out on the water, laughing and shouting good natured greetings to one another. He glanced over to his left, to the small cluster of cottages of varying shapes and sizes that nestled at the water's edge, hidden from view, until you walked towards the moored boats and looked back. One of those was William Harvey's house; his father's house.

23

A narrow cobbled pathway led him round to the back of the houses where there was a variety of small courtyard gardens in differing states of repair. Some had obviously had money spent on them and their bijou style reflected the many second homes he and Alex had already spotted. A couple of dwellings were unchanged, with damp bricks and tiles, cracked and peeling paintwork at the doors and windows. Perhaps older local people still lived in them. He scanned the buildings for house names. At the end of the pathway, standing back, up a slight slope, stood a larger house. Partly clad in wood, it was otherwise constructed in the local flint and brick. There were stone steps up to a wooden balcony and what he presumed was the front door. Underneath and raised up on newer stones was what might have been a garage at one time but now appeared to be a workshop – a studio perhaps. Tom read the slate sign attached to the wall at the foot of the steps. This was it. He climbed the steps and rang an old ship's bell hanging to one side of the door. No sound from within the house. Fighting a feeling of despair, he went down the steps just as the door of the workshop opened. He watched, fascinated, as a tall, lean, white haired man stooped to come out into the open. Tom reached the bottom of the steps and the man straightened up and looked towards him.

The shock rocked him so that he had to hold on to the wooden post at the foot of the steps. The gentle tinkling of the nearby boats and the call of sea birds over the marsh, the distant sounds of human voices, seemed to waft away, as Tom stared at the man. It was almost like looking into a mirror. He was older, lined and tanned, perhaps an inch shorter, but it was him. It was his father. There could be no doubt.

Bill looked at Tom. 'Good morning.'

Tom's voice croaked out, 'Good morning.' He cleared his throat. 'I'm ... er ... I'm looking for William Harvey.'

'Well, you've found him. How can I help?' His voice was deep and friendly.

Tom had rehearsed the words so many times but now could not remember them.

'Right ... I'm Tom Gabriel ... and I'm here ... on ... '

'Holiday?' suggested Bill.

'Yes, that's right. We're staying down the road actually.'

'Well, you've picked some good weather. How long are you staying?' Bill was making polite conversation but wondered what this man had come to see him about. 'You said you were looking for me?'

Tom knew he had to say something other than the stuttering words he had managed so far. 'Yes, that's right. You see, my mother grew up around here and I think you might have known her and ... ' He faltered once more.

Bill moved towards him. 'Oh really, what's her name?'

Here goes, thought Tom. This is the point of no return. 'Isobel Gabriel.'

Bill looked thoughtful. 'When would this be, would you say?'

'Oh, about 1960–ish ... 1963, maybe. But earlier, too ... when she lived around here with her parents. Oh, yes, of course, her second name then was Armstrong. Her father owned the chemist shop in the town.' Tom stopped abruptly.

Bill looked for a moment at Tom and then spoke carefully. 'Excuse me a moment, would you. I've left my glasses in the studio and I would be able to see you better with them. Then we could go up and have a coffee ... if you'd like one?'

'Yes. I'd like that. Thank you.' Tom watched as Bill entered his studio. He was wearing old brown cords and a faded blue denim shirt; battered, brown suede boots on his feet, splattered with paint and what looked like clay.

Bill emerged and without putting his horn rimmed glasses on, led the way up the steps. Once inside, he moved quickly to the kitchen, calling over his shoulder for Tom to take a seat. Tom stayed standing and took in the room with its huge window and spectacular view; the comfy sofas and armchairs, the paintings, stacked against the walls and some beautiful ones hanging around the room. This was surely an artist's dream home. He wondered how long William Harvey had lived here. After what seemed an age, Bill came into the room with a tray set with mugs, a pot of fresh coffee, a small jug of milk and a plate of digestive biscuits. He placed the tray on a low wooden table, moving a pile of books out of the way. He took a step away and put his glasses on. Tom remained absolutely still and returned Bill's look as steadily as he could. This was not easy as Bill had a piercing stare and because Tom was looking into his own eyes. It was startling afresh to look at those eyes. Tom had grown up with comments from everyone he met about his blue eyes. Alex said they were what he had fallen for in the beginning. Now, he was seeing them in someone else. Bill sat and leaned forward to pour the coffee.

'Please, sit down. Help yourself to milk and have a biscuit.'

'Tom accepted the mug of coffee. There was no way he could have swallowed any solid food. Eventually, just as he was beginning to think that Bill was never going to comment, the older man put his mug down and spoke.

So, you're Isobel's son. How is she?'

Tom had practised this too. 'I'm afraid my mother died last year.'

Bill gazed out of the window. 'Ah, I see. I am sorry ... ' Turning back to Tom he studied him for a moment. 'You don't look like her ... how I remember her.'

'No.'

'She was visiting with her daughter when I last saw her. She and my daughter, Caterina, played together.'

'Yes, my sister, Sarah, lives in Boston. She's a lawyer.'

'And you, Tom, what do you do?'

'I'm a doctor ... a GP ... in the Midlands.'

'I think I know why you are here, Tom.'

'Do you?'

'Yes. Right now, I am looking at a younger version of myself and you are seeing an older version of you. Am I right?'

'Yes.'

'Well, I can't say this has not come as bit of a shock ... for both of us ... except you have no doubt had longer to get used to the idea. If I were to have any doubts, I only have to look in your eyes to dispel them.' He smiled.

Tom smiled slightly. 'I guess so.'

They stayed in the room with the large window and talked. More coffee was poured. Bill rustled up some sandwiches and time passed. The light changed as the day wore on.

The shrill tone of Tom's mobile phone fractured the quiet conversation. He jumped up. 'I'm sorry.'

Alex's voice sounded anxious. 'Hi. Are you OK? I waited for a while but it's getting on and ... '

'Oh, Alex, I'm so sorry. Yeah, I'm fine. We've been talking. I didn't realise the time.'

'It's OK, as long as you're alright. When will you be back? I presume he's taken it OK or you wouldn't still be there?'

'Yes, I think so. There's just so much to talk about. I'll be back within the hour. OK?'

'That's fine. See you then.'

Tom stayed standing, hesitating, unsure what to say. Bill looked up at him and said gently, 'I gather you should be somewhere else.'

'Yes ... well ... in a little while. That was my partner, Alex. I hadn't really thought about the time.'

Bill remained silent.

'Well, thank you very much, William. Thank you for the food and drinks and ... thank you for listening. I seem to have monopolised the conversation rather.'

Bill stood and came close to Tom.

'No-one calls me William. Please call me Bill. It's been a pleasure ... I think! I'm going to need a little time to absorb what you have told me. Just as you did, after reading your mother's letter, I should think.'

His manner was perfectly friendly – in a polite sort of way. Tom could not imagine Bill being impolite to anyone.

'Yes, of course. I understand.' Arranging another meeting, he knew, needed to come from Bill. Bill moved to the table and picked up a sheet of paper and a pencil.

'Why don't you leave your number and perhaps I can call you sometime?'

There was nothing in his words to suggest that he would not call. Yet Tom felt deflated. He wrote his mobile number on the paper and left it on the table as Bill opened the door. They shared a brief but scrutinising look. Crystal clear blue eyes - behind which lay a lifetime of stories to resurrect – or to bury.

'Well, thanks again. I hope all this has not been too much of a shock for you.' They shook hands. Tom descended the steps and Bill watched this stranger as he walked away.

The sailors were packing up and heading into the clubhouse or to their vehicles, laughing, wind-burnt and tired after their spell in the fresh air. He felt completely alone. Quite irrationally, he felt as he had done as a teenager, when he knew he was gay and it seemed it was a secret he would never be able to reveal to anyone, but most of all to his father, Edward. The fear and confusion came reeling back into his mind. His feet felt heavy and his steps slow. A straggle of loud, brash young men and women, with stringy, salty hair and tanned faces, shouted and whooped around him. They were like the kids he remembered in the school playground – in gangs – confident, noisy, arrogant. He walked through the pack, his head pounding. His pace quickened as he walked up the slope to the road. His breathing was laboured and his pulse racing. He could hear them laughing. A few paces more would take him out of sight. There was an old oak bench at the side of the road. To his horror, Tom knew he had to sit down. He felt foolish and embarrassed. Common sense told him to breathe deeply and slowly. His tangled thoughts were sending strange, unsettling messages. He closed his eyes, aware anyone passing would be staring, but desperately needing to collect his thoughts and try to assemble them into something manageable. What the bloody hell had he just done!

He had not been able to imagine how he was going to feel meeting Bill but he had not anticipated this. He leaned forward and held his head, pressing his fingers into his temples. 'God, I'm like a child,' he whispered to himself as fear and alarm threatened.

After a time the panic subsided. His breathing and pulse rate slowed and the deeply inhaled fresh, clean air restored coherent thought. It had been a long time since he had experienced anything similar. Calmer and steadied, he continued slowly along the road to the cottage.

Alex was sitting reading in the garden. On the small table beside him stood a bottle of red wine and two glasses. He looked up at the sound of Tom's footsteps. On seeing his partner's face he stood up and limped over to him.

'Hey, what's up? You look awful!'

'Thanks.'

'Sorry, I mean, are you OK? You don't look it!'

Tom sat on one of the chairs. 'I think I'm OK, but a glass of that wouldn't go amiss!'

Alex poured them some wine. He watched as Tom took a deep gulp. He waited.

Tom drank some more. 'Sorry, I'm not exactly savouring this and I know it's a good one.'

'Right now, I think its effect is more important, so drink away,' Alex replied lightly. He stayed silent and waited as Tom gazed out to the sea. His glass drained, Tom looked at Alex and said, 'Well, I've met him at least.'

'What is he like?' Alex replenished their glasses.

'Me ... well ... me in twenty years or so ... if I stay fit.'

'Right, that must have felt strange.'

'Yeah, it was a shock ... for both of us. He's a nice guy; gentle, polite. His paintings are amazing. I told him about me, my family, work and stuff. Actually, I gabbled. He listened. And now I want to know more about him. There is so much to ask and I don't know if he will see me again.'

'I'm really sorry if my call stopped you from finding out more.'

'No, no, he was making it clear that it was time for me to go, really, by then. Oh, I don't know, Alex. I felt really odd on the way back ... like a panic attack. I haven't had one of those since I was a kid. Have I done the right thing? You know, I'm angry with Mum, in a way. Perhaps she should have kept her secret. I mean, what good has it done?'

'Well, none ... yet ... but the Isobel I knew was wise and kind and loved you to bits, so I can't think she would do anything to hurt you.'

'No, I guess not, but she couldn't know how this would work out. She probably just needed to confess her sins or something.' Tom sighed. 'Ah well, we'll see. You never know he might call tomorrow and we can continue our chat.'

Tom's words sounded hollow to them both. Over their supper and late into the night they talked it through. Alex saw the pain and confusion and tried his best to say the right thing. In the end, they collapsed into bed and fell into instant, red wine-fuelled oblivion.

The following morning, Alex persuaded Tom to join him and Jason on the boat. Tom felt a need to escape and pushed aside his nervousness about being out on the water. It was a gentle day and to be far away from the land, and Bill, appealed to him. He could not bear the thought of sitting around all day waiting for Bill to call; far better to distance himself for a while. Jason had been told the day before, that Tom was looking up an old friend of his mother's and, apart from asking if Tom had had a good day, nothing more was said about it. There was just enough of a breeze to carry them along and Tom was given various tasks to perform. Concentrating on them kept his mind busy, but in the quieter moments, as he surveyed the enormous panorama of water and sky, Bill was there.

After they had shared a drink together in the clubhouse and Jason had gone home, Tom and Alex walked past their house and on to the newly refurbished pub at the far end of the village. It was as they approached the garden, with its wooden tables and chairs occupied by early evening customers, that Tom's mobile phone went off. Tom had checked his phone when they had arrived back on dry land but there had been no messages.

'Hello.'

'Hi, Tom. Bill Harvey here.'

'Hello, Bill. How are you?'

'I'm fine thanks. I hope you are too. Look, I was wondering if you and your partner, Alex, isn't it, would like to come over tomorrow for a meal? Nothing fancy. I'm a pretty basic cook, but you'd both be very welcome.'

'That would be great. We'd love to come - thanks.'

'Good. Shall we say about seven?'

'OK. Thanks, Bill. See you then.'

Tom smiled at Alex. 'He's asked us over for a meal tomorrow evening, about seven. I said yes. Are you OK with that?'

'Sure. Let's go in. I'm hungry.'

'He doesn't know you're gay, does he?' Alex asked between mouthfuls.

'No, I never got round to talking properly about us. I'm sorry, Alex. He just knows we've been together for fifteen years and you're a GP too. I don't think I referred to you as, 'he' but, to be honest, I may have done, in which case, he knows.'

'Oh well, if he doesn't know, it will be interesting to meet him and gauge his reaction when he sees me!'

Tom did not want anything to cloud the strong feelings of relief and hopefulness that surged through him. He had tried to convince himself it did not matter whether he saw Bill again; that life would just continue as before - without him. Now, he knew it mattered a lot.

back the pictures. 'They are beautiful. Thank you for showing them to me.'

Bill rested them against the chair and sat down again. Alex broke the silence. 'You know, it is fascinating to see you two together. I have never seen such a strong likeness. With Tom's eyes Isobel must have been constantly reminded of you, Bill, all her life.'

'Yes, I was thinking about that. Tom, you must wonder how she managed to keep her secret.'

'I do. I can only think that she had the best interests of her family at heart. She was a loving and generous mother ... and wife ... which is the hardest part to understand I guess.'

Bill switched on the lamps. Through the window the last traces of the sunset were unbelievably beautiful. The clouds had blown away and the disappearing, burning colours, which had earlier illuminated the room, promised fine weather the next day. Bill's baked fish with tomato, basil and olive sauce was expertly cooked, the wine easily drunk and the conversation relaxed. Somehow having Alex there eased the tension and, as always, he was able to make people in his company feel at ease. Bill complemented him on his Irish accent. They shared a love of Italian opera and spent some minutes discussing their favourites. Tom felt a deep satisfaction seep into his body and was content to listen to them bouncing sparkling and witty remarks off each other. After the meal they settled into the sofas and chairs once more.

There was no embarrassment when Tom discovered that it was in this house that Bill and Isobel had spent their only night together.

'I expect in some people's eyes we were wrong, but Tom, you are the end result of two people who loved and needed each other very much. I should have hung on to your mother before she went away to do her nursing, but I was off to see the world, to lose myself in art and London and then Florence. It was my life and I needed to get away from this place. I saw it as dull and behind the times. The irony is that now I wouldn't choose to be anywhere else. We change in our needs as we get older, don't you think? I knew the owners of this house and they promised to tell me if they were ever going to sell it and they did. I let it out as a holiday home for years but now it is my own and it feels good.'

Tom told Bill more about his childhood. He spoke loyally of his father but Bill was wise enough to realise that more was being said by what Tom did not articulate than the carefully chosen words he did use. His heart went out to this sensitive man - his own son, unknown to him all these years. Bill explained that he never asked Isobel's married name. They had not thought about it in the short time they had been together. He had returned to Florence and thrown himself into his teaching. Caterina had been cared for by her grandparents while Bill worked at the university. Yes, there had been other women, but in the end no-one with whom Bill felt he could share his life. Caterina was now about to become a grandmother. She and her husband, Nico had gone on to have two children, a boy, Gianni and a girl, Flavia, named after Caterina's mother. Nico and Caterina now lived in London where Nico worked in the Italian Embassy. Flavia and her husband, Stefano, owned a thriving, Italian restaurant in Hampstead and it was their child who was expected soon. Bill visited them and they spent some holidays with him. Gianni, whom Bill had referred to earlier, had moved to London and was teaching Italian at one of the language schools.

Tom silently absorbed the fact that he had a family he had not known about. He had a half sister, other than Sarah, and a niece and nephew and he was about to become a great uncle.

'So, how did Caterina react,' he asked eventually.

'She was shocked and got a bit upset. We have decided to get the family together and talk about it. It's what Italian families do. I'm going to London tomorrow, so we will all meet at her home sometime in the next week, while I am staying ... and ... share our thoughts. Before we all meet, she will tell her children and Nico herself. It will give them time to process it, I suppose.' He smiled.

'I am very sorry if I have caused people to be upset,' Tom said quietly.

Bill gave a little shrug. 'What will be, will be. We are a close family. We will work it through. Don't worry, Tom. This is not your fault. You had no say in who your parents were to be.'

'Will you keep in touch?'

'Yes.'

When they were leaving, Bill held Tom's hand in both of his, but there was no embrace. He shook hands with Alex and waved them off cheerfully enough. They looked back to see his tall, lean frame, illuminated by the old lamp at the top of the steps and against a backdrop of the night sky. They did not talk much on the walk home. Alex had sensed Tom's need for contemplation and simply commented on what a pleasant and interesting person Bill had seemed.

'Yeah, I know, he is. I will talk about it, Alex, sometime. Right now I'm not sure what I feel.'

'Sleep on it, Tom. It has been a pretty overwhelming couple of days for you.'

'And him. One thing I was going to ask him was whether he would have wanted to be with us when we scatter Mum's ashes.'

Alex stopped and turned to look at Tom. 'Well, thank God you didn't! What a difficult situation that could have caused. He might not have known what to say. Tom, it is forty five years or more since they were together. He has lived a life of his own, as Isobel did. His memories of her are not of the woman you knew as your mother, or of the woman I knew, for that matter.'

'You're right.'

He did not slept well; thoughts churning his mind; questions unanswered; anxiety over whether he should have come to find Bill, should have told him. After all, Bill was not a young man and his quiet good manners had not convinced Tom that he was comfortable with the sudden arrival of a son he did not know he had. Why should he be? His peaceful existence in the place he loved had been shattered.

His restlessness persisted the next morning. 'Do you mind if we go home this evening? I mean, after we've done the ashes thing?'

Alex handed him a mug of coffee. 'No, if that's what you want. I'm easy.'

'It's just that I think I need to leave here in order to think straight.'

'OK.'

The day had started bright and hot. By late afternoon the weather had changed dramatically and the temperature had dropped. They drove to the beach car park, having packed and returned the house keys to a rather indignant owner. She gave them an appraising look but made no comment, except to ask if everything had been satisfactory with the cottage. They reassured her and made the excuse of someone being sick at work which meant they had to return early. People were driving in the opposite direction in droves; their sunny day on the beach over with the arrival of a sudden blustery wind and thunderous sky. They had planned to walk to the far end of the beach where the seals could be spotted and where there was more space and quiet. By the time they crossed the dunes it became clear that unless they wanted to drive home in sodden clothes it would be better to scatter Isobel's ashes where they stood. It was difficult to get a sense of the wind direction and they had heard of others performing this task and getting covered in wet ashes which clung ominously to their clothes. Tom had visualised shaking the ashes out from a height and watching them disperse into the wind as he said a final farewell to his mother. Today, he was far from sure how he felt about her. The elements seemed to him to reflect his own disquiet.

Alex stood beside him and waited. Tom opened the ugly brown plastic container, which reminded him of a catering-sized pot of mustard. Holding the pot at arm's length and with both of them turning their faces away he shook out the ashes. There seemed to be a lot. The wind whipped them up and carried them off. When it seemed safe to turn their faces back they saw some had settled amongst the dunes, the rest had gone.

'Goodbye, Mum.'

'Goodbye, dear Isobel.' Alex put his arms around Tom and held him close. They stood, leaning into the wind, with the rain cutting across their faces as the light faded and they grew cold.

The journey home was subdued. The weather improved as they left the coast and as they pulled up at their home, the evening felt warm and heavy with the scent of flowers. Tom's mood lifted as he carried their luggage past the lavender, breathing in the delicate, stewed apple scent of the old Albertine rose by the doorway. He felt safer here from the troubled thoughts still swirling around in his head. Later, after they had eaten, he sat at the piano and played away his anguish – as he had done all through his life.

Alex listened as he sat at his desk checking emails. He knew this consolation of music and the deep concentration it required were exactly the therapy Tom needed. He was still concerned about the possible effect their visit to Bill might have. Tom had devoted his time and energies to Alex since the accident, putting everything else on hold. Now that they had met Bill it would be interesting to see how it all panned out.

Tom stopped thrashing out some heavy piece that Alex did not recognise and switched to his favourite Debussy. When he finished playing he wandered out into the stillness of the garden. Alex left him as he turned off the lamps and prepared for bed.

25

The insidious progression had started with the reading of Isobel's letter and had grown slowly but inexorably. Alex had been watching, but because of his accident, even he failed to spot Tom submerging. For the first week after their return from Norfolk, Tom had been a bit edgy, waiting to hear from Bill. They had discussed the fact that Bill was talking to his family and would no doubt need time and so Tom had concentrated on his work. After two weeks, when there was still no word from Bill, Tom began to have even more difficulty sleeping. He would go for long walks by the river, asking to be on his own. He lost interest in eating and would waken in the early hours tense and unsettled. When Alex tried to talk to him, Tom would just say he was anxious about how the members of Bill's family were taking the news. The staff at the surgery began to notice little changes. He had always been a conscientious, reliable colleague; undemanding and comfortable to work with. Now he was vague about details he would previously have been on top of and he no longer engaged with the team but took his tea and coffee in his consulting room and left promptly at the end of the day.

Alex broached the subject one evening after Doug, the Practice Manager, had told him that Tom had reduced one of the receptionists to tears by telling her off in front of a waiting room full of people.

'Why don't you call Bill? The worst that can happen is that he'll tell you to get lost and don't you think you'd be better off knowing where you stand instead of tormenting yourself not knowing?'

Tom heard the impatience in Alex's voice. He was right of course. It would be better to know. He could put it behind him and move on. After all, life had been pretty good before he knew about Bill's existence. He tried the mobile number Bill had given him. It went straight through to his voicemail.

Alex spoke rapidly. 'Leave him a message. At least he'll know you've tried to get in touch.'

'Hello, Bill, it's Tom here. I hope you are OK. I was wondering how you ... I mean, I hope everything went OK with ... perhaps you could call me if you pick up this message?' He turned to Alex. 'Well, that was pretty slick, wasn't it! I can't even find the right words to say to him.' He left the room and disappeared to the bottom of the garden. No return call was made.

It was the following week when Suzie, their partner at the surgery, telephoned Alex at home.

'Hi Suzie, is everything alright?' It was unusual to get a call from any of the staff on his day off.

'I'm fine thanks but just wondering if Tom is OK. He's not turned up for morning surgery.'

Alex sat abruptly on the chair behind him.

'Alex, are you there? Alex? Alex, speak to me. Are you alright?'

He felt sick.

'Yes, I'm here.'

'Is something wrong? Where is Tom?'

He took a deep breath. 'Look, Suzie, I don't know where he is right now. He left at the normal time. Can you get the girls to rearrange the non-urgent appointments and find cover for the rest? Ring Frank if you need to. I know he'll help out if you need him. I'm going to drive the route we take to work ... just in case Tom's broken down ... or something. I'll call you as soon as I know anything.' His hands were shaking.

'Of course. We'll be fine. You go and find him. Don't worry about this place. We can cope. Good luck, Alex. Keep in touch.'

He tried Tom's mobile. It was switched off. He left a message anyway, asking him to call back. Why the hell had he not persuaded Tom to get help? He had been on the point of suggesting it so many times. He drove along the road dreading seeing the police clearing up after an accident. He cornered the bend where his car had left the road and where he never failed to think of that day every time he passed the spot. It was as he pulled into the surgery car park that his phone rang. He stopped and grabbed the mobile.

'Hello, Alex McKee.'

'Alex, this is Ronald Fairfax speaking.'

For a moment the name did not register and then he remembered Isobel's solicitor. Before he could summon up any words, Ronnie spoke again in his calm, authoritative voice.

'Tom's here with me, Alex. He was waiting for me when I got into work. He's alright; rather distressed. He wants to talk to me, which is fine, but I felt you should know his whereabouts as he seems a bit lost and confused about where he is meant to be. I presumed he was due at the surgery but I didn't want to involve them straight away. I hope that was the right thing to do.'

Alex closed his eyes. Thank God. Tom was safe. What on earth had made him want to see Ronnie he had no idea. All that mattered was that he was in a safe place.

'Thank you, Ronnie. Thank you so much for ringing me. I'll come over.'

'Actually, Alex, do you mind waiting until I ring you back? It's just that I had a bit of a job persuading Tom to let me ring you. He says he wants to talk to me alone – now. I'm due to see a client in half an hour but Mrs Pugh will sort that out. I promise I shall ring you as soon as Tom has finished whatever it is he wants to talk about. Is that alright?'

Alex suppressed the urge to drive straight over there. 'That's fine, thank you, Ronnie. Just one thing, can you make sure Tom is not left on his own? I'm worried about his state of mind right now. He's been a bit low recently.'

'Of course, I understand. I'll keep a close eye on him.'

The relief made Alex feel emotional. The stark realisation that Tom was in a bad way made him feel anxious and guilty. Typical bloody doctor – unable to see anything wrong with those closest to him – until it reaches crisis point, he thought grimly, as he walked to the back entrance of the medical centre, unseen by people in the waiting room. He checked with Doug that all the patients who needed a doctor that morning would be seen. He decided to keep it simple and told Doug to let the others know that Tom had felt unwell on the way to work and decided to return home. His mobile battery was low so he had not been able to ring them.

Doug sensed it was a difficult situation and looking at Alex's pale face, was genuinely concerned. 'Is there anything I can help with, Alex? I mean, is Tom OK? Are you OK? I don't want to intrude but I'm here to help if you need me.'

'Thanks, Doug, but right now I think we can manage. I'll call you later when I've spoken to Tom.'

Alex did not elaborate and Doug did not question his story. Alex drove home, thinking hard about how he could offer help to Tom. He had no idea why Tom had gone to see Ronnie, apart from the fact that, after himself, Ronnie was the person Tom most trusted. Maybe the old man would be able to help. He would certainly listen and offer wise counsel.

They sat, as they had on that previous occasion, in the old leather chairs by the window but Tom seemed agitated. He leapt up suddenly and paced around. Ronnie watched and listened.

'We went to Norfolk, you see. We tracked him down. I'm not sure we should have done that. He hasn't rung, even though he said he would, and when I try his number I get his voicemail message ... every time. I don't think he is going to call, Ronnie. I don't think we will ever meet again. God knows what damage I've done to him ... and his family!'

Ronnie stood. Taking Tom's arm he gently guided him to the chairs and quite firmly pressed him to sit. There was a discreet knock at the door.

'Come in.' Ronnie knew it would be Diana Pugh with the tea. She quietly placed the tray on the low table and moved to the door without making eye contact with either man.

Ronnie followed. 'Thank you, Mrs Pugh. I may be some time.'

She smiled at him. 'That's perfectly alright, Mr Fairfax. I've rearranged your client for another time. I'll make sure you are not disturbed.'

Ronnie closed the door after her and thought, as he often did, how quaint it was that after all these years he and Diana always referred to each other so formally. He knew that she would not have it any other way.

Ronnie was not without experience in dealing with distressing family situations and he was astute enough to know when the problems required other professional help. He poured the tea and handed the cup and saucer to Tom so that he had to take them.

'My dear Tom, I am sorry you are so low and so unhappy. It sounds as though you have been through rather a lot since Isobel died. You have had to come to terms with the loss of your mother, whom you

288

loved very much, and then Alex's accident, which was very serious, and now this meeting with Bill Harvey.' He paused, choosing his words carefully. 'Has it occurred to you that you may need a bit of help ... not from me ... to get through all this?'

Tom's gaze remained focused on the carpet. Ronnie sipped his tea and waited again. Tom placed his cup and saucer on the table. Ronnie went to speak.

'I will drink it, Ronnie ... just not yet. Yes, I have thought about getting help. Alex has been fantastic though. I was coping fine until we met Bill. I shouldn't have gone. It's a simple as that.'

'Tom, I can't make this better for you but I do think that talking to the right person would help you. Please allow yourself some therapy. If this was one of your patients, what would you be recommending?' Tom looked up. He saw the compassion in Ronnie's face.

'I know. You're right. Thank you, Ronnie. I knew you were the right person to come to, whatever you say. There is just one thing though. Why do you think Mum kept this secret from me ... and from Sarah ... until after her death?'

'Oh, Tom, if only we knew the reasons for other people's actions. The simple fact is we shall never know. Apart from her words to you in her letter, where, if I remember correctly, she told you that when she saw how full and happy your life had become with Alex and your work, she did not want to disrupt that. Then, I think she could not contemplate leaving you without telling you the truth. Was that a cowardly way to tell you? Perhaps, but were she alive now, I honestly believe her words would not be any different, and you would not have learned anything new from her. She has been very generous with the details of her life in that letter. She believed Bill was in Italy, probably with a new wife and family; possibly no longer alive. I am going to confess now that I was against her leaving the letter. Some secrets are best taken with us when we go, I feel. But, you never know, I may have been wrong. Bill and his family might just be taking some time to get used to the news. I do hope that is the case and all works out for you, Tom.'

Even through the fog of his confused thoughts, Tom sensed a subtle message, delivered gently and with tact, but which, put bluntly, was saying simply, 'get over it.' He drank his tea. He insisted he was fit to drive himself home. Ronnie called Alex to let him know and waved Tom off, feeling very old and rather inadequate.

Alex adopted a professional approach to Tom's depression and without much persuasion Tom agreed to some counselling. He carried on working and was encouraged to do as many normal activities as possible. Gradually he found stimulation once again in his work and he and Alex went for long walks. He went alone for more strenuous treks across the rolling countryside. His music soothed him and he became more sociable. Deep down inside, he felt a sadness, which he shared only with the therapist. Sarah emailed. In her typically blunt way she asked how it had gone in Norfolk and what Bill was like. Tom told her about their meetings and that he was waiting to hear from Bill. A week later she telephoned.

'Well, what's going on? You haven't told me anything. When are you getting together? Have you met your *other* half sister yet?'

Tom could not help a wry smile. Sarah was genuinely interested in his life for the first time – and curious enough to call him. 'Actually, I haven't heard anything at all. It's been a few weeks now so I guess he just doesn't want to know.' Something in his tone alerted Sarah.

'So, how are you about that?'

'What do you mean, how am I about that?'

'Just what I say. How are you about that ... all of this stuff ... you know ... finding your long, lost father, after all these years?

'I don't know, Sarah. I suppose I'm finding it all quite hard. I mean, I'm not sure about so much at the moment.'

'Well, I hope you're getting the right help, Tom, to sort all this out.'

Reluctantly, he told her about the counselling and was slightly taken aback when she laughed.

'My God, Tom! You mean to tell me you've got this far without therapy. Christ, I've been in therapy for years. You really are a stiff-upper-lip society over there still, aren't you?'

Tom was not sure what to say.

'Look, Tom, don't get hung up about it. Bill has every right to live his life without you. You've met him. Maybe that'll have to be enough. Anyway, I have to go. Ciao! Oh, and make sure you let me know if you ever do hear from him.'

There was a click and the line went dead.

Later the same evening Alex answered the telephone.

Hi, Alex McKee here. Oh, hi, nice to hear from you. I expect you want Tom. Hang on; I'll take this to him.' He went into the sitting room where Tom was playing the piano. He looked up and saw the wide grin on Alex's face.

'You didn't hear the phone. It's for you. It's Bill!'

Tom took a deep breath as he took the handset.

'Hello, Bill.'

'Hello, Tom. How are you?'

'I'm fine thanks ... and you?'

'Well, that's partly why I'm ringing. You must have thought I'd disappeared off the face of the earth. I'm sorry not to have been in touch.'

'That's OK. I wasn't sure if you would get back to me.'

Oh, yes, I would have got back to you sooner, but various things have been happening which have prevented me from doing that.'

'Right.'

'The first thing to say to you is that I left my mobile at my house in Norfolk. I hate the damned things anyway and only have one because Caterina insisted. Well, that was the only way I had your number. So, that was one reason. The other is that it took a while to gather my lot together and have the family discussion I told you about ... and ... for them all to get their heads round my news ... as I'm sure you appreciate.'

'Yes, of course.' Tom held back from asking what their reactions had been. Bill sounded as though he had more to say.

'Anyway, more of that later. I have to tell you that I am now a very proud great grandfather!' He sounded so excited Tom could not help smiling.

'Congratulations! Are they all OK?'

'They are now, but that is why I've only just got back home.'

Tom registered, with a huge rush of relief, that Bill had got in touch soon after returning to his own home'

'Unfortunately, Flavia had to go into hospital. She was suffering with pre-eclampsia. I'm sure you know all about that so you'll understand. Then they wanted to keep an eye on the baby, but all is well now, thank God, and they're home. She wasn't doing much heavy work in the restaurant and it was obvious they needed a helping hand from me. I am knackered! Enjoyed it, though. It's a great place. By the way, I just didn't have time to search for your Practice on the Internet. It was all pretty hectic down there and, as I said, they all needed time to think about what I had told them.'

Now, Tom could feel the tension, which had been holding him in its grip, begin to slacken. He felt a lightness lifting his spirits and yet, a desire to burst into tears. His body felt as though it was floating. 'I do understand. Congratulations! Is it a boy or a girl?'

'It's a little boy – Teodoro, William. That bit's after me! He is tiny and dark and very handsome!'

'Bill, I'm so pleased. I'm really delighted for you and your family.'

There was a pause.

'Tom ... if you want us ... we can be your family too.'

294

26

It was a month since the evening Bill had called to
tell Tom about his time in London. They had had a
couple of conversations since; each time a little more
relaxed. Tom's spirits had lifted. He was continuing
with his therapy for a few more sessions but the
communication with Bill had resolved many troubled
thoughts. He had tried Sarah's telephone number a
few times but typically got no reply, so he had
emailed her to tell her about Bill. She had replied
saying, 'Good, sounds interesting, but keep up the
therapy!'

The last time Bill had telephoned he had asked
Tom if it would be OK for Caterina to ring him. Tom
was surprised, delighted and nervous, all at the same
time. Bill had explained that his family was hosting a
birthday party for him at the restaurant on a Sunday
afternoon in late September. Caterina wanted to
invite Tom and Alex herself. A few days later she
rang. Tom heard a husky, deep voice. She spoke

perfect English with the appealing inflection of an Italian.

'Hello, Tom. This is Caterina. I hope you do not mind me calling you. My father gave me your number and said it would be OK.'

'Of course. It is lovely to hear you, Caterina. Congratulations on becoming a Grandmother!'

She laughed. 'Thank you, Tom. We are very happy. We were wondering if you and Alex would care to join us for a party in September. We will be celebrating my ... oh, but of course, I should say ... *our* father's eightieth birthday on the last Sunday of that month and we would all be honoured if you would share the day with us.'

Tom struggled to keep the emotion from his voice. 'We would love to come, thank you.'

'That way you can meet the whole family.'

'Are you sure they will want to meet me?'

'Oh yes. We have talked for many hours about you. Now, everyone is curious to meet Tom, the brother and uncle we did not know existed. Papa has said you are a very nice person. He would not say that if he did not mean it!'

'Thank you, Caterina. I am looking forward so much to meeting you – all of you.'

'Good. I will send you the details – time and date and so on. Perhaps you can bring a photograph of Sarah? She lives in America Papa said. Or do you think she would like to come too?'

Tom reacted instinctively. 'No ... I mean ... I don't think she would be able to leave her work at such short notice.'

'I see.'

'But ... I suppose I could ask her ... '

'I tell you what, Tom. I will send the details for you to give to her if you wish, but we will welcome you and Alex in any case. It has been lovely to speak to you and I know we will have much to talk about one day. Goodbye for now, Tom. Ciao!'

'Goodbye, Caterina – and thank you again.'

How strange that Sarah had used the same farewell 'Ciao!'

He emailed Sarah out of a sense of duty and tried not to sound too unwelcoming. Not known for her perspicacity, her intuitive reply surprised him.

'Good you are going to meet them - can't make it as I'll be away on my booked-ages-ago holiday in Maui. Anyway, Tom, perhaps better you meet them for the first time without me. S.'

He felt guilty relief.

'Which shirt do you think?' Tom was holding up two for Alex's opinion.

'Either. They both look good.'

'Thanks.'

'OK, the blue. Are you wearing your new trousers?'

'Yes.'

'Right then, that's decided.'

They rarely talked about clothes, both choosing what made them feel comfortable. Other people took more of an interest in what they wore. The staff at the surgery considered both men to be very stylish and often commented on a tie or a jacket, in the assumption that all gay men spent an inordinate amount of time choosing clothes.

Caterina had sent Tom directions to the restaurant in Hampstead. She had said it would be casual, and to expect the meal to go on for the whole afternoon, so there would be plenty of time to get to know each other. They were due to arrive at midday for drinks and gifts for Bill. This had presented Tom and Alex with a dilemma. In the end, and after much discussion, they decided to buy tickets for an Andrea Bocelli concert and to invite Bill to stay with them for the weekend. Tom felt confident enough to offer this and had mentioned it to Caterina in an email just to be sure. She had assured him that it would be perfect.

They organised a day off for the Monday and took the train. Tom checked that he had put in his jacket pocket a black and white photograph of Isobel, aged twenty five, the age she had been when she and Bill had met each other again in Norfolk. He did not have a recent picture of Sarah and when he had asked her for one she had refused. The only one he had was the one Isobel had kept on her desk. Sarah looking cool and beautiful in little black dress and pearls. It was just before Michael's death and she had a radiance about her. From what Tom had seen when she had come over for their mother's funeral, Sarah had not changed much, although she had lost some of her sparkle. It would have to do. He was not sure if he would show them to Bill. He would decide at the time if the moment was right.

They had been invited to stay the night with Gianni in his small house in Battersea. Caterina had said he was excited about meeting them. They had learned from Bill that Gianni had felt increasingly uncomfortable as a gay man in Italy, even in a city like Florence. Now, he was working and playing hard and relishing his freedom. He shared the house with two friends but they were on holiday so there was plenty of room.

They buried themselves in the Sunday papers on the journey down. Alex was keeping a careful eye on Tom. He knew how apprehensive he was. They walked from the tube. The day was bright and crisp, and leafy Hampstead, with its tall mansions and abundance of eating places, was looking particularly appealing. They turned off the busy street into a quieter area. The restaurant was called simply, 'Stefano.' There were a few tables and chairs on the pavement, under a green canopy. Seated at one of the tables was a young man, wearing sunglasses, smoking and reading a newspaper. He sipped his coffee and leaned back to survey the passers-by. Tom and Alex felt his shielded eyes watching them as they approached. He stood up, slim, elegant, looking like an Armani model. His white shirt dazzled and, with immaculately cut black trousers, tight around his snake hips, he oozed sensuality. Was it the clothes, the shoes, or just his demeanour? Whatever it was, he looked cool and confident – and Italian. He stubbed his cigarette out and drained his glass. As they reached him he smiled, displaying immaculate white teeth and dimples on either side of his mouth. His hair was the colour of molasses and curled around his smooth, tanned forehead.

'Buongiorno! I think that you are Tom and Alex, no? I am Gianni. Welcome. He shook their hands vigorously. 'Come, I will take you to meet my family.' Laughing suddenly, he added, 'But of course, we are *your* family too!' and ushered them into the restaurant. Inside, amidst the enormous mirrors and dark wooden furniture, a living family portrait greeted them. It was as if the world had turned to sepia and the tableau facing them assembled for a photograph. Alex and Tom stood just inside the entrance as their eyes adjusted to the change of light. The group suddenly broke up and beaming smiles appeared and lit the room. They were approached by Bill first and given warm embraces and kissed on both cheeks. 'Welcome, both of you. Come and meet the family.' One by one they were introduced; Caterina first. Tom looked at his half sister with fascination. He saw a small, softly rounded woman with auburn-tinted, dark hair, swept back into a chignon. She had dark eyes and smiled broadly. She wore an immaculately cut, olive green linen shift and heavy gold jewellery. She embraced them both and, holding his arms, stood for a moment looking up into Tom's eyes. 'Welcome, Tom. Welcome to our family.'

Before he could find his voice, they were introduced to Nico; a short, barrel of a man with a dark moustache and serious, caramel brown eyes, behind steel rimmed spectacles. Flavia, holding the baby, moved towards them next. She was a younger version of her elegant mother, with dark curls bouncing around her face. Dressed in a cream silk shirt and dark grey trousers and simple silver jewellery she held Teodoro for them to see. He lay in the crook of her arm, sleeping and blowing tiny bubbles.

'This is Teodoro. His name means 'God Given.'

'He is very beautiful,' Tom said gently. Alex handed a soft, floppy-eared toy rabbit to her. 'This is for Teodoro. We weren't sure what to bring for him but we couldn't resist this.'

'Thank you Alex. You are both very kind.' Stefano shook their hands as he rested one arm around his wife's shoulders. He was a long, lean man, bursting with pride and love for his wife, his new son - and his successful business. Without hesitation he had closed the restaurant for this family celebration. This was their gift to Bill.

Like the women, the men wore effortlessly chic clothes. Even Bill had abandoned his jeans for dark linen trousers and a cool white shirt. He was standing close to them when Gianni approached. His grandson had removed his sunglasses and it was with astonishment that Alex and Tom looked at his eyes. The blue was startling and yet so familiar. Gianni laughed. 'I know, I know. When I saw your eyes, Tom, it was like looking into a mirror. I have got used to seeing my grandfather's eyes looking back at me and now we have a third member of the family with the *occhi blu*!' Gianni was in high spirits. He was delighted to welcome two gay men into his family. His relatives all loved him and had tried not to be judgemental but had taken some time to accept the fact that he was gay. His father, Nico, had struggled with his conscience for a time. Now, here in London, seeing his beloved son embracing life and working hard, he had come to a sad but realistic acceptance. Gianni knew how fortunate he was compared to many of his friends, not just in Italy, but, he had discovered, in England too.

The afternoon was full of wine and exquisite food and a large, sweet birthday cake, all cooked and presented by Stefano, with Caterina as his assistant. Conversation flowed in a rich blend of Italian and English. They got to know one another a little. As the evening light filtered through the windows, the Murano mirrors and chandeliers reflected a gathering of vibrant, colourful people. Caterina found a moment to talk to Tom.

'When Papa told me about you, Tom, I was very upset. This was because I thought he had lost the love he had for my mother. I know now that this was not the case. I do have a faint picture, far back in my mind, of a beach and playing with a small girl and going to a house which had steps up to the front door. It is strange that Papa lives in that very house, don't you think?'

'Yes. It was a shock when he told us that was where they had spent the night together.'

'I think he was very lonely.'

'So was my mother ... for different reasons, I think. I have a picture of Sarah if you would like to see it.' He left the picture of Isobel where it was.

Caterina studied the photograph. 'She is very attractive. How does she feel about you having a different father?

'Well, it's difficult to tell. She doesn't say much, but she is interested in hearing how we get on, I think.'

'I think we will get on very well. Papa is happy and that makes us all happy. You and Alex are welcome and we will enjoy getting to know you. We are not young anymore and as we get older we learn what is and what is not important in life, don't you think?'

Enthusiastic embraces accompanied the farewells. Bill was delighted with his present and said he would be in touch as soon as he returned to Norfolk. Gianni whisked them off to the tube with shouted goodbyes and 'Arrivaderci!' echoing in their ears. They floated in an alcoholic haze to Gianni's house, laughing and joking on the tube and through the streets. Exhausted and euphoric, they politely but firmly declined Gianni's offer of a night cap. Gianni hugged them both hard. 'I am so happy to have you as my uncles. You are cool and I love you!' With resounding kisses on both cheeks he staggered to his own room.

He had gone to work the next morning and had left instructions about where to find things in the kitchen and to put the spare front door key through the letter box when they left. He signed the note,

'*Thank you for coming into my life. Vi amo - I love you! xxxx*'

The trundling train from Marylebone delivered them to their local station, so they had chosen it and not the faster service to Birmingham International. It was quiet and they easily found a table. Alex had been watching Tom, trying to decipher his mood; his reaction to the day before. They had not discussed any of it as they had travelled by tube from Gianni's house. Now, as they settled in their seats, facing each other, he broached the subject. 'So, how do you feel, now you've met them all?'

'I don't really know.'

'Well it was all very friendly and jolly ... and Italian!'

Tom laughed. 'Yes, it was, wasn't it?'

Alex waited. He had been trying to imagine how he would have felt if it had been him, meeting a family he had not known existed until he had reached the age of forty five.

'They are a kind and loving family by all appearances, and incredibly attractive. I guess with the mix of Bill and Flavia and then Caterina they were bound to be.'

Tom knew Alex wanted more but he found his thoughts confused.

'Are you glad we went?'

'I think so. You know, there's a part of me that is really excited that I have this new, extended family and there's a part of me that is thinking it might have been better if Mum had never written that letter. I mean, they were all lovely and more welcoming, to us both, than I could have hoped for.'

Alex smiled. 'I feel a big "but" coming on!'

'Yeah, there is one. Maybe it's just me but it was when Caterina said, "Papa is happy and that makes us all happy", that I wondered if they were all doing it just for Bill. They obviously adore him ... and who wouldn't ... I mean he is really quite special, don't you think?'

Alex had been expecting Tom to feel some insecurity. He was recovering well from the bout of depression that had knocked him back, but this was big stuff, even for someone more resilient. He said as much and Tom just nodded as he gazed through the grimy window at the gentle countryside rolling by. They talked about each member of the family. Gianni's exuberance and delight at finding two gay men in his family made them both laugh out loud and gradually, as they neared the Midlands, Tom's tension eased. With Alex's unquestionable logic and honesty about relationships in families, he began to feel more positive about his own. He smiled at Alex, grateful as always for his understanding.

'I don't think we will be meeting that often though. I mean, Bill spends time in Norfolk, London and Florence. He was talking about the fact that today he flies to Italy to visit old friends. Then he returns to the coast. He really relishes the peace there. I can see why now. It's easy to forget that he is eighty just because he looks about sixty! Caterina and Nico visit Nico's aged mother regularly. Flavia and Stefano were telling me they spend a few weeks every now and then with his parents. They live in the hills somewhere outside Florence – sounded idyllic! Apparently his chef and staff are quite able to carry on at the restaurant without him.'

Alex agreed. 'That's right. He was telling me about opening a second place in the city. I think he'll do very well. The food yesterday was superb, wasn't it? So, what will you say to Sarah?'

'Good question. I don't know. Tell it like it is, I suppose. I have no idea how she feels about all this. I mean, do we ever really know what Sarah feels, about anything?'

Alex laughed. 'Well, she has been known to make her feelings clear on occasions!'

'True, but this is a bit different, isn't it?' Tom was already planning to play the whole 'meeting the family' thing down as much as possible. Instinct told him that he needed to tread carefully and he said as much to Alex.

'Why, for goodness sake? It might do her good to be told that, actually, you have a family that welcomes you and wants you. God knows, she has rejected you often enough over the years, Tom!'

In the end, Tom emailed Sarah and said that it had been a good day and the family had been very welcoming. He was not sure when they would meet again but hoped Bill would come and visit in the New Year. There was no response from Sarah.

27

As usual, the surgery started to become busier as autumn approached. Everyone worked at full pelt. Patients took up most of the time but training students was still a commitment that Tom and Alex enjoyed and took seriously. Alex had started sailing again and continued to sing in the choir. Tom began playing the piano as part of a trio, with two young music teachers on violin and clarinet. They gave occasional recitals and every now and then played at weddings.

Bill and the rest of his family spent Christmas in Italy. Tom had wondered if they might all meet again but, although cards and small gifts were exchanged by post, there was no reunion. He and Alex worked right through to Christmas Day. It was their turn to give Suzie a holiday. She was now a full time partner and in need of time with her family. Many of their Christmases had been spent with Jessie and Ian at the farm, but this year they decided to be on call for the morning, handing over to the deputising service after midday. Alex based himself at the Out of Hours Centre in the town and Tom stayed at the house to take any calls to more rural homes. They had the offer of a driver but Tom, knowing how thin on the ground they were at Christmas, said he would drive himself. The morning was quiet. Outside the clouds were grey and rolling. The Centre was obviously coping as there had been no calls. It was Alex's fiftieth birthday. At their Christmas evening out, the previous week, the surgery staff had presented him with a smooth, black leather case, to replace his old Gladstone bag, after most of its contents had spilled out over the pavement outside the surgery. Alex had given a very plausible acceptance speech but Tom knew that he would part with his battered old bag reluctantly, even though he had to admit it was beyond repair.

Tom checked the preparations for the food as he drank his coffee. They had decided on duck, the plan being to go for a good walk and then to enjoy the meal in the evening. It was almost midday when the phone rang. Tom picked up the receiver and grabbed a pen ready to write down the details.

'Hello, Dr Gabriel. It's Kiran here at the Centre. We've got a bit of a tricky one, I'm afraid. Dr McKee is out with the driver and so are the others, but, in any case, this is out near you and it's one of your patients as it happens.'

'OK, do you want to give me the details?'

Kiran relayed the story. An old man had been found by his daughter, in his garage. He was in his car with the engine on and a hose running from the exhaust into the car. The emergency services had arrived and confirmed the death but they felt the daughter would probably need some treatment. 'Apparently, she's in a bad way.'

Tom took the details. The old man was known to him. As he drove past open fields to the house, the first one at the start of the large, mixed housing estate, he recalled seeing the man a number of times over the last year, since his wife had died from advanced cancer. She had eventually been found a bed in a hospice after it became too much for Harold to care for her at home and his family had persuaded him to be apart from his wife for the first time. Tom knew that Harold had not stopped grieving for his life-long companion, his first and only love. He had never stopped feeling guilty for not keeping her at home. They had been together for sixty five years. It had been pitiful to watch as the old man wasted away. This Christmas must just have been too much for him to bear without his beloved Vera.

As he approached the house he saw a small, shivering group of neighbours standing around, their breath visible in the cold air, as they talked quietly to each other. An ambulance was parked nearby. A police car was parked across the driveway of the house.

'Hello, Doctor Gabriel,' the young constable said. 'They're inside.'

'Thanks, Sean.'

The young man, one of Tom's patients, looked a bit shaken up.

Tom certified the death. The small group outside went back to their roasting turkeys and over-excited children. The police car waited. Tom was in the small, neat sitting room, with Jenny, Harold and Vera's daughter. He had given her a mild sedative and instructions to her husband about caring for her and, if they were able, to bring her to the surgery the next day. If not, Tom would visit them at home. The sad emptiness and the shock permeated through the worn, old fashioned room, from the small artificial Christmas tree in the corner to the taut face of Jenny.

'I came over for him you see. He was coming to us for the rest of the day. I knew something was up because the bedroom curtains were closed. Oh, Dr Gabriel, I can't tell you how scared I was when I heard the engine running in the garage. It was locked from the inside so I couldn't get in from the kitchen. I was screaming and then Colin next door came running and he took my keys from me. My hands were too shaky. I couldn't open the garage, you see. And that was it. There he was ... my Dad ... my lovely old Dad ... gone.' Her sobs were less now but she turned her tear-stained, blotchy face towards Tom and said softly, 'Why?'

Tom knew that whatever he said at that moment would not be adequate. He had spent time with so many bereaved people over the years and he knew one thing for sure. There was no point in speculating. Jenny needed comfort and compassion right now – not analysis.

'I don't know, Jenny. None of us does right now. I do know that this is very sad and difficult for you to understand and I am here to help you and your family in whatever way I can. Did Harold leave a note by any chance?'

arrive we will just have a few words out here and check that you and Gianni have the rings. Then I will go in and take my place.'

Half an hour later with all the guests seated, Jessie watched anxiously for the arrival of her two dearest friends. Gianni was practically jumping with excitement at being asked to support Alex and hold Tom's ring. He looked stunning, as usual, and smelt divine. He was deliriously happy in a relationship with Carlos, one of his mature students, whom he had brought to the wedding and wanted to show off to everyone. Jessie scanned the driveway for Ian's blue 1936 Morris 8 - his pride and joy. He had been doing it up for years and now relished the prospect of driving any couples who wanted him for future ceremonies. They were late. A soft breeze ruffled the hem of Jessie's crimson silk dress.

Walking briskly up the drive were two people – late arrivals she noted with mild irritation. The woman was elegantly dressed in a simple black shift with a cream pashmina around her shoulders, the exact colour of the pearls at her neck and ears. Her dark hair was held with a matching cream silk flower in a soft bun at the nape of her neck. She was immaculately made up and smelt expensive as her perfume reached Jessie's nostrils. Her companion was an equally distinguished looking man in a perfectly tailored dark suit.

'Hello and welcome,' Jessie smiled. 'You're just in time. They will be here any minute. There is a table plan just inside the door if you would like to be seated.'

The woman looked directly at Jessie and returned her smile. 'Thank you so much but I'm afraid we won't be on the list.'

Jessie studied the face before her and a tiny spark of recognition ignited. She hardly dared say what was in her thoughts but knew she had to. 'You're not Sarah, are you?'

'Yes, I am.'

'Oh, my God!' Jessie gasped. 'Does he know?'

'No. I wanted to surprise them.'

Jessie struggled to find words.

Sarah touched her arm. 'I'm so sorry to drop this on you but it really was a last minute decision and we do want it to be a surprise.'

'Oh, it'll be that alright! I'm Jessie, by the way. This is our farm.' And you are not going to spoil this day, she thought desperately.

Sarah took the arm of her companion. 'This is Elliot, my partner.' The kind looking man shook Jessie's hand. 'I'm afraid I'm to blame. I booked the tickets and then told Sarah we were coming. I knew she wanted to be here but she is stubborn and thought she wouldn't be welcome. I hope we are - even though you were not expecting us.'

From the road came the toot-toot of the horn on Ian's car. Jessie sprang into action. She dragged Harry out of the barn and told him to move two more chairs from the spares at the back of the barn and put them by the table on the far side which had room. It was too late to bother about who they would be sitting with – old medical friends of the boys she seemed to remember – as far away as possible from where Tom and Alex would be.

'Please don't tell Tom I'm here. We wouldn't want to shock him just as he is about to get married.'

'Oh, don't you worry. I'm not going to say anything!'

Harry ushered Sarah and Elliot to the seats as the Morris pulled up. Jessie took a deep breath and wished she had had a stiff drink. Tom and Alex looked very handsome in matching dove grey linen suits. Nothing, nothing was to spoil Tom's happy day. She would see to that. She loved him too much to let his ghastly sister ruin things.

'Gianni rushed to embrace both the men. 'Bello, bello!' Tom and Alex thanked Ian and hugged Jessie. Tom smiled down at his dear friend. 'You look stunning, Jess. Thank you for doing all this.'

She hugged him hard. 'It's my pleasure. Now let's go in there and have a wonderful ceremony. Gianni and I will be right with you.'

The registrar checked that everyone knew what they were to do and then she and Jessie and Gianni disappeared into the barn.

As the musicians played Debussy's hauntingly beautiful 'Clair de Lune', Tom and Alex looked at each other.

Alex raised an eyebrow. 'Happy?'

Tom laughed and said, 'Yes, very – and you?'

'Just a bit! Come on - let's get married!'

They wove their way through the tables to the far end of the barn. They were conscious of smiling faces, lit up by the candles, and of the intoxicating scent of country flowers and pungent herbs. Sylvia, the registrar, calmly guided them through the formalities. Jessie and Gianni handed them their rings and beamed proudly as Tom and Alex exchanged a few carefully chosen words of love and loyalty to each other; simple but heartfelt. They embraced and kissed each other to the sound of the musicians, accompanying one of Alex's fellow choir members, singing in a rich, smooth voice, the romantic words of 'Feeling Good', and the whole barn erupted into applause as they signed the register. The twinkling lights and the flames of the candles caught many eyes brimming with happy tears.

The plan was that everyone stayed seated, with champagne being served by Ellie, Ben and Harry, while the few speeches were delivered. Tom and Alex sat at a table with Jessie and Ian, Bill, Caterina, Nico and Isobel's oldest friends, Ronnie and Eileen. Next to them was a table with the rest of the Italian family and Gianni's Carlos. Tom had wondered if Alex would feel strange not having any family to invite but Alex was not in the least bothered. Jason and some other close friends of his were there and he and Tom had felt from the start that Bill's family were Alex's too.

Somebody rapped a table and silence fell. Jessie wondered when Sarah would make her presence felt and was not sure how to handle it. She could barely see Sarah at the far end of the barn. Alex and Tom stood. They thanked everyone for coming. They particularly wanted to thank Jessie and Ian for providing such a beautiful place to have their ceremony. Tom went on to thank his newly found family for being there and for their acceptance of him and of Alex. They had planned to keep any speeches

ABOUT THE AUTHOR

M J Knox lives in Warwickshire, is of Northern Irish heritage and has worked for many years in the National Health Service.

Continuing work is on a collection of short stories - the essential quick read for today's busy lives.